John Belushi Is Dead

KATHY CHARLES

GALLERY BOOKS   MTV BOOKS

NEW YORK   LONDON   TORONTO   SYDNEY

Sept. 2010

Gallery Books
A Division of Simon & Schuster, Inc.
1230 Avenue of the Americas
New York, NY 10020

Originally published in Australia in 2009 by The Text Publishing Company as *Hollywood Ending*

MTV Music Television and all related titles, logos, and characters are trademarks of
MTV Networks, a division of Viacom International, Inc.

First MTV Books/Gallery Books trade paperback edition August 2010

GALLERY BOOKS and colophon are trademarks of Simon & Schuster, Inc.

For information about special discounts for bulk purchases, please contact Simon &
Schuster Special Sales at 1-866-506-1949 or business@simonandschuster.com.

The Simon & Schuster Speakers Bureau can bring authors to your live event. For more
information or to book an event contact the Simon & Schuster Speakers Bureau at
1-866-248-3049 or visit our website at www.simonspeakers.com.

Designed by Jamie Lynn Kerner

Manufactured in the United States of America

10 9 8 7 6 5 4 3 2 1

Library of Congress Cataloging-in-Publication Data is available.

ISBN 978-1-4391-8759-3
ISBN 978-1-4391-8761-6 (ebook)

For Christine and Peter, who gave me life
And Evan, until death do us part

ACKNOWLEDGMENTS

THANK YOU TO MY wonderful parents, Christine and Peter, who encouraged me to write, gave me their love of books, and didn't take away my Stephen King novels when my teachers thought I was too young to be reading them. I am eternally grateful for your love and support, for all the sacrifices you made, and all the times you wouldn't let me give up. I love you with all my heart.

Thanks to my beautiful sisters, Elizabeth and Lisa, and my awesome niece and nephews, Jack, Victoria, and James. Thanks to my amazing aunt, Karin Paulsen, for looking after me in LA and keeping me out of trouble (for the most part!). You are a magnificent, inspiring woman and I am so grateful for everything you have ever done for me. Thanks to Barry and Loretta at the Beverly Glen Deli in Bel Air, for the free meals and fantastic company (if you're in LA you won't find better eating, and I can highly recommend the waffle fries). To my agent, Wendy Schmalz, thank you so much for all your tireless work, and for always believing in me. Finally, my immense gratitude to Jennifer

Heddle, an amazing editor who made this book so much better, and the whole team at MTV Books.

Various sources were used to draw information for this novel. They include *Wired: The Short Life and Fast Times of John Belushi*, by Bob Woodward; *Outrageous Conduct: Art, Ego and the Twilight Zone Case* by Stephen Farber and Marc Green; *Helter Skelter* by Vincent Bugliosi with Curt Gentry; *Hollywood Babylon* by Kenneth Anger; *Severed* by John Gilmore; *Sharon Tate and the Manson Murders* by Greg King; *This is Hollywood: An Unusual Movieland Guide* by Ken Schessler; *Laid to Rest in California* by Patricia Brooks and Jonathan Brooks; *Black Dahlia Avenger* by Steve Hodel; *Deadly Illusions: Jean Harlow and the Murder of Paul Bern* by Samuel Marx and Joyce Vanderveen; *The Night Stalker: The Life and Crimes of Richard Ramirez* by Philip Carlo; *The Chris Farley Show: A Biography in Three Acts* by Tom Farley, Jnr. and Tanner Colby, and *L.A. Exposed* by Paul Young. My infinite respect and gratitude to Scott Michaels and all the Death Hags at www.findadeath.com, without whom this novel would not have been written.

Lastly, heartfelt thanks to my husband, Evan Butson, for making every day above ground a good one. I adore you with all my heart. You're my Hollywood ending.

John Belushi Is Dead

1

WE HUNG OVER THE fence at the Ambassador Hotel, watching the demolition. Benji stood beside me taking photos with his digital camera, his mouth open in disbelief. He was determined to document every moment. As the bulldozers tore into the side of the hotel, the sound of crushing mortar made me feel sick. The Ambassador had a long, star-filled history. To us the building was a holy shrine, and watching its destruction was like watching a death.

For the past year we had attended protest marches and signed on-line petitions. During that time the hotel had been used as a movie set and a cheap location for sci-fi and comic book conventions. But finally the decision had been made. The Ambassador had no future, and the demolition was to go ahead. Los Angeles is a town that exorcises its demons—cursed properties are seized and razed.

Benji and I revelled in the celebrity history of the Ambassador. In the golden days of Hollywood, the Oscars were held there.

Marilyn Monroe lounged by the pool. In 1968, the allure of the Ambassador was tarnished forever when Senator Robert F. Kennedy delivered a heartfelt victory speech in the ballroom after winning the California primary, only to be gunned down as he tried to make his exit through the hotel pantry. Some people thought the CIA was in on it, but most believed that RFK was assassinated by a Palestinian immigrant with a beef against the Kennedys, just another run-of-the-mill nut job in a town full of them. I preferred the theory that the Palestinian was just a patsy, that he'd been hypnotized and ordered to kill the senator, like something out of *The Manchurian Candidate*. Benji said he had a piece of the floor from directly beneath RFK's head. He bought it off eBay from a seller who claimed to be one of the workers hired to tear the building down. Benji said the dark stain on the corner that looked like barbecue sauce was actually Kennedy's blood.

Our mission for the day was to remove something from the demolition site, this time with our own two hands. Benji had dressed in combat fatigues, convinced it would help him blend into the scenery. A couple of ex-cops in black T-shirts patrolled the perimeter, German shepherds on short leads trailing beside them. We looked for ways to get through the fence undetected but couldn't maneuver around the guards. After we'd stood around for an hour, hands in our pockets and staring through the chicken wire, one of the guards came over. He was wearing aviator sunglasses and had a gun in his holster.

"Can I help you kids with something?" he asked.

"Good morning, officer," Benji said politely, pointing at the crumbled ruins of the Ambassador. "Any chance we could come in and watch history unfold up close?"

The guard shook his head. "Private property," he said, tipping his head at a sign that read WARNING—DEATH. "Dangerous, too. Why, a piece of rock could come flying off one of those bulldozers and hit you—bam!—square in the eye." He threaded his thumbs through his belt, chewed his gum with the gusto of a cowboy, and stared into the sun like the sheriff of *Deadwood*. It was then I knew we would get what we needed.

"Can I make you a proposition?" Benji suggested. He removed a black, studded wallet from his back pocket, snapped it open, and pulled out a ten-dollar bill. The wallet rattled on its chain. Benji lived to negotiate.

"What do you mean, proposition?" the guard asked, adjusting his cap.

Benji handed him the bill: clean, crisp, and freshly minted.

The guard paused for a moment, then took the bill and examined it. He held it to the sun as if the light could confirm it was real. "What the hell is this all about?" he asked, looking around to make sure no one had seen the exchange.

A crane crashed through the ceiling of the hotel and a dust cloud made its way across the lot, shrouding everyone in dirt. Benji coughed and brushed dirt from his clothes. "We want some bricks," he said.

The guard stared at him. "Bricks?"

"Flooring, too, if you can find any. But bricks would be a good start."

The guard gazed out across the site, incredulous. His boss was sitting in the watch house taking a nap, feet hanging out the window.

"Make it twenty," he said, turning back and licking his lips.

Benji had been expecting this, too. He took another ten from his wallet and handed it over. He always carried many denominations, always started small. Once people knew what we were after they would jack up the price—capitalism at its finest.

"All right, then," the guard said, and grinned. He folded the bills and put them in his top pocket, then set off at a jog across the lot. Benji let out a high-pitched whistle and the guard turned around.

"Not that way," Benji yelled over the bulldozers and cranes. "That way."

He pointed toward where the ballroom had been, and the guard changed direction. A minute later he was running back, two whole bricks in his hands. He carried them against his chest, puffing and wheezing all the way. He dropped the bricks on the ground and started to cough.

"Careful," Benji complained. "I paid for those."

Just like you paid for the one off eBay, I thought. Only this time he could authenticate it.

The guard spat on the ground, then composed himself. It had obviously been some time since he'd been chasing criminals around the streets of LA.

"What the hell do you kids want those for, anyway?" he asked. "What's so special about a couple of bricks?"

Benji picked up the bricks and cradled one in each hand. He held the rough, red surface against his face and breathed in, then cast a victorious glance in my direction.

"Feel this," he said, handing the brick to the guard, who gave me a quizzical look.

"Take it," I said. "It won't bite."

He took the brick, sniffed it, weighed it in his hand, then handed it back to Benji. "It's a brick," he concluded.

Benji shook his head. "It's not just a brick. This piece of building, this element, is a living, breathing organism. This brick has witnessed some of the most amazing events in American history. It was there when *Gone with the Wind* received the Oscar for Best Picture. It watched Marilyn Monroe being photographed by the swimming pool. Perhaps it made up part of the room where Jean Harlow stayed, or Howard Hughes, or Nixon. Listen."

He held the brick up to his ear as if it were a shell. The air was suddenly still and the crash of demolition momentarily ceased.

"It's telling us its secrets," Benji said. "These pieces of building, they are part of history. They talk to us. They tell us stories. Robert Kennedy might have been our president if he hadn't died here, on this very site. And what do we do? We tear the place down, as if what happened here doesn't matter one bit. We just tear it down and forget it was ever there."

There was an explosion and rubble rained down. The guard jumped and spun around as if he'd seen a ghost. Benji took a plastic bag from his pocket. I took some newspaper from my backpack and handed it to him. He wrapped the bricks in the paper, lovingly folded down the edges, and placed them in the bag. The guard scratched his head.

"You kids are crazy," he said, and started to walk away.

Benji looked at me and smiled, pleased with himself.

"Did you have to freak that guy out?" I asked.

Benji laughed.

We walked back to his car. He put the bricks on the backseat.

"You wanna put seat belts on them, too?" I asked.

2

WE DROVE TO BARNEYS Beanery in West Hollywood, where we sat at Janis Joplin's booth and ordered poached eggs with hollandaise. The food at the Beanery wasn't the greatest, but the ambience more than made up for it. In the old days the Beanery was a hangout for Hollywood's rock elite, like Jimi Hendrix and Jim Morrison. Now it was full of tourists and frat boys with their girlfriends, playing pool. No one cared about the significance of the place anymore, no one except a few educated tourists and us. Jimi Hendrix and Jim Morrison were now members of the Forever 27 Club, along with Kurt Cobain and Janis Joplin. It would have sucked to have died at twenty-seven, and it was so damn creepy how many awesome musicians had lost their lives at that exact age, but at least they were in good company.

Benji drank coffee and loaded photos from his camera onto his laptop. I looked at the ceiling, where an old table from the Beanery had been nailed up so that everyone could see it. Someone had scratched their name into the table larger than the others. The lettering was messy and jagged but the name was unmistakeable: Janis. It was rumored she'd had her last screwdriver at the Beanery, one final drink before departing this world in a pool of her own vomit. I imagined her in all her junked-up glory, plying her face with pastrami on rye and hacking at the table with a bread knife. I felt honored to be sitting in her booth.

Although it was only ten in the morning, the frat boys were drinking Coronas and the stereo was cranked to the hilt with an Elvis Presley song. A few tourists wearing Hollywood T-shirts with cameras slung around their necks waddled through the doors.

"Oh, Harold," a woman said to her husband as she hooked her arm through his. "They say Jack Nicholson used to drink here with Dennis Hopper when they made *Easy Rider*."

Her old hippie husband looked around in awe. "Far out."

These people should have annoyed us just as much as the frat boys did, but the truth was they were just like us. They were scavengers feeding off others, obsessed with lives that were not their own. They were our people.

Benji pierced his eggs with a fork, looked at me, and took a bite.

"You look stupid with that pink hair," he said through a mouthful of food. In a fit of boredom I'd dyed my hair the night before. It seemed like a fun idea at the time, but the pink hadn't really taken and my head looked like Hello Kitty threw up on it. I tossed my napkin at Benji.

"You said you liked it this morning."

"I've changed my mind. It looks stupid."

"Well, you look disgusting. Finish your food before you open your mouth."

He stuck out his tongue, revealing the saliva-coated remnants of his meal. "Have some respect at Janis's table," I said.

"Janis wouldn't care." He snickered, chewing loudly. "She would fully appreciate someone enjoying such a hearty, lard-laden meal."

He reached over and grabbed my orange juice.

"Your aunt Lynette's gonna be pissed when she sees your hair," he added, swallowing a mouthful of food and juice.

"No, she won't. She won't even care."

The waitress refilled our coffees and I ordered another OJ. I looked out the window. There was surprisingly little traffic on Santa Monica Boulevard. When the road was clear you could imagine it was the 1960s and the Beanery was filled with beatniks and poets, rather than drunken sorority girls. I finished my juice and watched Benji eyeing the girls at the bar. One of them bent over, exposing pink frilly panties beneath her tight leather skirt.

"Do you mind if I check something, seeing as how you're so distracted?" I asked, pointing to his computer.

Benji unplugged his camera and spun the laptop around to face me. Another great thing about Barney's was that it had free Wi-Fi. I logged on to my favourite website, the Celebrity Autopsy Room, and checked my profile:

NAME: Hilda Swann
AGE: 17
LIVES: Encino, CA
MOOD: Apathetic

I opened my personal preferences and changed my mood to excited. Summer vacation had finally arrived, and Benji and I were going to spend it doing what we loved best.

Summer vacation means different things to different people. To the popular girls at school it meant three months of hanging around the mall, playing beach volleyball in string bikinis, and being screwed by jocks under the boardwalk. To the neglected kids it meant being packed off to summer camp to battle the bugs and basket weaving. For Benji and me it meant days and days of glorious death.

FAVORITE MOVIE: *Harold and Maude*
FAVORITE MUSIC: Nirvana, the Ramones, the Carpenters
FAVORITE BOOK: *Hollywood Babylon* by Kenneth Anger
INTERESTS: Dead celebrities, living in LA, books about serial killers

MY Favorite Dead People (in no particular order):
1. Sharon Tate
2. John Belushi
3. Chris Farley
4. James Dean
5. Marilyn Monroe
6. Phil Hartman
7. Kurt Cobain
8. Elizabeth Short (the Black Dahlia, for those not in the know)
9. Jayne Mansfield
10. My parents

"Are you done?" Benji took the laptop back. "I'm waiting for this dude to contact me."

I called the waitress over. "Can we get the check?"

"There it is," Benji said, smiling. "Bingo."

He took a napkin and scribbled on it, then stuffed it in his pocket.

"What's that?" I asked.

"You'll see. Come on. Let's head up the hill."

It was a beautiful day, so we decided to walk all the way from the Beanery to Janis's place. Janis OD'd at the Landmark Hotel on Franklin Avenue—now the Highland Gardens—on heroin that was cut too pure. The batch killed a whole lot of people in LA, but Janis was the only famous one. Benji had stayed in the room once before, but every time I tried to make a reservation it was already booked. Sometimes it was booked solid for weeks in advance. People wanted to be close to Janis. They wanted to sleep in the same bed she'd puked on before dying on the floor. When we got to the hotel we tried to see in through the windows of her ground-floor room, but the curtains were closed. We walked back to the car, disappointed. Benji checked the backseat to make sure his bricks were still there.

"What next?" I asked.

"You up for a little adventure?"

"Sure," I said. "What did you have in mind?"

Benji leaned over. "You ever heard of Bernie Bernall?"

Bernie Bernall? "I don't think so," I said. "Was he in *Plan 9 from Outer Space*?"

Benji rolled his eyes. "God, you're such a lightweight, Hilda. Bernie Bernall was a silent movie star whose career was ruined when they introduced the talkies. Apparently his voice was so bad he became the laughingstock of the industry. They tried dubbing another voice over his, but it didn't work. He became a junkie and an alcoholic, then killed himself in his apartment."

"How?"

Benji leaned in close. "He stabbed himself."

"What do you mean, 'stabbed himself'? Like with a knife?"

Benji shook his head. "Scissors."

Scissors. What a way to go. I whistled. "That's awesome."

"Not only that, they were small sewing scissors so blunt you could barely cut your toenails with 'em. He just gouged that shit straight into his heart and moved it around till the hole was big enough to kill him."

"Wow. How could I not have heard about this?"

"It gets worse. His wife was in New York when it happened, and apparently she didn't give a shit. She didn't even come back to town for the funeral."

"Damn."

"She didn't even send flowers. She sent a telegram saying how "regretful" she was that it had happened, or some crap like that. When he stopped being famous, no one gave a shit about him anymore, you know? Everyone forgot about him, even his wife. Suicide was his last stab at being famous."

"Literally."

Benji held up the napkin he had scribbled on at Barney's. "I just found out where his apartment was."

My eyes lit up. "Where?"

"Echo Park."

Echo Park. One of the oldest neighborhoods in LA, home to junkies, freaks, and bohos. Jackson Pollock and Ayn Rand once lived there, as well as Tom Waits and Frank Zappa. Gentrification had turned Echo Park into a trendy suburb, but there was still a good amount of squalor in its rambling Spanish homes and overgrown gardens. I took the piece of paper from Benji and held it in my hands.

"I want to get inside," he said.

"Oh yeah?" I laughed. "How are we going to do that? Breaking and entering?"

He put the car in gear and pulled out from the curb. "Simple," he said. "We'll just ask."

I looked at Benji, with his military clothes, dark sunglasses, and black army cap. "You think some little old lady is gonna let you into her apartment?"

"Hilda, you have seen my methods of persuasion. I can charm myself into anyone's good graces."

We drove down Hollywood Boulevard, past Grauman's Chinese Theatre and away from the busloads of tourists and faded stars on the Hollywood Walk of Fame. We headed east toward downtown LA, where the road became cracked and pitted with potholes and the most colorful sights were the prostitutes outside the Rite Aid.

"Can't remember the last time I was this far downtown," I said.

"Did you know Echo Park was actually the center of the movie business during the silent era?"

"Gee, Benji, you're a wealth of information today," I said a little sarcastically. Benji loved to show off how much he knew about Hollywood.

"I just read a book about it," he continued. "All the major studios were in Echo Park before they moved out to the Valley. Mack Sennett's studio was there. Can you imagine how cool it must have been? Charlie Chaplin and Fatty Arbuckle and all those guys making all those fantastic films, pioneering the medium. It would have been magic. Fatty Arbuckle raped a girl with a Coke bottle, you know."

"Now, that I *do* know."

It was one of the most famous stories from that era: the fat movie star in the bowler hat who allegedly held the studio bit player down on the bed and rammed the bottle inside her, causing massive internal injuries. There were rumors that Fatty wasn't even in the room at the time, and that the actress was really a prostitute who OD'd during a party in his hotel suite, and somehow Fatty got blamed. The actress died, and even though Fatty was acquitted by a jury, his career was ruined by the scandal. Ten years later the studio he had worked for all his life finally took pity on Fatty and cast him in a movie. Fatty proudly proclaimed it was the happiest day of his life. That same night he died of heart failure.

"Hang on," I said. "Didn't Elliott Smith die in Echo Park, too? In a similar way?" I remembered a newspaper article about the Oscar-nominated folksinger who took his own life under very suspicious circumstances.

"That's right!" Benji said, excited. "He had an argument with his girlfriend, and she says she went to take a shower, and after the shower she opened the bathroom door and found him standing in the middle of the kitchen with a knife in his chest."

"Maybe he was possessed by the ghost of Bernie Bernall?"

"Maybe his girlfriend was lying to the cops and stabbed him herself."

"Who knows. Have you ever heard his music? He seemed pretty miserable to me."

"Knife-through-the-heart miserable?"

"More like emo, self-harming miserable."

"Huh."

"So what's the game plan today?"

"No game plan. We'll just knock on the door, ask if we can go in and take a few photos."

"What if some crackhead opens the door and wigs out on us?"

Benji gestured to the glove compartment. I opened it and took out a small aerosol can.

"Pepper spray?"

"You can never be too careful, Hilda. This town's full of psychos."

I put the spray back. We'd done some crazy stuff before, but knocking on someone's door and asking if we could take a look inside was a new one. There was the time we trekked through the Hollywood Hills trying to find the mythical ruins of a movie star's pool, said to be on vacant land wedged between two properties. What made the pool so special was the mosaic tile work on an adjoining wall that depicted a large spider sitting in a web, a creepy remnant of old-time Hollywood we were desperate to see. We climbed down a cliff face and pushed our way through the undergrowth, but when Benji saw a snake we screamed and ran out of there as fast as we could, our mission thwarted.

One night we climbed the fence at the Hollywood sign and slept under the stars, the enormous D towering above us, Los Angeles teeming below. We hid under the letter so we wouldn't be seen, curled into its side with pillows and blankets and talked about all the people who'd OD'd up there and the actress who'd leaped to her death from the H. In the middle of the night I felt a tugging on my sleeping bag and woke to find a coyote tearing at the fabric.

I stared into its black eyes for a few seconds before it took off, running silently into the scrub.

I watched Benji as we drove. He was stealing proud glances at the bricks on the backseat, his precious artifacts to add to his vast collection of strange objects. He liked to think of himself as the Indiana Jones of the macabre.

"Stabbing yourself in the heart with scissors," Benji said with admiration. "Now that takes balls. Did you know Elliott Smith's girlfriend told the cops she found him with the kitchen knife already in his heart and pulled it out. Her prints were all over it. It's so messed up. People should know better than to pull out the weapon if someone's been stabbed. It's the dumbest thing you can do."

"I don't think that's something they teach you in school, Benji."

"They should. It's useful shit to know."

We drove down a dead-end street full of crummy apartment buildings and bungalows with faded pink paint. There weren't many sprinklers on this side of town, and the lawns were dead and covered in weeds. Benji pulled up in front of a white stucco apartment block, the name DISTANT MEMORIES emblazoned on its side in wrought-iron cursive, the letters chipped and rusted.

"Distant Memories?" I said. "How depressing."

It was hardly a fitting place for a movie star to live, and I figured Bernie Bernall must have been really down on his luck when he moved here. The building was two stories with a flat roof, and a sign advertising vacancies was hammered into the ground outside. Thick bars covered the windows of the lower level, giving the building the look of a prison. Old catalogs that had fallen from mailboxes were scattered across the front lawn, the edges eaten by snails. Benji shut off the engine.

"If you were gonna kill yourself," he asked, "how would you do it? I'd jump off a building, so I could sail through the air and watch the pavement rushing up toward me."

I thought for a moment. "Pills," I said quietly. "It would be the most painless way to go."

"Bor-ing." He opened the glove compartment and took out the pepper spray. "We'll be needing this."

We walked up the sun-bleached path to the apartment building, Benji up front, the spray concealed in his jacket. He stood in front of the mailbox looking for the right apartment number, and when he found it he took a photo.

"The death certificate says the apartment was on the ground level," he said, nodding toward an apartment with its blinds open, rock music blasting from inside. "But this guy online told me the death certificate is wrong and it's actually that apartment right there."

He pointed at the second-story apartment at the front of the building, facing the road. The windows were open but I could see that heavy brown curtains were drawn against the sun. It did not look inviting.

"Are you sure?" I said. "Shouldn't you go by the death certificate?"

"Nah. This guy said he actually lived here when it happened, and that Bernie's apartment was definitely up there."

"Huh. Did he tell you he knew Elvis, too?"

Benji ignored that comment and started to make his way down the cracked concrete path. We walked past the ground-floor apartment with its blaring rock music and I saw the silhouette of someone inside sitting hunched over a computer. I wondered how anyone could concentrate on work with a stereo at that volume.

"I think he needs to turn the music up louder," I said sarcastically to Benji. "The rest of the neighborhood can barely hear it."

Benji didn't answer. He was firmly fixed on getting into the apartment upstairs, intent on his mission. I trailed behind him as he made his way up the old concrete steps, hands at my sides so as to avoid the sharp, rusty railing and the possibility of needing a tetanus shot later on. The upstairs apartment had a big wooden door and a flywire screen that was falling off its hinges. To the left of the door was a large window with bars that was also open, the same heavy brown curtain drawn. A wicker mat said WELCOME in big black letters.

"See?" Benji said. "'Welcome.' There's probably some real nice folks living here."

I looked along the row of apartments. A couch with torn upholstery sat on the balcony, and an ashtray on the ground was overflowing with butts. A strange odor hung in the air, like home cooking gone horribly wrong. It smelled like somebody was boiling a dog. I gagged.

"Can you smell that?" I whispered. "That's rancid."

Benji lifted his fingers into claws. "Perhaps it is the votting vemains of the late, great Bernie Bernall," he said, giving his best Bela Lugosi impersonation.

"Can we just get on with this, please? Let's get your shit and get out of here."

Benji banged on the door with a heavy fist. "Anyone home?" he yelled.

"Jesus, Benji," I whispered, pulling on his arm. "They'll think it's the cops."

"You don't get what you want in this world if you don't show strength, Hilda."

"Why thank you, Tony Robbins."

He banged again. Inside the apartment nothing stirred. A dog barked in the distance. I could feel someone's eyes on my neck and turned around to catch an old woman peering at me through her curtains. I gave her a small wave and she ducked back inside.

"No one here," I said, throwing up my hands. "Let's go."

It was then we heard the sound of a dozen locks turning inside the apartment. We waited as bolts and chains were slid and un-hooked. I held on to Benji's arm and instinctively reached for the pepper spray concealed inside his jacket. He patted my hand away and gave me an annoyed look.

"Jesus Christ, calm down," he whispered.

"Gimme the pepper spray," I said, grabbing for his jacket. "Give it to me!"

"No!"

Before we could say another word, the door opened a crack before one final chain caught it, and a bearded face gazed out, a wrinkled eye looking us up and down. Benji tapped my hand away and I crossed my arms, trying to act casual, and gave the man a smile. The smile was not returned.

"WHAT?" the old man thundered from behind the door. "WHATTA YOU WANT?"

"Good afternoon, sir," Benji said, holding out his hand and trying to slip it through the slit in the door. When the man didn't take it, Benji withdrew his hand, dismayed. "We were wondering if we could talk to you for a moment?"

"WHAT ABOUT? WHAT THE HELL DO YOU WANT?"

Benji looked at me. I looked at the old man, our eyes meeting.

"Well," Benji started to say, "you, sir, live in a very unique property—"

"I AIN'T SELLIN'! I AIN'T GONNA SELL, GODDAM-NIT!"

"No, sir, you misunderstand me. Something very interest-ing happened in your apartment once. We were just hoping you would let us inside so we could have a look around and take some pictures."

Benji held up his camera.

"You gonna give me that camera?" the old man asked, a hint of a smirk on his face.

"Ah, no, but I can give you something for your trouble."

Benji pulled out his wallet and removed a ten-dollar bill. The guy was obviously poor and lonely. He'd be a pushover.

The old man stood there for a moment, considering the propo-sition. I could feel the vilest heat radiating from inside and figured he didn't have an air conditioner. I would have been just as happy had he turned us away on the spot.

"Do you know me?" he finally growled. Benji looked at me and we both shook our heads.

"No, sir, we don't."

"You don't know me?"

"No. Should we? Are you famous or something?"

Another pause. "You wanna come in and take some photos. That's it?"

"That's all we want to do, just take some photos of your bath-room."

"You ain't from the real estate agency?"

"No."

"The government?"

"No. We are . . . private operators."

The old man extended a spotted hand through the crack in the door. Benji handed him the bill and he snatched it out of Benji's fingers.

"Any chance of some bath tiles?" Benji asked.

"Benji!" I said, sure the door would be slammed in our faces, but instead the man grinned and extended his hand again. Without hesitation Benji pulled out another ten-dollar bill and stuck it in the man's scrawny fingers. The old man shut the door and we heard the sound of the last chain unlocking. The door opened. The old man stood in front of us in boxers and a stained white T-shirt, his thin, spindly legs covered in hair. He had long, ragged blond hair that was flecked with gray and stuck out on the sides of his head like he'd put his finger in an electrical socket. His face was drawn and gaunt, and his eyes were tiny black pinpricks in his head. In his right hand was an unlit, gnarled cigar, and he brought it to his mouth and jammed it between his teeth as he stepped aside to let us enter. I immediately thought of Nick Nolte's mug shot and wondered if Benji did, too.

"Thank you very much, sir," Benji said, wiping his feet, the very model of good manners. The man put his hand roughly on Benji's shoulder.

"The name's Hank, son," he said. "You call me sir again, I'll knock your teeth through your goddamn head."

"Okay, dude, it's cool," Benji said, holding up his hands. He looked back at me and grinned. I waited outside, frozen to the welcome mat. Hank looked at me as Benji made his way around the apartment, picking up items and snapping pictures of light fittings and doorknobs.

"It's not really our kind of scene."

"You coming in?" he barked.

I scurried inside, racing over to be close to Benji. The apartment was nothing more than one large room with a kitchenette; there were two doors off to the side that I assumed led to a bedroom and the bathroom. It was also a mess. The walls, once white concrete, were now a dull, faded yellow. There was an old torn sofa, a matching chair next to it that was just as beat-up, and a low wooden coffee table stained with bottle rings. An old black-and-white television was propped in the corner, a coat hanger for an antenna. Empty bottles lay strewn on the stained beige carpet, which had been darkened by what looked like spilled wine and cigar ash. Next to a small wooden desk by the window were stacks of newspapers, yellowed and faded by the sun. The ashtrays were full, and in some the embers were still smoldering. I glanced over at the kitchenette, which looked like it hadn't been cleaned since the seventies. Behind the chipped linoleum countertop was a rusty old stove and an enormous old refrigerator that hummed so loudly it sounded like it was about to take off. Dirty dishes were piled high in the sink, and the overhead cupboard doors hung open, exposing their sad emptiness. Hank watched with curiosity as Benji took photographs, touched the surface of the walls, and looked at the view from the window. The old man scratched his head and stuck the cigar between his teeth, sidling over to me.

"Are you reporters?" he asked me suspiciously.

"Not reporters exactly," Benji butted in. "More like enthusiasts. Is the bathroom through here?" Benji gestured to a closed door.

Hank nodded and smiled, amused. "You wanna photograph my shitter, too?"

"Would that cost me extra?"

The smile disappeared from Hank's face and was replaced by an icy stare. "Are you some kind of wiseass?"

"He's just playing around," I said. "The truth is, a very famous movie star once lived in this apartment."

"No shit?"

"His name was Bernie Bernall," Benji interjected once again. "He was one of the biggest stars of the silent era. Valentino had nothing on him."

"I ain't never heard of him."

"Maybe he was before your time."

"So he lived here?" Hank looked around his disheveled apartment, disbelieving.

"Sure did. And he died here, too. In there."

Benji pushed open the bathroom door and went in. I waited in the living room while Hank went into the bathroom and looked over Benji's shoulder. This was taking too long. I wanted to be out of that dirty apartment and back in the sunshine, away from the flies and the heat and the squalor. Hank came back and stood beside me. I looked at the floor.

"Gee, that guy's music is pretty loud," I said, motioning to the apartment below.

"The walls here are paper-thin," he grunted, stomping his foot. "Shut the hell up!" he yelled, and abruptly the music switched off. "Damn kid, always plays his music too loud. So you're not in school?"

I shook my head. "No. Well, yeah, we go to school, but it's summer vacation."

"So why ain't you at the beach, or the pool?"

"That's not really our kind of scene."

"Oh," he grunted. "And this is?"

I shrugged and offered him a small smile. We stood for a moment in awkward silence.

"So what's with your friend?" he asked. "Is he in the military or something?"

"No, he just dresses like he is."

"What for?"

"I think he just likes it," I offered. "Maybe it makes him feel more masculine."

"Well, he looks goddamn ridiculous if you ask me."

"Hilda, come look at this," Benji called out. I walked into the bathroom, grateful to be away from Hank and his questions. The bathroom was as old as the rest of the apartment. There was a large bathtub with an enormous, old-fashioned showerhead above it, and the shower curtain, which had once been white, was almost black with dirt. Benji was staring at the sink. "It's the original one," he whispered. "It hasn't been replaced."

I leaned forward. It was definitely the original. There were even dark splatter stains along the rim. I looked at the linoleum floor, the cracked edges curling up where it met the sink. There were spots there, too.

"I want this," Benji said, bending down to tear at the linoleum.

"Benji! You can't tear his floor up!" I whispered, but he continued to pull unsuccessfully on the flooring, ignoring me.

"Whatcha lookin' at?" Hank asked, suddenly appearing at the door. Benji leaped up.

"Oh, nothing," I said nonchalantly. "Just looking around. Benji, you got what you need?"

"Uh, yeah, just a second," he answered, snapping off a few more shots as if that was what he had been doing all along. Hank wandered back out to the kitchen, looking bored. I followed and watched him fill a kettle and place it on the rusty stove.

"You like tea?" he asked.

"Tea? Uh, sure."

He took three mugs from the cupboard and placed a tea bag in each. I was amazed he had any clean dishes left. The plates in the sink looked like they had been there for a week, and a few flies were buzzing around excitedly, feeding off the scraps. I was just starting to consider the possibility of mice when Benji walked out of the bathroom. When he saw the cups on the counter, tea bags hanging expectantly over the sides, he practically recoiled.

"Oh, no thanks, man. We gotta get going."

Hank held a small spoon in midair, ready to scoop sugar from a jar.

"You sure? Ain't no trouble. You ain't from the government or the newspapers, I ain't got no beef with you."

"Maybe we could stay for one cup?" I asked Benji.

"No, we can't," he replied quickly. "We have that thing we have to get to, remember?"

"Oh, of course," I said, playing along, although I felt a pinch of guilt for skipping out on Hank so fast. We had barged into his home and taken photos and now we were going to leave without having so much as a cup of tea. He was obviously lonely, and staying would have been the nice thing to do. But nice wasn't in Benji's repertoire, and he was my only ride home.

"So, Hank," Benji said, holding out a business card, "if you ever decide to get a new bathroom sink or sell the one you got, give me a call. I'll take it off your hands, and for a reasonable price."

"Now, why the hell would I get a new bathroom sink?"

Benji shrugged. "Any number of reasons. Just, if it happens, give me a call, okay?"

Hank took the card. I watched him study it, as if he could extract some greater meaning from what was printed on it, an answer to why we were there.

"All right," he said, and slid the card into his boxers. "All right."

Benji walked out the front door and I followed close behind. Just as I was about to step out onto the balcony Hank caught my hand, making me jump. He leaned in close, spoke quietly into my ear.

"That movie star," he said. "How did he die?"

I hesitated. "He killed himself."

Hank nodded slowly, as if digesting the information, and I gave him a small shrug. He let go of my hand, mumbled something that I couldn't hear, then went back inside, slamming the door and turning the locks once again. Benji was already down the stairs and out on the dead lawn, photographing the front of the building. I ran down to be with him in the sunlight, where it was warm and you could see the blue of the sky.

"DAMN." BENJI LAUGHED AS we drove back toward Hollywood. "And I thought Bukowski was dead."

"You didn't have to be an asshole," I said, annoyed by Benji's cavalier attitude. "He was an old man. You didn't have to make fun of him."

"The guy was a freak, Hilda. 'Do you know me? Do you know who I am?' He was like something out of a James Ellroy novel."

"*He* was a freak? You told the guy someone died in his apartment!"

"And that's probably the most exciting thing that's ever happened to him. Did you see all those empty bottles? By the rate he's putting it away, he'll have forgotten we were even there by tomorrow."

I picked up Benji's camera and started scanning the pictures. The bathroom in Hank's apartment was small and cramped, tomblike. In one photo I could see Benji's reflection in the mirror, imposing and out of place in his army gear. In another photo Benji's detached, floating arm pointed out an original light fixture while Hank lingered at the edge of the frame. In the next photo, taken just seconds later, Hank had raised an arm to cover his face. I turned the camera off and put it in the glove compartment in the spot where the pepper spray had been.

"Such an angry way to die," I said, returning to the story of Bernie Bernall in an effort to try and shake Hank from my mind, the sadness of his situation. "You know, stabbing yourself with a pair of scissors. It's not like pills, or even shooting yourself. It's like Bernie was still trying to say to the world, 'Hey, I'm different, I'm special,' even as he was dying."

"All suicide is angry," Benji said in a dismissive tone. "Suicide by its very nature is a hostile act, an affront to the natural order. It's an offense against God."

I looked out the window at the tourists walking down Hollywood Boulevard, disposable cameras in hand, taking photos of the shiny metallic stars on the sidewalk and the footprints in the cement.

"I read an interesting theory the other day," Benji continued. "Some religions believe that when we die we are reincarnated, and some souls just aren't ready to come back. They haven't dealt with all the things in their past life and they aren't at peace, and when they come back into the world they can't handle it. People who are crazy or killers are souls that weren't ready to come back and just can't adjust to the world again. It's the same with suicides."

"So suicides are lost souls?" I asked. Benji didn't look at me.

"I don't know. That's just what I read."

3

BENJI LIVED IN A large house a few blocks from mine; it was all glass and steel surfaces and reminded me of Cameron's house in *Ferris Bueller's Day Off*, where everything was cold and beautiful and he wasn't allowed to touch anything. Benji's dad was some kind of banker who worked long hours and was never home. His mom's job was to make sure the house always looked perfect. Benji's dad wouldn't let them hire a maid, and Benji ordered his mom around the house as if she were a servant, but she didn't seem to mind. I guess it made her feel useful.

We lay on Benji's bed listening to Nirvana, hands in our pockets, heads barely touching. Next to us was a tray of freshly baked cookies Mrs. Connor had just served us, the chocolate soft and warm. Benji's cat, Freddie, was curled at our feet. The CD was a bootleg of Kurt Cobain laying down tracks in the studio, strumming an acoustic guitar and trying to work out what chords to use. We preferred to listen to bootleg recordings. They were raw and real, the distilled essence of the musician before the mixing desk came in and smoothed everything over. In the half light from Benji's lamp it was easy to imagine Kurt sitting in the corner of the room, head down, chipped fingernails picking at the strings of an old Martin guitar; but if you turned to look at him, he would disappear, dissolving into the air, and all that would be left were the last picked notes, floating into the night.

Benji sighed. I knew what was coming.

"I can't believe she got away with it," he moaned.

I groaned. "For the last time, the evidence pointing to Courtney is entirely circumstantial."

"How can you still believe her? Even after that documentary where they interviewed the bounty hunter? He swore Courtney hired him to kill Kurt."

"Benji, the dude had no teeth."

"Even so—how do you explain the amount of heroin that was in Cobain's system? He was so doped up that even medical experts say there is no way he could have lifted that gun and pulled the trigger."

"Ever heard of functioning junkies?"

"There's functioning and then there's superhuman. The woman's as guilty as OJ."

"Okay, hold up," I said, getting agitated. "You're just persecuting her because she's a strong woman who acts the way she wants to and doesn't give a shit what anyone thinks of her. You and the rest of society have cast her as the murdering wife because you don't know how else to handle her. She scares the crap out of you so you cut her down. She's not a murderer—she's a survivor."

Benji stretched back and pouted. "Yeah? Well her solo album sucked."

I sat up and looked around. Benji's walls were decorated with restraint, a poster here or there of one of his favorite bands, carefully framed. Green Day. Fall Out Boy. A large portion of the space was taken up by a glass cabinet filled with memorabilia and illuminated by spotlights. It was here that he kept his most prized possessions. A stone from Sharon Tate's fireplace. Phil Hartman's welcome mat, still dirty with his footprints. Pride of place was a script for the movie *Animal House* signed by John Belushi. The scrawl was barely recognizable, but Benji explained it away by saying Belushi must have been high at the time he signed it, which made the script worth even more to him. For Benji, Belushi under the influence and living on the edge was more valuable than the healthy, sober version.

I had my own collection at Aunt Lynette's, but it was much smaller and not as well organized. Lynette had not been expecting another occupant in her house, at least not one who would require an entire bedroom, so my living space was cramped compared to Benji's spacious quarters.

"What's your favorite Nirvana song?" Benji asked.

Another Benji trait. Always cataloging, passing a critical eye over everything. It was the disease of our generation. We were constantly distilling the world into lists, classifying our lives according to what was hot and what was not. Music. Movies. TV shows. Countries you most want to visit. A hundred and one things to do before you die. Ironically, the more obscure the list item, the greater the chance it had of being considered hot, which in turn would inevitably make it mainstream. It was a vicious cycle.

"'Smells Like Teen Spirit,'" I answered after some consideration.

"Amateur hour. Only people who have no understanding of Nirvana's work would make such an obvious choice."

"And what's yours, Lester Bangs?"

"'Radio Friendly Unit Shifter,'" he replied, citing one of their most obscure singles. He put his hands behind his head with smug satisfaction.

"You're a dick, Benji."

He leaped up and went to sit at his desk. Annoyed by Benji's sudden movement, Freddie the cat jumped off the bed and saun- tered off. In front of his PC and its enormous twin monitors, Benji squinted with concentration and clicked the mouse furiously. Mov- ing rapidly from one screen to the next were album covers that he'd cut and pasted and dumped into folders.

I turned on the TV and watched America's Next Top Models strut across the screen. I glanced down at my own body, not exactly chubby but definitely a little dumpy. I'd been wearing the same plain black T-shirt for days, and my jeans were tatty. Grooming had never been a priority with me. I usually threw on whatever was comfortable. With hippies for parents, I guess it couldn't have turned out any other way.

"What the hell are you doing?" I asked as Benji cursed under his breath.

"Looking for cover art," he said, not taking his eyes off the screen. "For my iPod. If the artwork is missing it ruins the effect, you know that."

"How many more covers do you have to download?"

"About five hundred."

"Five hundred! How long is it going to take you?"

"Not sure. I've been working on it for a few days. I reckon in a few more hours I'll have them all."

"Is it really that important?"

Benji swiveled in his chair. "Well, it's not cover *flow* if all the covers aren't there, is it?"

For a supposed punk, Benji was the most pedantic person I knew. He made sure his mom ironed his band T-shirts perfectly and that his cargo pants had creases. I stared at the ceiling. Sometimes when Benji and I were talking like this, a splinter of despair would work its way into my heart. I could feel the wasted moments ticking away, and wondered whether large portions of my life would be lost to inane conversations about cover art and whether Nirvana's mainstream hits were better than their B sides. Sometimes I felt like my head was so full of trivia, there was no room for anything of substance. I didn't care too much about it. The noise kept out things I would rather not think about, the dark thoughts that crept in all too often since my parents' accident.

"You wanna stay the night?" Benji asked, scratching at his arm as he spoke, like it was no big deal. Benji was always asking me to stay over, but I didn't anymore because I didn't want him to get the wrong idea. I used to stay over all the time. Mrs. Connor would make up the spare bedroom for me and fill my private bathroom with little unopened toiletries. It felt like staying in a hotel, and I'm sure if I'd picked up the phone in the middle of the night and asked for a sandwich I'd have probably gotten one. But I didn't stay over anymore.

"Nah, it's cool," I said. "Lynette's expecting me for dinner."

"Since when have you cared about that?"

"I don't care. I've just got shit to do. *Comprende*?"

"Whatever. You still up for tomorrow?"

Was he kidding? I had been looking forward to this expedition for ages. "Cielo Drive," I said.

"Cielo Drive," he repeated, and the name hung between us like a talisman.

"Benji?"

"Yes, Hilda?"

I looked at my nails, which were chewed and sore. "What do you suppose that guy was so nervous about today?"

"Nervous?"

"You know, the guy in Echo Park. Hank. The way he freaked out when we knocked on the door, it was like he was hiding something."

Benji didn't look up from the screen. "I dunno. Maybe he's got some unpaid bills. You know they can't turn off your electricity unless they tell you in person. They have to make sure you're not on dialysis or something. An electric company once cut off the supply to this old woman's house in winter, and she froze to death in her chair."

"No . . . it was something else. He seemed really scared, like he was expecting someone else."

"Maybe he's the Unabomber. Or a serial killer. Maybe he had pieces of dead bodies in his fridge. Anyway, what do you care?"

"I just think that maybe we should have stayed a bit longer. He seemed lonely."

Benji didn't respond. I looked over again at his collection of artifacts. The stones from Sharon Tate's fireplace were in a little Ziplock bag on a shelf by themselves. I stood up and walked over to the cabinet and emptied the stones into my palm.

"I saw an episode of *Ghost Chasers* last week," I said. "A woman bought a piano that turned out to be haunted. From the moment they had it in the house, all sorts of strange stuff started to happen.

They think the piano belonged to a gangster who used to slam people's fingers in it."

"So?"

"So maybe having all this stuff in our houses is bad luck."

"Hey, Hilda," Benji said, turning back to his computer. "You should see this video. It's a girl getting screwed to death by a horse."

I am the first to admit that my interests border on the macabre, but Benji's obsessions were without boundaries. I put the stones down and grabbed my bag.

"I'm out of here," I said, and Benji waved to me halfheartedly. As I walked to the door I heard the sound of a girl moaning in ecstasy; then the moans became groans, and then screams. I closed the bedroom door behind me, and smiled at Mrs. Connor on my way out.

4

THE DAY BENJI AND I became friends was the day the cat died.

Stanley Dale was the first to notice it. No one saw it happen but we all heard the sound, the sickening squeal of tires as the car slammed on its brakes, then sped off again.

"You guys! You've gotta come and see this!" Stanley yelled, gesturing toward the road. A small crowd gathered around him, screaming and pointing. I was on my way to the library when I heard the shouts. I followed the sounds, convinced Stanley was going to show us a dead bird or rat, or something equally disgusting. What he showed us was much worse.

The cat was still moving, flopping around on the roadside like a fish out of water. I couldn't tell if it was still alive or in the last throes of muscle spasm: its body was literally jumping into the air, and its blood was flying in thin spurts onto the asphalt. I squealed and put my hand to my mouth. Stanley hung over the fence like a monkey, and soon a large group of kids had gathered to see what the fuss was all about.

"Somebody do something!" I heard someone scream.

"What do you want me to do?" another kid yelled. "I'm not going to pick it up!"

There was nothing we could do. The cat was jerking so violently that there was no way anyone could have caught it. All we could do was hang over the side of the fence and stare.

"This is so awesome!" Stanley yelled. Someone punched him on the shoulder.

"Shut up, you retard. It's not funny!"

I looked around. Half the kids were laughing and pointing, the other half gazed on in shock.

"Look at the blood!"

"Is it dead?"

"Holy shit. Its guts are on the road."

"Should we get a teacher?"

Then I saw Benji. He was standing quietly at the edge of the crowd, his hands on his head, a look of horror on his face. We were in the same classes but had never spoken to each other. Benji was quiet and mopey, and would sit in the back on his own and stare out the window, only speaking when called on. He didn't stand out in his tight jeans and Morrissey T-shirts, but he didn't fit in, either.

I had my own problems. Everyone thought I was strange. I was the tragic girl whose parents had died suddenly, the one everyone whispered about but didn't know how to talk to. I wasn't interested in making friends, and spent my lunchtimes in the library, reading celebrity bios about tragic stars like Marlon Brando and Marilyn Monroe and staying away from groups and conversations, not revealing anything about myself and what had happened to me. So Benji and I had sailed past each other week after week, oblivious to each other's presence, until today.

The cat started to tire, its flops becoming heavier, until finally it lay on its side in the dirt, took a few shallow gasps of air, and died. I looked back at Benji. Two fat teardrops were making their way down his cheeks. Everyone quieted down, and an eerie silence descended on the scene. Suddenly Mr. Barrett appeared, blowing his whistle and trying to disperse the crowd. Mr. Barrett was a gym teacher who always wore short shorts, even in winter, and was known for picking students up by their sideburns.

"What's going on over here?" he bellowed. "Get away from the fence, all of you!"

"There's a dead cat on the road!" someone yelled.

Mr. Barrett made his way to the fence and peered over. Then, without a word, he strode off in the direction of the teachers' lounge, returning minutes later with a black garbage bag.

"Okay, show's over," he shouted. "All of you get out of here. Now!"

We began to wander off, a few of us lagging behind to take one last look at the carcass on the road. Mr. Barrett picked the cat up with his bare hands and threw it in the garbage bag. Benji didn't move. I heard some of the other kids chatting excitedly as they walked away.

"I've never seen anything dead," one of them said.

"I saw my grandma."

"I saw my uncle in a coma."

"Yeah, but he wasn't dead, was he? Doesn't really count."

Mr. Barrett swung the bag over his shoulder and strolled off toward the Dumpsters without a glance in our direction. I walked over and stood beside Benji, the tears now streaming silently down his face. I felt bad. Not because he was upset, but because he was doing what I desperately wanted to do. I wanted to curl in a little ball on the ground and cry for that poor cat, its beautiful tabby fur now hardened with dry blood. But I couldn't bring myself to. I had cried so much over the past few years, I was empty. But Benji cried openly and without fear. He cried as if he were alone.

"Are you okay?" I tentatively asked.

He didn't say anything. He turned to look at me, his eyes glistening. Then he ran off.

Lying in bed that night, all I could think about was the dead cat. I thrashed about in the heat, a tiny fan blowing ineffectually into my face. I thought about the Dumpster, how hot it was in there during summer. One day the other kids had thrown me in, amused by my indifference to their taunts and my refusal to fight back. They had closed the lid and suddenly everything was silent, black, and hot, like the inside of an oven. On an excursion to the Holocaust museum one day, an old lady told us about the furnaces, the places where they burned children alive, and I pictured that rustic green Dumpster at the back of the schoolyard, crouched in the sun, its mouth open.

I imagined that night what would happen when the trash was collected, how the cat's body would be compacted with soda cans and candy-bar wrappers until it was all one compressed block of rubbish. I wondered who its owners were, and whether someone was tapping on the side of a can with a spoon, calling its name. I remembered that Dumpster collection happened only once a week, and that the next collection was days away. I still had time.

The next day, under a blistering hot sun, I related my plan to Benji. We stood in the middle of the playing field watching our classmates play baseball. Mr. Barrett always sent the worst players as far away from the diamond as possible, where there was nothing to do but run after balls hit so far out that it didn't matter how slowly we threw them back. I was more than happy with this arrangement.

I sat on the grass, patted the ground next to me, and Benji reluctantly moseyed over, squatting beside me among the dandelions. We didn't say anything, just picked at the flowers and watched the players run in circles. Then Benji started to scratch at his face. Under the sun his pale skin was turning lobster red.

Someone hit a ball out of the field and everyone cheered. The boys ran to the fence and started climbing it. Mr. Barrett chased them from behind and yelled at them to get down.

"That was horrible yesterday," I said to Benji. "You know, what happened to that cat."

He waited, and for a while I thought he wasn't going to say anything. Then he spoke.

"I have a cat," he said. "Freddie Prinze."

"Freddie Prinze? You mean after the actor? The one who killed himself?"

Benji nodded. A loud *chock* sound echoed across the field and another ball sailed over our heads. Neither of us made any attempt to get up. Mr. Barrett yelled in our direction. I gave him a wave, and, defeated, he went to get another ball from his gym bag. Benji laughed. He tore at the dandelions in the ground and crushed them between his fingers.

"I hate Mr. Barrett," he said, his voice cold. "He deserves a bullet in the head."

"Teachers like him make you understand why Dylan Klebold and Eric Harris did what they did," I replied, not even thinking before the words tumbled out. "Columbine wasn't a very nice place to begin with, from what I've heard. I mean, killers aren't made in a vacuum, you know? I'm not saying what they did was right. It wasn't. I just hate how people call them evil and don't think about why they did it."

I didn't know whether he was going to call me crazy for sympathizing with the Columbine killers.

"Columbine had a history of bullying and repression," he said, as if reciting from a textbook. "The teachers had established a hierarchy that kept the jocks at the top and everyone else on the bottom. What they did—Dylan and Eric—was a political act, like in the French revolution."

I was stunned, and kind of relieved. I had never heard anyone say something like that about Columbine. My aunt Lynette always said the world was a better place now that "those sociopathic monsters" had blown their own heads off.

"This place is just as bad," Benji continued. "Nothing but a bunch of jocks and cheerleaders."

I thought again of the cat baking in its metal coffin. "Would you be interested in coming on an expedition?" I asked.

Benji looked suspicious. "What kind of expedition?"

"I'm going to help the cat that got hit by the car," I said. "I'm going to save it."

"How can you save it? It's dead."

This was true. Still, I believed that dead things were not beyond dignity. And I was still alive and could do something about the way the cat had been literally thrown away. The whole incident had made me feel indescribably dirty, like a rubbernecker at the site of a car crash. I wanted nothing more than to get clean.

"Are you in or are you out?" I asked. Benji looked at his classmates, all the jocks and princesses and people we would never be like.

"I guess I'll help you," he muttered, as if he were doing me an enormous favor. "There's nothing on TV tonight anyway."

Benji met me at the Dumpster after class. We waited until the other students had left and the school was deserted. The Dumpster was hot to touch, but luckily the handles had been shadowed by the towering oaks above it. I took this as a sign that the natural world was pleased with my plan, that it too knew the importance of setting things right.

If Benji was nervous, he didn't show it. As I struggled to lift the side of the lid, he took the other end without being asked, and together we hoisted the Dumpster open and let the top bang noisily against the classroom wall. Immediately we smelled the cat, a cloying, decaying stench that slapped our faces. I covered my mouth with my hand. Benji heaved himself over the side and stuck his head in.

"I can see it," he yelled. "Its paw's sticking out of the bag. I'm going in."

He threw his legs over and disappeared into the darkness. I waited in the cool breeze until the garbage bag appeared over the side, wet and torn, fur poking from a hole. I took the bag from Benji and gently laid it on the ground, trying not to look at the contents. Benji vaulted over the side of the Dumpster and landed with a thud in the dirt.

"Careful," I said as he steadied himself inches from the bag. "You nearly jumped on it."

"My cousin accidentally jumped on a puppy once. He was on the top of his bunk bed and the puppy was on the floor and he didn't see it. He landed right on its stomach and its guts came out of its mouth."

"Benji! That's horrible."

He frowned. "Well, it happened. Just 'cause you don't wanna hear about bad stuff doesn't mean it doesn't happen."

This I knew. Another reason I never talked about my parents' accident was to spare myself and everyone around me the gory details. I knelt and opened the bag carefully, sticking my hand inside. The cat's head lolled out, limp and lifeless. I jumped back and shrieked.

"Geez, what a girl," Benji said. "Give it to me."

He pushed me aside and crouched over the cat, lifting the head gently. Its eyes were closed and it looked peaceful, like it was asleep. I'd had nightmares about its eyes being open and was terrified that if I tore open the bag it would be staring at me. Benji felt around its neck for a collar and discovered a small blue name tag.

"Oscar," he read. "Twelve Paige Street."

We spoke little as we walked, the cat in the bag swinging between us. I started to feel a little like someone who worked for the government and was going to tell someone that their son had died at war. We arrived at the address to find a cozy little bungalow with a small front yard and no fence. As we walked up the path to the front door, my heart sank. On the stairs were a plastic water dish and a ceramic food bowl, some tuna still in it. I rang the bell. The door opened and a young woman stood in front of us, a friendly smile on her face.

"Yes?" she said politely. "Can I help you?"

"Do you have a cat named Oscar?" I asked.

"Sure do. Didn't come home last night. Don't tell me he's been pestering you for food. He's such a cheeky boy."

I handed her the bag. I explained how Oscar had been hit by a car, and told her he had not suffered. It was just like with my parents' accident: it was best to spare the gory details. Gory details never made anything better. The woman cried, but she was brave and tried to hide her tears by smiling through them. She stepped forward and hugged me, then Benji, who cringed at her touch.

"You are both such good kids," she said. "Good kids. Thank you so much for bringing home my baby."

She closed the door, and Benji and I started the long walk home. I didn't feel like a good kid. I knew we had done the right thing, but something was niggling inside, a worm burrowing its way through my core. I hated to admit how exciting it had been to stand outside that Dumpster, breathing the fetid stench of the cat's remains. The smell was familiar, comforting. After my parents died, Aunt Lynette had tried to get my life back to normal as quickly as possible, and for a while everything *did* seem normal. I went to school, did my homework, watched TV. But something inside me had changed. In quiet moments I could feel it, a creeping anxiety that would overtake me—the realization that everything was temporary, fleeting, and no one was safe. In the shadow of my parents I had felt protected, but once they were gone I was horribly exposed, and as much as Lynette tried to make me feel safe, she couldn't erase what I knew to be terrifyingly, irrevocably true: that any one of us could be taken at any moment, and I sometimes couldn't help thinking that in escaping the fate of my parents, I had somehow cheated death, and that death would now always be with me.

It could have been my imagination, but I was sure Benji had lingered awhile in the darkness of that Dumpster, taking his time before returning to the fading sunlight of the afternoon. I watched him as we walked together. He was immersed in thought, staring at his sneakers as they hit the pavement. Like archaeologists excavating a tomb, Benji and I had crossed over an unspoken boundary and emerged forever changed by the experience. He looked at me, eyes ablaze, and somewhere in the distance a dog howled.

"So why did you name your cat Freddie Prinze?" I asked.

Benji shrugged. "Don't know. I'm just really interested in that stuff, I guess. You know, dead movie stars and all that."

"Me too! I'm reading a book about Marlon Brando right now."

"Oh man, Marlon Brando had such a shit life."

"I know. His son shot his daughter's boyfriend, then his daughter committed suicide. It's horrible."

Benji gave me a wry look. "You ever seen the house where it happened?"

"You mean the house on Mulholland Drive? I think I drove past it once. The numbers are confusing."

"I know exactly which one it is," Benji said, sounding excited for the first time since we met. "We should go check it out."

"Totally," I said. "That would be so cool."

We walked along in silence, hands in our pockets, and even though I felt that familiar darkness starting to swirl around me, for once I didn't feel so alone. I knew I had found a kindred spirit.

5

I LEFT BENJI TO THE video of the girl getting screwed by the horse and started to walk the few blocks to my house. The warm air, coupled with the start of summer vacation, had brought people out of their homes. Across the road a couple walked a teacup poodle on a thin leash. A group of kids skateboarded past me, the wheels of their boards making a long, rolling sound like an incoming wave, building to a crescendo and then disappearing as they sped away into the dark.

My mind wandered. I looked into the windows of houses, some in shadow, others illuminated by the light of television sets. I thought about the Manson Family. On nights like this they would go out and do what they called a "creepy crawly." A group of four or five Family members would target a house entirely at random, break in, and proceed to "creep" around the place. The idea was to move around the house unnoticed, making sure not to wake the occupants. Occasionally they would take something, like cash, if it was left lying around, or food to feed the Family back at the ranch. But it was more about moving around undetected—the excitement and power that came with infiltrating someone's house as he slept in his bed.

Richard Ramirez—the Night Stalker—was one of Los Angeles' most infamous serial killers, and also favored neighborhoods like this. The neatly trimmed hedges and manicured front lawns were a far cry from the bleakness and despair of downtown LA, where he regularly scored drugs at the bus terminal and slept in whatever car he had stolen at the time. The suburbs made the Night Stalker angry, just like they did the Manson Family. The warm little houses in tidy rows were a reminder of every comfort Ramirez didn't have. The order of suburbia affronted his need for chaos.

Aunt Lynette's house was a spacious beige California bungalow with a large front yard and an old-fashioned porch. The light was on in the living room, and I could just imagine Lynette bent over her books, a glass of red wine in her hand. From a distance she looked just like my mother, with her hair hanging loose and those thick-rimmed glasses. It wasn't until you got closer that her features became her own. Green eyes instead of brown. A mole on her chin where my mother had none. From a distance I could imagine it was my mother, and for a brief moment everything was as it used to be. But the closer I got, the more reality came crashing back.

Aunt Lynette and I were always being mistaken for mother and daughter, something that made us both equally uncomfortable. It was easier not to correct people, as that would involve going into details, something neither of us wanted to do. But there was no denying the family resemblance. The same round face, the same large, Kewpie-doll eyes. I didn't get much from my dad's side of the family, except a healthy suspicion of authority that my teachers liked to call an "attitude problem."

Aunt Lynette was an assistant district attorney. She prosecuted people on behalf of the county, regardless of whether or not she thought they were guilty. This didn't seem to bother her. She'd worked hard all her life to make it this far, and whether or not clients were guilty was largely irrelevant to her career. She had prosecuted battered wives and mothers, and sent innocent men to jail. But still she slept well at night. All that seemed to matter to her was that she was doing her job effectively.

Lynette also had the alarming habit of flashing her DA badge. Once when I was nine she took me to Disneyland, and two guys got into an argument in the line at Splash Mountain. She pushed through the crowd, walked straight up to them, flipped open her little leather wallet, and watched the blood drain from their faces. No one even looked closely enough at her badge to see that she was an assistant DA and not actually a cop. The two men held up their hands and stepped back as if she was going to taser them or perhaps cuff them to the fence, where they'd have to listen to "Zip-a-Dee-Doo-Dah" all day long. I remember being mortified and hiding behind a corn dog stand as everybody stared at her. Lynette wasn't fazed by the attention. She was proud of working for the county.

As I walked in the front door, she looked up from her casebooks. Next to her on the dining table were two plates, one stacked high with some kind of casserole, the other scraped empty.

"I've already eaten," I said as I kicked off my shoes. Lynette looked at the casserole, brown and congealing on her fine china. I watched her swallow her anger.

"What did you and Benji get up to today?" she asked, choosing to ignore the casserole situation.

"Just stuff."

"Oh, really?" She put her pen down. "What kind of stuff?"

I opened the fridge and took out a carton of milk. "Went to Universal Studios, took the tram tour. Can I take this?"

She didn't say anything, just nodded, then looked down at her books. "I saw the most horrible thing on *Oprah* today."

"Hmmm?"

"They had a story about a woman whose car was stolen, and her baby was still in the backseat. She tried to grab the baby, but the car sped off, her child still hanging out, attached to the car seat. She watched her child being dragged along the side of the road."

"That's a repeat."

Lynette pursed her lips. "Stories like that make you put your life in perspective," she continued. "Make you realize how lucky you really are."

"Just another day for you and me in paradise."

She examined me through her thick, black-rimmed lenses. "Have you done something to your hair?"

"It's pink."

"So it is. Do you like it?"

"I just love it."

"Good. As long as you're happy."

I leaned over her casebooks. "What are you working on?"

"It's a murder case," she said as she scribbled something down on her notepad. "It's gang related."

"Cool. Got any crime-scene photos?"

She put her pen down and adjusted her glasses. "Hilda, I find your fascination with murder a little disconcerting. This is a very sad and horrific crime."

"But you said it was gang related."

"So?"

"So then he probably had it coming."

She took her glasses off and rubbed her eyes. "Life isn't as black and white as that, Hilda," she said, sounding annoyed. "It's not fair for you to judge other people when you have no idea what they've been through, the social and economic circumstances they were born into—"

"All right, you don't have to give me a sermon. I'm not the jury."

"Thank God for that," she said, putting her glasses back on and straightening up. "Then the poor boy would have no hope."

"Anyway, you're the one obsessed with murder, not me. You made a career out of it."

"I'm not obsessed with murder, Hilda. I'm helping people."

"Come on, just one look . . ."

I tried to slide one of the case folders away with my finger, but Lynette snatched it back.

"No, Hilda. Trust me when I say you are better off not seeing this."

I had never viewed any of Lynette's case files. She kept them under lock and key and never once made the mistake of accidentally leaving one out. She obviously had no idea what I had access to on the Internet.

"You're probably right," I said, giving up. "Wouldn't want to warp me now, would we?"

I was halfway out of the room when Lynette spoke again. "You know, we could feed a third-world country with the amount of dinners I've made for you and you've never eaten. It's very wasteful."

"Sorry."

"I hope you had a proper meal at the Connors."

"Sure did," I lied, my stomach still full of Mrs. Connor's chocolate-chip cookies.

"Well, I hope you're more thankful toward Mrs. Connor than you are to me. I'd be very embarrassed if you weren't."

I went back over to where Lynette was sitting and gave her a kiss on the forehead. "I said I'm sorry."

I felt her soften. "Next time call," she said, still trying to sound mad.

"Okay," I yelled over my shoulder as I left the room, taking the milk carton with me.

6

OHN BELUSHI ONCE SAID that happiness is not a state you want to be in all the time. I knew what he meant. He was talking about the uncontrollable urge to fuck it all up, the desire to put a knife in the toaster of existence just to see what would happen. To put a bomb under your blessings and watch them blow sky-high. To swan dive off the precipice and give in to the free fall.

Belushi had it all: money, fame, a wife, a home. But he didn't want to live in the safety of these creature comforts. He wanted to exist on the knife's edge, the sharpest point of the blade, where you could fall either way—the only guarantee being that you will inevitably get cut. He rolled the dice, tossed the coin, shook his tail feather in the face of death until the reaper lost his sense of humor. The punch line was a big fat speedball to the heart, a massive dose of heroin and coke that left him dead in an expensive hotel room in Los Angeles, bloated and bleeding on freshly laundered linen thousands of miles from home.

I sat down at my desk and watched footage on the Internet: the old CBS newsreel—all grainy and washed-out—from the day Belushi died, posted on a fan's website. A swarm of photographers milled outside Belushi's bungalow at the Chateau Marmont; the coroner, grim-faced, wheeled his body out on a gurney. That famous toga was now a death shroud: a thin, white sheet covering his body and pulled up over his head in an attempt to give dignity to the unmistakable girth beneath. For some people this unpleasant image would have been enough, but I wanted more. I wanted to see autopsy photos: the incisions made by the coroner's blade, the thick, careless stitches that left the deceased looking like Frankenstein's monster. But what I wanted to see most was an image from the inner sanctum: the photographs of Belushi lying dead in his hotel bed, his naked body seeping gas and fluid onto the sheets. This was the money shot, the point of impact where life abruptly ended. To see how a celebrity looked at the very moment of passing, that mysterious instant where life just stopped. This was what I lived for.

Before my parents died, I never even knew pictures like that existed. It was at their funeral that I heard someone whisper it, a family friend who I barely even knew. He leaned over to the person sitting beside him and said, "Kinda like Jayne Mansfield, huh?" At the time I had no idea what he was talking about, but his words stuck with me. In our first few weeks together, Aunt Lynette took me to the local library to get me some books to keep me occupied, and instead of staying in the children's section, I somehow found my way over to the movie star bios and checked out a book called *Hollywood Babylon,* which told me the whole story about what had happened to Jayne Mansfield. It was then that I realized what the person at my parents' funeral had meant, but strangely enough, knowing that Jayne Mansfield had been through what my parents had didn't make me feel bad at all. It made me feel strangely comforted. Jayne Mansfield was a *Playboy* Playmate and actress, a cheaper, gaudier version of Marilyn Monroe. She died when the car she was traveling in hit the back of a truck in poor light, allegedly decapitating her and killing the two men beside her while her children sat in the backseat. Now, when I started to feel that familiar anxiety starting to grow, that feeling that death was upon me, lurking, I would look at a picture of Jayne Mansfield in the front of that car, and everything would seem okay. Death didn't just come for me, or my parents, it came for everyone: the rich and famous, the beautiful and privileged. The thought made me relax, and I imagined the relief I felt was similar to the feeling some people got when they cut themselves. I didn't have it in me to be a cutter (too squeamish), so this was my anxiety release. Looking at these pictures kept me sane.

I checked in at the Celebrity Autopsy Room. The website was run by an anonymous webmaster who called himself the Coroner. He had set up a Frequently Asked Questions section to try and impede the flow of disgust leveled his way. *Yes,* he posted, *I can live with myself. No, I don't know what it's like to lose a loved one, but I'm sure it's terrible. No, I am not being disrespectful to the dead, if anything I am preserving their legacy by showing the truth of their final days. No, I will not post a photograph of myself on the website, as it will only assist those of you with vigilante justice in mind to track me down and beat me with a baseball bat, as you have threatened to do so many times before. Yes, if you have any photos of dead celebrities, please send them to me. No fakes, please—after so long in the business, I can tell the difference.*

I logged on to the chat room and posted a question asking

whether anyone had seen a photograph of John Belushi dead. There were some high-profile celebrities who were fortunate enough never to have photographs of their bloated, distended corpses find their way onto the Internet. Phil Hartman was one, which I attributed to the fact that he was so well liked in the press and no one had the stomach to publish photos of such a likable guy with his head blown off. Another was Kurt Cobain. Sure, there was that famous shot taken through the window of the greenhouse in which Kurt's dead, lifeless leg can clearly be seen, a Converse sneaker on his foot. But actual photographs of his full dead body had never surfaced. I'd read that the impact of the shotgun blast blew half his head off. I guess it would be difficult to prove that the exploded head in a picture was actually Kurt's and not some other poor, unfortunate individual's.

I checked the message board. A couple of people claimed they had seen photographs of Belushi's autopsy on the Internet, but when I clicked the links to take me to the photos, I was redirected to porn sites. Most people pointed me in the direction of photos of Chris Farley's death, which had been readily available on the Internet for years. Chris Farley was a *Saturday Night Live* comedian who wanted to emulate his idol Belushi in any way possible, even if it meant dying like him. Farley died of a drug overdose at the age of thirty-three, exactly the same age Belushi was when he took the speedball that ended his life.

The photos of Chris Farley showed him lying on the floor of his Chicago apartment, his face purple and bloated, a large, white bubble coming out of his mouth. The bubble was so solid-looking it resembled a mouth gag, so people often mistook his death for an S and M ritual gone horribly wrong. In reality the white stuff was his stomach coming out of his mouth, pushed up by the toxicity of the drugs. The photos were good and graphic, but still a distant second to the footage of Belushi's body being wheeled from the Chateau. Belushi was an original that Farley had failed to measure up to, no matter how hard he had tried. Their deaths had both been sad and pointless.

MY ROOM DEPRESSED ME. Lynette wouldn't let me stick posters up because she didn't want the wallpaper ruined. As a compromise she bought me a corkboard, which hung like a lonely blank canvas in the middle of the room. To show I wouldn't be placated, I'd never stuck anything on it. Occasionally I'd find a note from Lynette pinned to it about remembering to do my homework, or wishing me a good day at school, but I always took it down. The only thing she pinned up there that I hadn't thrown away was a recent article about the Manson Family parole hearings that she'd cut from a newspaper. I kept that, another slice of LA's morbid history, in a drawer.

My own little collection of artifacts wasn't as carefully laid out as Benji's, or as well presented, and I didn't have lights or even a cabinet, just a single shelf on my wall that once housed Lynette's case files. I picked up my treasures one by one. A jar of dirt from underneath the Hollywood sign, a T-shirt that a guy at a flea market told me belonged to Karen Carpenter. I carefully handled a single long-stemmed rose that was now all dried and flaky. I'd taken it from Marilyn Monroe's grave. There were hundreds of them there, and it wasn't as if she could enjoy them anyway. I'd grabbed it and run, while the other tourists tutted behind me, and some angry lady told me to stop. But I kept running. It wasn't like they really cared about Marilyn, not the way I did. I figured Marilyn would understand why I did it, and that was all that mattered to me. Everyone else was just a hypocrite.

I picked up a bracelet of tacky plastic beads, all different colors, and put it on. At one time it had been way too large and would hang off my wrist like a hula hoop, but now it nearly fitted. Mom didn't care that they were cheap and gaudy beads, she just loved the colors: the blues and reds and oranges that danced on her wrist. She didn't care what anyone else thought about her. As long as she was enjoying herself and wasn't hurting anyone, everything was fine. I wanted to be just the same way. I was never going to let anyone tell me how to live, what I could and couldn't do, what was *acceptable*. I took the bracelet off, placed it gently back on the shelf, and went to bed.

7

THE NEXT MORNING BENJI and I once again made our way toward Hollywood. The heat was stifling, the sun blazing like it was the apocalypse. I wound down the window and breathed in the city air, a familiar mix of smoke and gasoline. Brush fires in the north had left a brown haze across the horizon and smoke drifted dreamily over the surrounding hills. We didn't give it a second's thought. Something was always burning in Los Angeles.

I leafed through Benji's copy of *Hollywood Hell*, the pages yellow and well thumbed. It was a pocketbook guide to LA's seedier tourist attractions, offering tourists an alternative to the corporate, predetermined tourist traps like Disneyland and Universal Studios. Listed in its pages was information on Hollywood's sordid, secret past, with detailed maps to guide the way. There was no listing for Grauman's Chinese Theatre, no directions to Knott's Berry Farm. Instead you could find the location of the Beverly Hills house where Lana Turner's daughter killed her mother's boyfriend, the infamous standover man Johnny Stompanato. The apartment where the actor from *seaQuest* hanged himself. The street where Robert Blake's wife was shot.

We drove to Leimert Park, where the Black Dahlia's body was found in 1947. The Black Dahlia was a young actress struggling to make it in Hollywood. She was a transient floating from one lonely part of Los Angeles to the next, hanging out with sailors and letting strange men buy her meals. Her naked body was found in a vacant lot close to the side of the road, severed at the waist and drained of blood. Cigarette burns covered her breasts, a piece of flesh was carved from her side, and her mouth had been slashed into the shape of a grin with a sharp object, most likely a straight razor. It was the most horrific crime Los Angeles had ever seen, and it haunts the city to this very day.

Benji and I got out of the car and stood next to the spot where her body had been found. The vacant lot had been replaced by a neat row of family homes; the exact spot where her body was discovered was now a driveway. A kid's bike lay on its side on the front lawn, its back wheel spinning slowly in the air. Benji and I stood side by side, entranced. Benji was infatuated with the Black Dahlia. Many were. She was the epitome of the untouched innocent destroyed by the evils of Hollywood. With her ravishing black hair and full, pouting lips, her mysterious death was an obsession Los Angeles couldn't quite shake off.

Benji stared at the spot where her body had been discarded. An old man walked his dog across the road, watching us with suspicion, and the tiny dog started yapping in our direction. The man was old enough to know what had happened here and why two teenagers dressed in black where standing at the side of the road, staring at the sidewalk. He could see right through us. The little dog kept yapping and I felt the urge to flee, ashamed that we had roused such awful memories on such a beautiful sunny day. I didn't blame him for being angry. Wherever we went we stirred up memories people had been trying to forget, brought darkness back to what were now nice neighborhoods. Benji pulled out his camera and took a picture of the sidewalk.

"Time to go," I said. The old man and his dog were still watching us. Benji took one more photo, then reluctantly got back in the car.

"Did you hear about that new book?" Benji asked as we drove away. "Apparently John Huston was involved in the Black Dahlia's murder."

"John Huston?"

"Yeah."

"The director of *The Maltese Falcon*?"

"Yeah."

"Father of Anjelica and the perpetually underrated Danny?"

"What's your point?"

"My point is, every day there is a new book about who killed the Black Dahlia. One day it's an evil abortionist, the next it's some vagrant who later burned to death in a hotel room."

"But Huston could have done it. You could see it in his eyes. When he was in *Chinatown* he totally freaked me out. That guy is one evil dude."

"Benji, he was playing a role in a movie! Do you think Anthony Hopkins really bites people's faces off?"

Benji found a spot of dirt on the dashboard and wiped it off with a wetted finger. "All I'm saying is, to play a role like that in

Chinatown, a guy so evil, and to do it so well, you've gotta have something going on inside. He had it in him. He could have done it."

"Yeah, and Christopher Reeve was faster than a speeding bullet in that wheelchair."

Many of the sites listed in the guidebook were now gone or had been altered forever. Hotels were now car parks. Schwab's Pharmacy, where a young composer scribbled "Over the Rainbow" on a napkin while Lana Turner sipped malts in the back booth, was now a strip mall. The last place that James Dean ever lived, a large house in Sherman Oaks, had been renovated until it was unrecognizable.

We stopped at a food stand on Ventura Boulevard and bought French dip sandwiches for lunch. The stand was next to a florist that was used in our favorite TV show, *Six Feet Under*. We sat beneath an umbrella and watched the cars come and go, loading up with bouquets and posies. Benji dripped mustard on his Nine Inch Nails T-shirt and swore.

Our next stop was the highlight of the day, the one we had been waiting for. We drove through Laurel Canyon and past the Canyon Country Store, an iconic grocery shop frequented by rock gods like Jim Morrison, who would drink orange juice on the patio before scoring drugs from the neighborhood dealer in the parking lot. We only caught a glimpse of the ruins of Houdini's mansion, set high up on Laurel Canyon Boulevard above the racing traffic, obscured by trees. The staircase that led to the mansion fell haphazardly down the cliff face, the servant quarters the only part of the house still remaining. I had read on the Internet that many believed Houdini still haunted the ruins of his mansion, and that the walls of his Hollywood Hills home would forever be the only ones he would never escape.

To me the Hollywood Hills were beautiful, wild, and deadly. This was where coyotes attacked the pets of movie stars, where George Reeves went upstairs during a party at his house on Benedict Canyon Drive and shot himself. Errol Flynn held orgies at his infamous House of Pleasure, and speeding cars regularly ran off the road along Mulholland Drive, plunging down the cliff face. As we drove up Laurel Canyon, cars hurtled back down the hill at terrifying speeds, and a passing truck nearly took off one of our side mirrors. On the radio Courtney Love sang about flying away to Malibu. There were always songs about our town on the radio. Even with the murders and the rapes and the car jackings and the earthquakes, the radio played songs like "L.A. Woman" and "California Dreaming," convincing us that this was the only place we would ever want to be.

We drove past quaint chateaux and larger, more extravagant homes. Cielo Drive was easy to find. A brand-new street sign had been erected higher than the others, to discourage theft. Another sign, NOT A THROUGH STREET, was erected next to it. The houses were inconspicuous in their plainness; lawns were trimmed and walls whitewashed. Two neighbors stood on the corner, coffees and papers in hand, oblivious to the scrutiny of the world and the prying eyes of curiosity seekers. One of them tipped his cap to the other and set off at a jog, sneakers hitting the pavement. Above them the sky turned gray and threatened rain.

"Here," Benji said, pointing to a concealed driveway. "This looks like it."

We made a tight turn onto a dirt road with a sharp and steady incline. After a few houses, we came across a wooden sign that read PRIVATE DRIVEWAY and listed five house numbers, each one carved on a quaint piece of oak and hung one above the other. The house number we were looking for changed every six months, moving up or down a digit, and Benji had been careful to check the latest incarnation on the Internet before our trip. We came to the end of the road and stopped at a set of gates higher than the others, the walls flanked by security cameras. Benji shut off the engine and picked up his camera. I sat back in my seat, overwhelmed.

"Are you coming?" Benji asked impatiently. I opened my door, hoisted myself out into the gray day, and shivered.

On a hot August evening in 1969, actress Sharon Tate and four other people were murdered in her home by the Manson Family. Sharon was pregnant, and her baby did not survive. All that remained of the house where she lived and died was the original telephone pole; everything else had been leveled. I touched the stone of the gate with an outstretched hand. It was still warm from the morning's sunlight, had not yet cooled under the rain clouds that had started to gather. I placed my face against it, felt the thick texture, and ran my hand along its surface. Sharon Tate was only twenty-six when she died. A millionaire had bought the property a few years ago and destroyed the old house, erecting a modern structure in its place. I had seen photographs of Sharon Tate and her friends dead in the front yard and the living room. Now the places where their bodies had lain had been smoothed over, purged of demons.

I listened. The canyons loomed around us, silent and patient. I was sad that so little remained in the spot where it actually happened. Since my parents died, I had come to believe that life was made up of energy. When someone committed a violent act, that energy would become even stronger, fueled by anger and hatred, fear and desperation. That energy wouldn't dissipate. It could hang in the air, even years later. The canyons were the perfect place for that kind of energy. The hills trapped the impulses inside, where they fermented, growing stronger every day. I could feel it in the ground. It ran through my hands like bolts of electricity. It reminded me of the day my parents died, the static that hung in the air that night, the darkness that had followed me ever since, and for one brief moment I felt closer to them. I was back there.

I shook my head, trying to clear my thoughts. I heard the whir of a surveillance camera as it zeroed in on me.

"Better go," Benji said, putting the lens cap back on his camera. We got back in the car and drove away. My head didn't clear until we were back amid the noise and traffic on Sunset Boulevard.

8

LATER THAT NIGHT I sat in my bedroom browsing through websites about the Manson Family. Leslie Van Houten was up for parole again. There was no way she would be released, even after thirty-seven years in prison. All the Manson Family murderers who were put on death row had their sentences commuted when California abolished the death penalty, but there was no way any of them would ever get paroled. Murderers like that became part of the public consciousness, part of our collective nightmare. Kill an unarmed grocer in a robbery gone wrong and you might get twenty years. But if you kill John Lennon, you can be pretty sure you're never seeing the light of day again.

Lynette was working late as usual, and the house was quiet. All the lights were off except for a small desk lamp above my computer. I was looking at a photo of Leslie Van Houten in her jail manacles when the phone rang.

"Hello?" I said.

A voice filled with gravel snapped back. "HUH?"

I waited. "Uh . . . hello?"

"Is this Hilda?"

"Yes it is. Who's this?"

"This is Hank."

My mind was blank. "I'm sorry, who?"

"HANK!" the voice boomed back. "From Echo Park."

"Echo Park?"

"You came to my place, you and your friend with the camera. You took photos of my bathroom."

My mouth went dry. I sat there for a moment, stunned, the receiver frozen in my hand. "How did you get this number?" I asked, already knowing the answer.

"I called that wiseass friend of yours," Hank said. "He left his card with me. I called and he gave me your number."

"I'm sure he did," I said under my breath.

"So I was thinking I'd call," Hank continued, now sounding a little unsure of himself. "I figured I had something you'd like to see."

Great. Now I was getting obscene phone calls from senior citizens. "Not interested," I said. "I mean, really, I'm flattered, but you're not quite my type, get what I'm saying?"

"No! Not like that, for Christ's sake," Hank yelled, and I jerked the phone away from my ear.

"All right, all right," I said. "Calm down."

"I meant like the sink," he said, sounding frustrated. "The sink in the bathroom you wanted to see. I got something like that for you."

"Then why don't you give it to Benji, you know, the guy who

was with me?" I suggested, not really relishing the idea of going over to the apartment in Echo Park on my own. "He said he was interested if you ever wanted to sell anything."

"'Cause it's not for him! It's for you!"

"You know what? This is very nice of you, mister—"

"HANK! MY NAME'S HANK!"

"—Hank, but I can't come over. I don't have a car."

He sighed. "Well, uh, why can't you get a cab?" he said, looking for alternatives. "There's plenty of cabs in this town."

I scrambled for excuses. "It's more complicated than that," I said, hoping my vagueness would make him give up. I was wrong.

"It's as complicated as you wanna make it. What I got, I think you'll like. I think you'll like it a hell of a lot."

I don't know what came over me, whether it was the darkness of the house, the silence, or merely curiosity about what was on offer. Maybe it had something to do with the feeling that after the accident I had no control over what happened to me in this life, so I might as well throw myself over to fate. Hank waited on the other end of the line, his breathing raspy. Jesus, I thought. He'll probably kill me. Chop me up over all those old newspapers in his apartment.

"Well, all right," I said, against my better judgement. "Just don't try anything. I'll be telling people where I'm going."

"I said it ain't like that. You will get a kick out of this. Trust me."

"When?"

"I'm an old man. I ain't got all the time in the world."

I rifled through an imaginary diary in my head, every page blank. Benji had mentioned a dentist appointment he had the next day. "I suppose I could squeeze in some time tomorrow."

"Done!" Hank cried, and slammed down the phone.

Done. I looked around my room, the sound of the dial tone still echoing in my ear. I looked again at the photograph of Leslie Van Houten. When she was first convicted, she was just another gangly hippie teenager with scraggy brown hair, a glint of mischief in her eye. Now she was an old lady, her face gaunt, gray hair pulled back in a tight, old-fashioned bun. She had put a pillowcase over dress-shop owner Rosemary LaBianca's head, tied it with electrical cord, and held her down while another Family member stabbed her in the stomach with a knife.

I wondered if she thought it was all worth it now. Fate or no fate, I wondered if in agreeing to meet with Hank I was getting myself into something I was going to regret.

9

THE NEXT DAY I took a cab to Echo Park. It was going to cost a fortune, but I couldn't bring myself to take the bus. There was something unsavory about riding public transportation in Los Angeles. All I could think of was the song by Billy Idol about the killer traveling on the bus, reading books about murder and thinking about his next victim. It was the Night Stalker's favorite song. He'd play it on his Walkman as he skulked through people's yards, looking for an unlocked window or open pet door. Anyway, I didn't really have to worry about money. Lynette made enough as an assistant DA to give me a healthy allowance that kept me quiet and out of her hair.

The driver turned on the radio and the Ramones were playing. I couldn't believe that three of the band members were dead already. It sucked.

"Can you turn it up?" I asked. The cabbie turned a knob, and the Ramones and their special brand of frenetic punk rock blasted throughout every corner of the cab.

"Pretty rockin', huh?" the cabbie yelled over the music.

"Hell yeah."

"Most girls your age, they like the pop music, you know? Britney Spears. Christina Aguilera. They don't like the good stuff. They think Maroon Five is rock and roll. I got more if you like."

The cabbie put in a CD of hard rock hits—AC/DC, Nine Inch Nails, Metallica. We drove down the freeway, the music battling against the sounds of traffic. Fifteen minutes later we pulled up outside the drab apartment building in Echo Park. The same mail catalogs were still on the lawn, dry and brittle like fossils. As I paid the driver and handed him his tip, he looked at me with concern.

"You okay?" he asked, looking up at the apartment building. "You need me to wait?"

I considered it for a moment. "No, I'm fine. Thanks for the tunes."

The cabbie shook his head and drove off, which didn't make me feel any better about this little expedition. I looked up at Hank's apartment. Unlike the day before, the curtains were wide open, which made me feel a little better about being there. At least if I screamed it would be carried on the wind.

"YOU!"

I jumped. Hank was hanging out the window, waving.

"Hello," I called, waving back.

"Come up! Come up!" he said, motioning with his arms. "For Christ's sake, don't just stand there!"

"Uh, okay."

I walked up the stairs. The front door was already open when I got to the top; Hank was standing there in a pair of white shorts and a blue Hawaiian shirt. He looked better than the first day I met him. His hair was wet, like he'd just jumped out of the shower, and he smelled of aftershave. He waved me in. "Hurry. Come one, get inside. Quickly."

"I'm Hilda," I said as I stepped inside, knowing it was a dumb thing to say as soon as it slipped out of my mouth, but I couldn't help it. I was nervous.

"I know who you are," he barked. "What the hell you think I've been standing up here waving my arms for? Get inside, quick!"

Hank threw the door closed behind me, but not before giving one last look outside as if he suspected I'd been followed. The apartment, much like Hank, was cleaner than it had been the day before. The bottles had been cleared away and the ashtrays emptied, but for all the effort that had been made, the smell of alcohol still hung in the air. I had to admit, though, that with the curtains open and the breeze coming in, the place seemed much nicer, more inviting. I stood in the doorway as Hank dashed to the kitchen and scooped the kettle off the stove. On the counter were two matching cups and saucers, and I noticed the dishes had been washed and were sitting in a rack by the kitchen window, drying in the sun. Hank poured us tea and brought the cups carefully into the living room.

"Don't just stand there like a freakin' hat rack," he growled as he balanced the two cups in his hands. "Sit down."

I took a seat on the edge of the dusty old couch, not wanting to get too close. I was still unsure of Hank's intentions, and decided it was best to play it safe. Again I looked around the room. No easy exits. The door was locked, but if I needed to I could jump out the window, and the worst that could happen is that I'd break a few bones. As death became an everyday part of my life, I began to be curious about people who put themselves in situations where their demise seemed almost inevitable. The wife who gives her violent husband a second chance. The girlfriend who lets her ex-boyfriend visit late at night to return a paperback, a knife concealed in his jacket. I always thought I was much smarter than that, but here I was in a strange man's apartment with the door locked and only an open window for escape. Maybe this had something to do with my death obsession. Maybe I was deciding to tempt fate.

"Tea?" he said, handing me a cup of hot, milky liquid.

"No thanks. I can't stay long."

"Sure you can. Take the goddamn tea."

I took the cup.

"Everyone's always in a rush," Hank said, settling back down into the couch. "Rushing here and rushing there. No one takes the time to sit anymore."

"I really can't stay long," I repeated. "I'm due back—"

"To what?"

"Well, I have stuff to do."

"What have you got to do that's so important?"

I swallowed. "Excuse me?"

Hank's lip curled. "You heard. A girl who spends her time going into strangers' houses to take photographs of bathroom sinks ain't got a lot going on in her life, if you get my meaning."

I nodded. "Kinda hard to miss it," I said wryly.

"You know that friend of yours?"

"Benji?"

"Yeah. That kid, he's some kinda asshole," Hank said, starting to get agitated. "He ain't as smart as he thinks, I can tell ya that."

I frowned. As far as I was concerned I hadn't come to chat, especially about how much of an asshole he thought my best friend was. I wanted this transaction over with as quickly as possible. "You said you have something for me?" I asked, my voice stern.

Hank's eyes, so black and tiny the first day we met, now seemed gray and dull. The skin on his legs was dry and scaly and had flecked off only to get stuck in the spindly hair that grew there. His voice softened. "What are you doing with someone like that?" he asked sadly.

"There's nothing wrong with Benji," I said defensively.

"Sure there's not. Comes in and tells an old man someone died in his bathroom."

"Look, I'm really sorry about that," I said, taking a mouthful of tea and swallowing hard even though it was scalding hot. I was eager to get through the cup as fast as possible. "We shouldn't have done it. We were just curious."

"Yeah, well, people do things, and once it's done you can't take it back," he said philosophically. "Now here you are. Ain't nothin' but consequences in this life."

"Consequences, huh?" I tried to sound like I didn't care, like what he was saying wasn't creeping under my skin and taking root in my veins. I didn't like the sound of "consequences," the way his eyes glazed over when he said it, like a murderer reminiscing about his last really satisfying kill. I wondered whether I could smash the teacup right there on the table if I needed to, pick up a sliver of ceramic and drive it into his throat just as he lunged for me, or whether I should just throw the whole cup at his head, praying to God I hit a temple or some other magic spot that would make him black out. A hundred different scenarios raced through my mind from movies and TV shows: Dan Aykroyd getting a TV smashed over his head in *Grosse Pointe Blank*, the scene from *Single White*

Female where a guy gets dispensed of with a high heel to the forehead. I stood.

"I gotta go. My brother's gonna be outside. I told him to pick me up. He'll be looking for me."

Hank laughed. "You ain't got no brother pickin' you up. What the hell is wrong with you? You think I'm gonna attack you?"

"I don't know," I said. "When you sit there talking like Hannibal Lecter about "consequences," you can really start to freak a girl out."

"What the hell do ya think I'm gonna do? My cock's been useless for years. I'm lucky to get any piss out of it, let alone make it stand to attention long enough to get my rocks off."

"Gee, uh, thanks for the comforting thought," I said, feeling a little nauseous.

"Just sit down, will ya? Believe it or not, you're makin' *me* nervous. I don't get many people around here, you know."

I stayed standing, not knowing what to do. "Listen, I know we did kind of a shitty thing," I said, trying to explain myself. "It was not a cool thing to do. But if you think you're going to hold me hostage because I feel bad about it, and make me do some kind of forced community service by coming here to visit you to make up for it, you're mistaken."

"I ain't holdin' no one hostage. You came here of your own volition. And it's because I have somethin' for you. I wasn't lyin' about that. Just wait."

"You know what? It's cool. I don't want anything."

"No. Wait."

He pushed himself up off the sofa and struggled to his feet. I watched him slink into the kitchen and take something off the counter, and when he came back I saw that it was an old brown paper bag, crinkled and stained. He handed it to me.

"What's this?" I asked.

"Open it."

I hesitated. "It's not some dude's severed ear, is it?"

Hank cocked an eyebrow, then scratched his ass. "You're a weird kid, anyone ever tell you that?"

I couldn't help laughing. "Only every day," I said, thinking about Lynette and the way she just rolled with my eccentricities now, not even batting an eye when I walked into the kitchen with bright pink hair. I opened the bag an inch and started to peer inside, then closed it again, convinced that something was going to jump out at me. I handed it back to Hank.

"You open it," I said. "I don't feel like getting my finger ripped off by some bizarre booby trap."

"Oh, for Christ's sake," he said, snatching the bag away. "Give it here."

He turned the bag upside down and tipped the contents out. In the middle of his liver-spotted hand sat a piece of blue ceramic tile. It was a perfect square, the edges sharp and exact except for one corner that was chipped, the whiteness exposed beneath. I carefully picked it out of his hand.

"What is it?" I asked, turning it over in my fingers.

"A pool tile."

"So why do I want this?"

"It's from Jayne Mansfield's swimming pool."

My heart skipped. I held the tile up to the light.

"Are you serious?" I almost squealed. Hank smiled. It was too good to be true. Jayne Mansfield's heart-shaped pool was a Hollywood icon, torn down by some unfeeling developer who didn't much care for history. A couple of looters had managed to retrieve a few tiles from the demolition site, but mainly they were the stuff of legend. And now I had one, right in my hand, and it was blue and beautiful and filled with mystery. "Is this for me?" I squeaked.

"Sure is. You can have it. I ain't got no use for it."

I turned the tile over. It was so special, unique, perfect. "How did you get it?"

"I helped build Jayne Mansfield's pool in the fifties. She was a real sweet girl. Terrible what happened to her. When we were done building it, she gave each of us a tile from the pool. And that pool, shaped like a heart, what a sight. Such a shame."

"Did you know her dog was decapitated in the car accident, too?" I asked. "A little Chihuahua sitting in the front seat on her lap."

Hank made a face. "Christ girl, how old are you?"

"Seventeen."

"Seventeen and talkin' like that. What is it with all this death crap? Do your parents know you're into all this shit?"

"Sure," I lied. "They don't care what I do."

"Well, I don't see no reason why a young, pretty lass like you gotta be fillin' your head with all this morbid stuff."

I shrugged like it was no big deal. "It's just a hobby."

"Strange hobby. Sure ain't stamp collecting."

"No, I guess not," I said quietly.

"Aw shit," Hank said, sounding a little embarassed. "I feel like I got this all ass-backward. How about we start again? I'm Hank. Hank Anderson."

"Hilda Swann," I said, and held out my hand to shake his. "You really don't know how much this means to me."

There was no way he could know. I already had something

in common with Jayne Mansfield. To own an item that once belonged to her just brought us closer together, made our fates even more entwined. Hank reached forward and took my fingers, shook my hand with a soft but firm grip, and it was then that I noticed the black smear on his arm that had once been a tattoo, and looked as though it had been scrubbed down until it was nothing but an indistinguishable blob on the inside of his wrist.

"You know what, Hilda Swann? You look like a young Louise Brooks. At least you would without that pink shit in your hair."

"I'll try and take that as a compliment."

I let go of his hand and acted like I hadn't seen the mark on his arm. I noticed some old VHS tapes with no covers on top of the television set. "You like movies?" I asked, picking one up.

Hank groaned as he sat down in an old armchair, splayed his legs, and scratched at the rim of his shorts. "Sure, I like movies. If they're good."

I read the tape labels. *Gilda. Gone With the Wind. Gentlemen Prefer Blondes.*

"Classics, huh?"

Hank heaved himself up. "The trouble with Hollywood these days is the women have no grace. No style. All those sluts down on Sunset with their cooches hanging out. Goddamn tramps."

"What about Julia Roberts? Reese Witherspoon?"

"Bah—it's not the same. Back in my day, actresses were elegant. *Refined.* They were more than women; they were apparitions on the screen. We feared them, adored them."

"So you haven't seen Lindsay Lohan in *Herbie Fully Loaded*?"

Hank frowned. "Today, everyone finds it so easy to laugh at things. Everything is a big joke."

"Oh no, Lindsay Lohan is no joke. She's a terrifying reality."

He tilted his head at me. "There is something about you that is too familiar. You make jokes, but they don't come from a place of joy. A joke from the heart lights up an entire room. When you joke, there is no light. Your face goes dark."

I put the tape down on the television set and crossed my arms. "You wanna talk darkness? How's it feel living in a place where a guy killed himself?"

"I've lived in worse."

I looked toward the bathroom. The door was open and inside I could see small shafts of light from the tiny window illuminating the tiles. "So you're quite happy to brush your teeth at that sink every day?"

"Brush, floss, hell, I'd probably beat off if I still could."

I looked again at the mark on his arm. "Do you believe in ghosts?"

"Sure I do."

"But you're not scared to go in there?"

"Shit no," he said defiantly. "If there's a ghost in there, at least I'll have someone to talk to."

I walked over to the bathroom and pushed the door open. There were a couple of dirty towels on the floor, moldy and smelly. The mirror above the sink was so rusty you could barely see a reflection. I opened the little brown bag and peeked inside to make sure the tile was still there, that I hadn't imagined it. I walked back to the living room and collected my bag from the sofa.

"Well, I should be going," I said.

"Fine. Go," Hank said, suddenly sounding cold. "People always have somewhere else they have to be. Never here. Never now."

"Thanks for the tile," I mumbled.

"Don't mention it."

I made my way to the front door. Hank didn't get up. "You gonna open this for me?" I asked, and for a minute I got scared, but I needn't have because Hank got to his feet and undid the dead bolt, then stood behind the door as I walked outside. I hesitated, seized by a genuine desire to spend more time with this strange old man who had given me such a special gift. Maybe it was because as I took a last look around his apartment, with the matted carpet and brown curtains, I was overcome with immense sadness. All I knew was that as I prepared to step off his front doorstep, I became seized with incredible panic. Everything felt unfinished. More than that: it felt like we'd only just begun.

"Well," I said, holding up the paper bag with the tile in it. "Thanks again for this. You were right. It's pretty amazing."

"I got no use for it." Hank scowled, his expression suddenly cold. "It's just a piece of tile. Silly to think a piece of tile is so special. Ain't nothin' in that bag but dust."

"Well, I think it's beautiful."

"That's good for you," he said, stepping forward. "Now, if you've gotta go, you go."

And he slammed the door in my face.

10

Mom and Dad had loved movies. My earliest memory was of the soothing flicker of a television screen, the interplay of light and dark bathing me in warmth as I lay on the carpet of our living room. Over time the shadows took shape. People, streets, a puppy running toward the screen, then sprinting off again—all the things I had seen outside now contained in one magical window just for me. Slowly the images joined and became stories: an alien stranded in a giant forest, a talking yellow robot and his little robot friend on wheels, a witch with an apple in her hand. I saw visions I would never see outside, and could never hope to, images so fantastic they transfixed me for hours. And always in the background was the comforting sound of my mom's and dad's voices, the clink of dishes as Mom cleared away the breakfast table, the romantic chattering of Dad's old-fashioned typewriter.

I remembered growing up in Topanga Canyon, a place for "alternative lifestyle" seekers who thought the hippie haven of Laurel Canyon had been destroyed by coke and rich music execs. Mom wore beads and sarongs and dyed her hair with henna. Dad was once a teacher but now worked at a factory, but only to support his "art." He wrote poems and articles about astrology for magazines. He smoked rolled cigarettes, and the house was covered in ash. You couldn't open a book without having tobacco spill out from between the pages. Dad had terrible problems at the factory where he worked. He said the Manson Family had ruined everything for the hippies, even though the murders had happened decades ago. He said that everyone thought he was crazy.

I remembered our watching movies together. Every night after Dad had finished an article (or the article had finished him, Mom would joke), we sat down on the couch to watch a VHS tape from our vast collection. Sometimes whole weekends were gobbled up by movie marathons, and summer vacations flew by without my getting so much as a tan. Aunt Lynette didn't like it. One day I was sitting on the couch, Dad on the sofa behind me, and I could hear her arguing with my mother.

"Aren't you worried she'll be socially inept?" I overheard her say as they drank tea in the kitchen, although she wasn't making much of an effort not to be heard. I was watching *Animal House* for what must have been the tenth time. I didn't fully understand the jokes, but I knew that John Belushi was loud and funny-looking and made me laugh. Lynette looked tight and uncomfortable in her office suit and high heels, surrounded by coffee mugs made of clay and glowing incense sticks.

"Nonsense," Mom said. "You should let children do what interests them. One day she'll be the first great female film director."

"Or illiterate," Lynette continued. "Martha, it's not healthy for her to watch so much television. And the stuff you let her watch."

"Like what?"

Lynette pointed at the TV. "Like that! Have you even seen that movie yourself? It's full of sex. There's drug use in it, and naked women."

"So? Hilda can decide what she wants to watch for herself. Sex never hurt anyone—it's the most natural thing in the world."

"But at her age? She's only eight years old!"

"I'd rather have her watching sex than something that was horribly violent. I mean, what's wrong with this country? It's okay to show people getting their limbs blown off, but sex is a problem?"

It seemed like a good argument at the time, but looking back I'm not so sure it was the greatest excuse for letting me watch movies like *Porky's* and *Bachelor Party*, movies we watched mainly because Dad wanted to. Still, that wasn't all I watched—I also loved Disney films and musicals like *West Side Story*. It just seemed an unfortunate coincidence that campus comedies were the kinds of movies Dad liked to put on when Aunt Lynette was around for her weekly visit (or inspection, as he liked to call it).

"The film ratings are there for a reason," Lynette went on.

"Aunt Lynette," I said, joining the conversation, "what does 'socially inept' mean?"

"It means brilliant and unique," Dad chimed in, and I didn't understand why he sounded angry.

"Jim," Lynette started to say, but Dad cut her off.

"I think you've said enough for one afternoon. Lay off Hilda. She's fine."

"How do you know that, Jim? Did you read it in the stars?"

"Yeah, I did, and I've got a prediction for you, too."

"Sweetheart!" Mom snapped. "We do not have negative energy in this house."

"Only on Saturday afternoons," Dad said, glaring at Lynette, who barely flinched.

My only friend at primary school was Janey, a redheaded loner who was all gangly limbs and awkwardness. The kids teased Janey because she had knots in her hair and smelled like cat food. They teased me because I hung around her, but I didn't care. We were outsiders, dangerous outlaws like Martin Sheen and Sissy Spacek in *Badlands*, misunderstood like Beatty and Dunaway in *Bonnie and Clyde*. Apart from Janey, there was no one but Mom and Dad and the movies, and the occasional game of Scrabble. Dad loved Scrabble almost as much as he loved movies. I don't think Mom and I were much competition, but he enjoyed it nonetheless, probably for exactly that reason. We weren't good enough to make him feel like a failure.

"See, a master's in English *is* good for something," he would say with bitterness after a triple-word score. "It's not like they appreciate it down at the factory."

"Why do you work at the factory if you don't like it?" I asked.

"Because he can't work as a teacher anymore," Mom replied, not looking up from her letters.

"Why?"

"Because he was fired."

"Why were you fired, Dad?"

"Because, Hilda, I tried to teach something that was about real life. Something you couldn't find in a syllabus."

"Jim, smoking dope with a group of ten-year-olds behind the basketball courts was not the best decision of your career."

Dad threw up his hands. "Goddamnit, Martha, it was their dope!"

Janey and I would play in the canyons that ran alongside our neighborhood. We would climb the trees and tear our pants and talk about what we wanted to be when we grew up.

"I want to be a movie star," Janey would say, twirling a ratty string of hair between her fingers. "Like Drew Barrymore. What about you, Hilda? Do you want to be a movie star?"

"I want to work in an office," I told her, thinking of my aunt Lynette with her nice clothes that didn't smell like incense. "Where everything is shiny and new and I have to wear a suit to work. I want to be a businesslady and make lots of money."

"Lame!"

Once when I met Janey in the canyon she was so upset she was shaking. She told me she had just found out that one day we were all going to die. She told me our bodies would be put in the ground, and we would rot, and worms and maggots would eat our flesh until all that was left was our skeletons. I still remember how my brain tried to digest the information, letting it swirl around before settling with heaviness in my heart. I was terrified. My bowels loosened. I ran home crying. I was angry at Janey, angry that she wanted to make me feel bad by telling me such awful things. But now I know that Janey wanted someone else to share her revelation, to feel her terror. She was looking for someone to commiserate with. I burst through the back door of our run-down cottage and fell into Mom's arms. With heaving sobs I told her all that Janey had told me, and asked her if Janey was lying, asked with growing panic what it all meant. Mom sat me at the kitchen table and made me a hot cocoa. She poured herself a green tea and sat down, folding her hands in front of her.

"What Janey told you was true," she said, "but there is no reason to be afraid."

"But I don't want to die!"

"It's a very natural part of life, Hilda. Everything dies, so new things can be born. It's very beautiful."

"It's not beautiful!" I screamed. "It's scary!"

Mom laughed. She reached out and took my hand. "It's not scary, honey," she said, rubbing my fingers against her cheek. "Some people think it is, and spend their whole lives worrying about it. Many people are too scared to even talk about it. But you should never be scared, Hilda."

"I don't want you to die, Mommy!" I sniveled.

"Well, your father and I believe that when we die, our spirits go to another place. Our bodies may die, but our spirits live forever. And when that happens, we will all be together. Doesn't that sound wonderful?"

"I guess."

"I'm not going anywhere for a long, long time, Hilda. But when I do, won't it be comforting for you to know that someone is waiting for you on the other side? That your mom and dad are there waiting for you?"

"But how will I know you are there?"

Mom took my face in both her hands. "When I die, I will give you a sign," she promised. "Even though I will be dead, I will still be with you. I will always be with you, Hilda. Everything you do, everywhere you go, you will feel me with you. I promise."

My mother had lied. Sitting in my bedroom in my aunt's house, listening for Mom's voice in the night, I felt nothing from her, not even the vaguest whisper of her presence. She was gone, Dad was gone, and all that remained was my fear that in surviving the crash that took my family, I had somehow managed to cheat death, and one day, when I least expected it, death would come to collect.

11

I LAY ON MY BED, turning the tile over in my fingers. It was without a doubt the most beautiful thing I had ever seen. I'd heard stories of people jumping the fence around Mansfield's house to retrieve whatever they could from the wreckage of the demolition: tiles, concrete, even the pool handrails. But I didn't know anyone who had a tile that Jayne had held in her hand and actually given to someone to express her love, gratitude, and respect. Maybe I was romanticizing Jayne's relationship with Hank and the men who built her pool, but it seemed such a personal gift to give someone, such a symbolic gesture.

At least, that's the way I felt when Hank handed it to me, *bestowed* it upon me. I felt like I'd been given a portal to another time, a key to history. Sure, Mansfield was a chick with big boobs and a bad peroxide job, but she grabbed this town by the balls, shook down Hollywood and took whatever she wanted, and went out like a true legend. I couldn't help admiring someone with that much ambition. At least she knew what she wanted and did everything it took to get there.

I wrapped the tile in cotton wool and placed it in a small, wooden heart-shaped jewelery box on my shelf with the rest of the collection. That night I had a terrible dream: the earth in front of Grauman's Chinese Theatre had cracked open, an enormous canyon running the length of Hollywood Boulevard. The entire sky turned from blue to pink, and the sun was a flaming red ball hovering above the Hollywood sign. Tourists flung themselves into the gaping hole, disappearing into the center of the earth, clutching their cheap souvenirs to their chests. Photographers lined the edges of the hole, snapping pictures with archaic cameras that had enormous flashbulbs and yelling after the tourists to give them their best look. The people smiled and positioned themselves midair for the photographers, striking exaggerated poses during their descents, and I flung myself in after them, flashing a winning smile on the way down. When I looked up I saw Benji at the edge of the canyon, snapping photos of my descent with his digital camera, and I screamed for him to help, but he didn't hear me, or wouldn't.

The next morning when I woke up, all I could think about was Hank and the tile. I leaped out of bed, pulled on jeans and a T-shirt, and called a cab. The morning sun was strong; I thought of babies left to bake in cars, dogs tied to chain-link fences with no water bowls. By the time the cab arrived at Hank's, I was in a daze, propelled by a sense that there was nowhere else I wanted to be, nowhere else I was *meant* to be. When I got to the top of the stairs, the door was already open, and I could see Hank inside on his sofa in front of the television. I tapped on the door and he looked up.

"You're here early," he grunted, as if he'd been expecting me all along.

"I know. I, uh, wanted to ask you about Jayne Mansfield."

"Why don't you come in, then?"

I stepped inside. I heard familiar dramatic music coming from the television, then the wail of an ambulance siren. I looked at the screen.

"*Rebel Without a Cause*," I said as I sat down. It was the end of the film: James Dean was standing outside the planetarium, defeated; his best friend was being wheeled away in a body bag. "This is my favorite James Dean movie."

"Humph," Hank snorted. "Everyone goes on about James Dean being this big legend and all, but he was nothin' but a little freak. Seriously, that kid was messed up in the head. I used to clean rooms at a crappy two-star hotel down Sunset Boulevard. I caught him crawling into one of the room windows one night, buck naked. He saw me and just laughed, basically swung his prick at me so I'd get a better look."

My eyes widened. "Wow."

"Yeah. Wow."

On the television the ambulance drove off, siren blaring, and the words THE END appeared on the screen. Hank stood up, his back creaking, and shuffled into the kitchen, where he put the kettle on.

"Did you meet anyone else famous?" I asked.

"Sure. Humphrey Bogart, James Cagney, Lauren Bacall, Jerry Lewis—"

"Holy shit," I said, impressed. "I've lived here all my life and the best I saw was Paris Hilton at a frozen yogurt stand."

Hank brought two cups of tea over and handed one to me. He was about to sit down when something stopped him. He glanced at the front door, hesitated, then wandered over and snapped the lock shut on the screen door.

"They weren't anything to get excited about," he said, groaning as he finally settled back down. He was wearing boxers and an old T-shirt, and his hair was sticking up at an angle, like he'd fallen asleep, or passed out, somewhere he shouldn't have. "Just 'cause you're famous doesn't make you less of an asshole, or a bore."

I fanned my face with my hands. The apartment felt like the inside of an incinerator. "It's so hot in here," I said. "How can you stand it?"

"Heat don't bother me one bit. Where I grew up, it was so cold your balls would crawl up your ass just to get warm."

"Where was that?"

Hank turned the TV to a news channel and cranked the volume up loud. A police chase was taking place a few blocks from where we were, the news helicopter trailing a red station wagon as it swerved and jackknifed its way across town.

"Idiot," Hank snarled. "I hope he crashes and kills himself before he gets a chance to kill anyone else."

We watched the car chase for a bit until the driver was brought down by a strategically placed stop stick. "So you wanna tell me more about this guy who knocked himself off in my bathroom?" Hank said. "This Bernie guy?"

"Bernie Bernall," I said, remembering all that Benji had told me, and what I'd found on the Internet. "He was a big movie star for a while, but his voice was no good for the talkies. His career went downhill fast. No one would even talk to him anymore. Apparently he ended up working at a hot dog stand outside the studio where he used to be a big star. I guess he had plenty of good reasons to be depressed."

"Yeah, well, the guy was a pussy if you ask me," Hank said.

"People have had to live with much worse than what he went through. So your face gets a little singed, so what? No reason to carve yourself up like a Christmas turkey."

"People have killed themselves over less."

"Boo-hoo."

"Just because he was famous doesn't mean his life was great. The studios were really evil in those days. They got Judy Garland hooked on drugs and drove Marilyn Monroe to suicide. Well, them and the Kennedys."

"If I had all that money, I wouldn't have a goddamn care in the world."

"Was Jayne Mansfield happy?"

"As far as I could see, she was having a ball. She enjoyed every minute of her life."

"So do you think it was her time to go?"

Hank gave me a peculiar look. "You driving at something?"

I looked at the floor, avoiding his gaze. "You know how when people die we always say it was meant to be? No matter how terrible or out of the blue it was, we say that it must have been their time to go. That it was meant to happen."

"That's a pile of BS. There weren't nothin' poetic about her death," he said. "There was no goddamn reason in the world that a lovely lady like that gotta be taken in such a horrible way. Did you see what happened to that car she was in? I'm surprised anyone survived that. Those poor damn kids in the back."

"You got a wife, Hank?"

He made a face. "Nah. Don't need the aggravation."

"No wife. Kids?"

Hank cocked his eyebrow at me. "You think I'm father material?"

I smiled. "I don't know. I guess I don't know you well enough yet to make that judgement call."

"What you see is what you get."

I doubted that. Hank thought I hadn't noticed him change the subject when I asked where he was from. I made a note to ask about it again later, when he couldn't stray so easily from the topic.

"What about you?" he asked, turning the tables again. "I suppose you got a family?"

"Sort of. I live with my aunt Lynette. She's a pain in the ass."

"She's probably fed up with you bringing that creepy kid home."

"There's nothing wrong with Benji," I said, once again leaping to his defense. It seemed like I spent half my life defending Benji.

"Yeah, and I'm pitching for the Yankees at the next World Series."

I thought for a moment. "She does try, though," I said. "I don't know. Sometimes I think I just push her away because she's not my mom. Maybe I'm just scared I'll lose her, too."

I shook my head, startled by how much I had just revealed. Hank could sense my discomfort at the sudden shift in tone of the conversation and graciously turned us toward something more innocuous.

"You wanna watch a movie?" he suggested.

"Sure," I said gratefully.

"Pick one."

I looked at the small collection of old VHS tapes. Some of them had been purchased from video stores and still had price stickers on them. I couldn't imagine what kind of state they were in.

"You haven't thought of upgrading to DVD?" I asked as I crouched down to get a closer look at what was on offer.

"Do I look like I got money for DVDs?"

We watched *Double Indemnity*, one of my favorites, and whatever discomfort may have existed between us melted away. I was a firm believer in the unifying force of art in all it forms: a shared love for a movie, book, or song could transcend all other obstacles in a relationship. Hank reminded me of a song by Tom Waits, or a novel by John Fante. For all his cragginess, there was an underlying soulfulness, and his words floated on the air like the music of a raspy trombone or a wailing saxophone. There was something poetic about his absolute disdain for the world, a view based not on ignorance but experience, the experience of living so many years in a world that was indecent and deceptive. I wanted to know what had happened to make him that way. I wondered if it was as bad as what had happened to me.

The movie ended. "Hey, Hank," I said, turning away from the television as the credits rolled. "Tomorrow Benji and I are going to check out a house where a writer died. It's just downtown. Maybe you wanna come with us?"

"And why the hell would I wanna see a thing like that?"

"I don't know. I just thought, downtown isn't that far from here, and you might find it interesting. The guy who was murdered used to write for *Alfred Hitchcock Presents* and *Lassie.*"

"*Lassie*, huh? How'd he die?"

"Someone cut off his head."

Hank grimaced. "I'll pass."

12

THE NEXT DAY BENJI and I were standing outside a white weatherboard home on a quiet street in Hollywood. The house had large French windows, Roman-style columns framing the front door, and a small green lawn running to the sidewalk. There was a FOR SALE sign with the words SEE AGENT REGARDING DISCLOSURE. In the world of real estate that was bad news. Real estate agents were required by law to fully disclose the history of a property to any potential buyers. I imagined this unassuming bungalow was proving to be a tough sell.

A woman emerged from the house next door, pushing a baby carriage and struggling with an assortment of diaper bags and baby toys. Benji moved toward her, his camera as always around his neck. "Excuse me, ma'am?"

She flung a bag over her shoulder. "Yes?"

"Can you tell us how long this house has been on the market?"

The woman put one hand on the carriage and the other above

her brow, shielding her eyes from the sun. "It's been a while. Are you interested in buying it?"

She looked down at Benji's T-shirt, which featured a picture of Charles Manson with the words BEING CRAZY USED TO MEAN SOMETHING in bold lettering. "No, we're just having a look," Benji said, and you could almost see the relief on her face.

"Oh, okay, well, you have a nice day," she said, and hurried off down the street, casting a concerned look back in our direction. Benji pointed his camera at the house and started taking photos. He handed the camera to me.

"Hey, get a pic of this," he said, bending over and pointing at the FOR SALE sign with a cheesy grin on his face, as if he were standing beside Walt's statue at Disneyland. I took a photo. He leaned casually on the sign, looking into the distance. I took another photo.

"Pretty hard to offload a house where a guy had his head cut off," he said, scratching his neck.

"How old was he again?"

"Ninety-two."

Benji walked up to the windows, put his hands around his eyes, and peered in. The hardwood floors were bare and a pile of real estate brochures was stacked high on the kitchen counter.

"Imagine surviving being blacklisted in Hollywood, clawing your way back into the industry, watching your wife die of cancer, and then finally you're in your twilight years and bam! Some LSD-crazed psycho breaks into your house and cuts off your head for no reason."

"Didn't that guy kill someone else, too?" I asked. Benji turned around and sat on the front lawn and I joined him. The grass was freshly cut, and the smell tickled my nose.

"Sure did. The guy broke in here, cut the old man's head off, then climbed over the back fence carrying the head, and killed the guy in the next house. Cut off his *dick*."

"God. What a bummer."

"Totally. He dumps the head with the other body, then makes his way over to the Paramount studios and tries to get in but is taken down by some security guards who can sense something is seriously messed up with this dude."

"No shit."

I pulled at the lawn with my fingers. The earth felt warm beneath me. Sometimes I didn't mind that one day I would become part of the soil, that we all would. It seemed like the only logical way to keep the human race ticking. Other days it frightened me beyond words. But not today. Today it felt natural and right. I watched the ants crawl up my leg, and Benji scanned through the photos on his digital camera. He pointed the lens at me.

"Smile."

"Benji, don't," I said, putting my hand in front of my face.

"Oh, come on," he moaned. "Just one picture."

"I don't like having my picture taken," I replied, but that wasn't it. I just didn't want Benji to have any photos of me. I couldn't shake the feeling that I wouldn't like what he would do with them.

"Maybe one day we could have a place like this," he said, giving up on taking my picture. "After school finishes we could get a bungalow in West Hollywood or Laurel Canyon."

"I thought you were going to college in New York? Remember? You wanted to walk the streets in a trench coat like James Dean."

"I said that when I was, like, sixteen."

"And that was soooo long ago."

"I don't know what I want to do anymore. I just wanna do this."

"This?"

"You know, drive around, look at stuff. Hang out with you."

"Sounds like a great way to make a living."

Benji busied himself with his camera. I could tell he was hurt. He had talked about us moving in together before, and every time he brought it up, I dodged the issue. It wasn't that I didn't want to live with Benji; I just wasn't sure how much of him I wanted in my life on a day-to-day basis. I had my own demons to contend with and couldn't handle his as well. Anyway, I still didn't know what I wanted to do after school. I wasn't even sure I would make it that far. I felt like death was still riding my back.

A car drove past, the driver honking the horn. Benji put away his camera and lay down in the grass. I wondered what I could do to make amends and decided to tell him about my adventure from two days ago. I hadn't been sure about whether I would mention it to Benji, but if I planned on visiting Hank again, which I did, it would be difficult to keep it from him. I picked at my chipped nail polish and tried to act casual.

"Hey, you know that old guy from the other day? That guy called Hank?"

"You mean the creepy guy from Bernie Bernall's place?"

I paused. "I went to see him two days ago."

Benji sat up. "What do you mean, you went to see him?"

"I went back to his place."

"What? Why? Why the hell didn't you tell me you were doing that?"

"You were busy getting your teeth whitened."

Benji got up on his elbows, his face reddening. "What the hell would you do a stupid thing like that for?"

My mouth dropped open. "Well, why would you give him my phone number?" I stammered.

"It was a joke! A stupid joke because you like *Harold and Maude*! You know? And we'd laugh it off and not be having this conversation about you going alone to some sleazy old dude's place. I didn't know you liked *Harold and Maude* that much. I didn't think you'd go on a fucking date with the guy."

"It wasn't a date, you dick. He said he had something to give me."

Benji scoffed. "I'm sure he did."

"Here. Look."

I took the heart-shaped jewelery box from my bag and pulled out the tile. Benji snatched it from me and examined it closely.

"Is this from his bathroom?"

"No. It's from Jayne Mansfield's swimming pool."

Benji looked at me, disbelieving. "Bullshit."

"It's true. He worked on her pool when he first came to LA. Be careful with it."

Benji put the tile in the palm of his hand, almost shaking.

"Can I have it?"

"You've gotta be kidding me."

I snatched the tile back and put it carefully in the box. Benji lay down again, sulking.

"That was still a stupid thing to do," he said. "That guy was nuts. The way he freaked out when we knocked on the door. He's hiding something. You said so yourself."

Benji was right. I could feel it, too, something about the way

Hank looked at you, as if he was always trying to decide whether he could trust you.

"He had a mark on his arm," I blurted out, not sure if I wanted Benji to know but not able to help myself. "It was all blurred and burnt, like someone had tried to take it off with acid. It was near his wrist."

"Russian mafia."

"But he didn't have any others. Don't the Russian mafia have tattoos all over their bodies?"

"Maybe he wasn't that high up. Maybe he only made it to single-tattoo status."

I thought about the size of the mark, the blueness of the ink. "I think he was in a concentration camp."

"Naaaah. If he was ever in a concentration camp, there is no way he would try and get rid of that number. It's like a badge of honor among those people."

"Those people?"

"Yeah. It's a sympathy ticket."

I let it slide. Benji was always saying things purely to be controversial. At least, I hoped that's what it was.

"Anyway," I said, "I was thinking I'd go see him again. He seems lonely."

"Do what you gotta do, but I don't think the dude's got piles of cash hidden under his mattress, if you know what I mean. When that guy pops off, he's leaving a big fat zero, so if you're planning some kind of Anna Nicole Smith agenda, I think you've backed the wrong horse."

"You're disgusting. It's not like that."

"Okay. I'll come, then."

I realized I had unconsciously tightened my grip on the grass. Hank had been something I wanted to keep to myself, something just for me, but now I had no way of telling Benji I didn't want him there. I was worried about what he might say or do. But there was no way I couldn't let him come. Hank would be fine with it, I figured. He was a tough guy. He could handle a kid like Benji.

"Okay, sure. I mean—you don't have to. It's pretty boring over there."

"On the contrary, it sounds like there's a mystery afoot."

I couldn't fault him there. I had to admit I was intrigued by Hank, by what he said and what he didn't say. He seemed eager to have visitors and at the same time uncomfortable with their presence. I reasoned to myself that we were doing a good deed, that visiting Hank in his old apartment and keeping him company was akin to community service. But in my heart I knew it was the dead cat all over again. Something about Benji's eagerness also made me anxious.

An expensive car pulled up in front of us and a man in a business suit got out. He was followed by a young couple with anticipation etched on their faces, and they looked at us curiously as they started to walk up the path. The man in the business suit looked at me and gave a confused smile.

"Can I help you?" he asked. He looked at Benji lying on the grass, eyes closed. The couple locked hands nervously.

"No," I said, getting up and dusting myself off. "We were just leaving."

"Hey," Benji shouted from the ground. "You interested in buying this place?"

The guy held his girlfriend's hand tighter. "Don't know yet," he said with a forced smile.

"Oh, this place is great," Benji said, getting up, and the real estate agent smiled with relief. "It's the kind of place you could really lose your head over."

The agent stopped smiling. The couple looked at him for an explanation, and I dragged Benji off, begging him to shut up as his laugh echoed down the street.

13

YOU DIDN'T TELL ME you were bringing *him*." Hank scowled, refusing to open the door more than an inch. Benji saluted like a captain and tried to get his hand through the door, almost getting his fingers chopped off as Hank tried to close it on him.

"I can't catch a cab every day," I said. "He gave me a lift. It's cool."

"Good afternoon, Mr. Anderson," Benji said, beaming. "Lovely day."

Hank looked over our shoulders. "You got anyone else with ya? Huh? Any more of your little friends?"

Benji looked behind himself. A Korean woman stepped out of her apartment and threw a saucepan of hot water onto the concrete.

"There's one!" Benji cried as she scampered back inside. "No, wait, she's gone."

I kicked Benji in the ankle. "It's just us," I assured Hank, "and I got you these."

I held up a bag from Blockbuster, filled with tapes. I took one out and shook it at him. "*Psycho*? I've got *Lawrence of Arabia*, too. The uncut version."

Hank closed the door in our faces, and for a moment I thought we'd been given our marching orders. Then we heard the sound of a chain unlocking, and the door opened. We slithered through the crack Hank had made for us.

"Wipe your feet," he snarled at Benji, who did a little tap dance on the welcome mat before stepping inside. Hank walked to the kitchen to prepare some tea. I put the bag of tapes on the coffee table and sat on the sofa. Benji slid over and whispered in my ear.

"Looks like you're not the only do-gooder who pays him a visit," he said, referring to the apartment's cleanliness. "Jealous?"

"You promised me you'd be nice," I whispered. "And anyway, he probably cleaned it himself."

"Doubtful. The dude can barely stand up. By the way, I am being nice. I just want to know what time we give him the sponge bath. Or should I leave for that? Give you both some privacy?"

I didn't bother dignifying Benji with a response, but he was right about one thing: the apartment was really clean, even cleaner than the last time, when I'd arrived to find all the dishes washed and the ashtrays emptied. I couldn't imagine someone Hank's age having the energy to do all of that and figured maybe there was some kind of service like Meals On Wheels that cleaned old people's apartments. Benji put his boots on the coffee table and looked around with a smug expression. Hank brought the tea over on a little tray and stopped suddenly.

"Hey!" he yelled with such force that I jumped.

Benji looked at him calmly. "Are you talking to me?"

"Yeah, I'm talking to you. Get your feet off my table."

"Oh, I'm so sorry. I thought it was a footrest. My mistake."

If there was any doubt in my mind that it had been a bad idea to bring Benji, it had now evaporated. He seemed intent on behaving badly. I stared at him, imploring him with my eyes to be civilized, but he was already helping himself to tea, filling his cup with a ridiculous amount of sugar. Hank stared at Benji, incredulous, as he put in four lumps, then five, then six. He stirred the tea with a spoon and took a mouthful, closing his eyes as if it were the most glorious thing he had ever tasted.

"Mmmmm," he moaned. "Now that is a perfect cup of tea. Where do you get your tea, Hank?"

"Supermarket."

"I mean, who gets it for you? Do you have someone who comes here and cleans up, runs errands?"

Hank fixed himself a cup and leaned back. "Somethin' like that, yeah. I got someone who helps out."

I sat between them feeling like the meat in a macho sandwich. I could practically feel them peeing in their seats, marking their territory.

"Look at all this great stuff I got," I said, leaning forward and rifling through my bag from Blockbuster. "I thought you could do with a few more tapes. And I found this."

I handed him a copy of *The Girl Can't Help It*, starring Jayne Mansfield. On the cover she was wearing a tight red dress, her enormous breasts busting to get out.

"She was a nice lady," he said, "but she weren't no great actress. I prefer Janet Leigh." He picked up the copy of *Psycho* and read the back cover.

"Hilda tells me you knew Jayne Mansfield," Benji said. "That you worked on her pool."

"That's right. I did."

"I get it. You were the sexy pool man, giving her what her husband never could?"

"Benji!" I almost shrieked. "What the hell?"

"It's cool, Hilda. It's just guy talk. Hank knows what I'm talkin' about. He knows what goes on with the hired help. Am I right, my man?"

Hank grinned, saying nothing.

"Yeah, he knows." Benji said, pleased with himself.

"We were thinking maybe you'd like to go out," I offered. "Benji has a car—we could take you someplace if you wanted."

"Why would I want to do that?"

"To get some fresh air."

"Plenty of air in here."

"Come on, Hank," Benji said, slapping his knees. "Let's go cruising."

Hank stayed in his chair. "Ain't nothin' I can see out there that I can't see in here," he said, motioning to the television set and the tapes.

"You don't wanna drive on down to Pink's, get some hot dogs?"

Hank sank into his seat and muttered an almost inaudible no. This was not the Hank I was familiar with. It was as if Benji had him cornered. All his bluster and bravado were gone, and in their place sat a frail old man being interrogated in his own home and scared to go outside. For a moment I forgot Benji was there. I leaned toward Hank and put my hand gently on his arm.

"Are you nervous to go outside?" I asked softly, and Benji leaned forward in his seat and pointed at Hank's arm.

"Hey, man, what's that?"

Hank swiftly placed his fingers over the blurry ink blob. "What?" he cried.

"Under your fingers, man. What's that on your arm? Is that a tattoo?"

"It's nothing," Hank said, talking fast. "Got it when I was a teenager. Just a stupid mistake. Take it from me, sonny, when you fall in love for the first time, don't be dumb enough to have her name tattooed on your person. Sure, they got laser surgery these days. But in my day, well, let me just say, acid hurts like a son of a bitch."

I laughed, relieved. Benji sat back, his eyes darting around, unsatisfied. "Believe me, I wouldn't be stupid enough to do that for a girl," he said, shooting me a look that could have withered a vine. "So tell us a story about Jayne Mansfield. Seeing as how you knew her so well."

Hank poured himself another cup of tea, made himself comfortable. "Frankly, I didn't know her that well. Just saw her coming and going, in and out of the house, sometimes in her bathing suit, sometimes . . . well, not in her bathing suit. If you catch my meaning."

"Oh yeah." Benji whistled.

"She was a beautiful woman but had no self-respect. Didn't care who saw her naked. Me, I was just off the boat, and, well, I was damn impressed by her. By the whole town. I'd never seen anything like it."

"Off the boat?" I asked. "From where?"

"Norway," he said without hesitation. "Came out when I was eighteen."

"Was your family with you?"

Something passed through Hank's eyes. "No. Just me."

"What was it like back then?" Benji asked, and to my surprise he sounded genuinely interested.

"You mean Hollywood? You're asking the wrong person. I only ever saw people's pools, or their hotel rooms as I was cleanin' them."

"Did you know any other famous people?" Benji asked, almost drooling into his cup. It was alarming how fast he could turn from interrogative bulldog to salivating sycophant.

"I once built a mailbox for Mickey Rooney."

Benji put his cup down. "Awesome."

"More tea?" Hank asked.

"No, it's cool. I'm not much of a tea drinker."

"How about a beer, then?"

"Now you're talking!"

Hank stood, walked back over to the kitchen, and grabbed two cold beers from the fridge. "Your boyfriend's pretty cool," Benji said, leaning in. "You two have my blessing."

Hank handed Benji a beer and sat back down. Benji tore the cap off and drank a little too enthusiastically, showing his age. "Take it easy, tiger," I said. "You're driving, remember? If we get pulled over, you'll lose your license."

"Hey, Hank," Benji said, wiping foam from his mouth with the back of his hand. "Hilda's got something in common with Jayne Mansfield."

"Benji, don't!"

Benji fixed me with a cold stare.

"Do they?" Hank said, looking at me. "And what would that be?"

Benji took another drink. The room filled with the smell of alcohol. "Don't flip your lid, Hilda. I was just gonna say you both dye your hair."

I downed my tea. "We have to get going," I said, standing. Benji stood as well, finishing his beer.

"That's right, old man. Places to go, people to see. It's a big world out there—you should try it out sometime."

"Maybe I will," Hank said, not standing, taking another drink. "I just might take you up on that, *boy*."

"WHAT THE HELL WAS that all about?" I asked as I put on my seat belt. Benji started the engine and laughed.

"What? What's the problem now?"

"Why do you have to be such an asshole?" I said.

"I have no idea what you're talking about."

Benji plugged his iPod into the cigarette lighter and busied himself with making a song selection. I looked back at Hank's apartment in time to see him closing the curtains, shutting himself in once again. Benji slammed his foot on the accelerator and we roared off, tires squealing.

"Slow down!" I yelled over the music, AC/DC at their rowdiest. I turned the volume down and Benji scowled.

"I just wanna get the hell out of this dump. I don't know how people can live like that."

"People live the best way they know how, Benji. You wouldn't know a thing about it. Your mom still presses your underwear."

"What's your problem, Hilda? You got something to say?"

"Yes," I said, turning to him, angry. "Yes, I have something to say." I breathed deeply, forming the words in my head before saying them aloud. "I am not a specimen."

"What?"

I balled my fists, defiant. "I am not a specimen. I am not something you can keep in a jar and poke with a stick whenever you feel like it."

I caught something in Benji's eye that told me he knew what I meant. Instead, he tried to laugh it off with a joke.

"Is this *The Elephant Man*?" he said, slurring his words as he added, *"I am not an animal, Benji! I am a human beeeeing!"*

"You know what I mean," I said, not letting him off the hook. Benji knew exactly what I was talking about—the fact that he had made it look like he was going to mention my parents' accident to Hank, even though he knew how I felt about telling people. "You're supposed to be my friend, Benji. That's my private business. That's *my* story. It's not for you to tell."

"As if I'd say anything about it," Benji said defensively. "God, give me a little more credit, Hilda."

"It sure sounded like you were going to."

"Look, I'm sorry, I really wasn't." He gave me a small smile. "Truce?"

I didn't say anything. I didn't tell him that sometimes I thought he was friends with me only because he was fascinated by what had happened to me. It was as if he wanted to see how I developed and grew, if I was going to be normal or turn into one of those people who walks into McDonald's with a rifle and starts shooting. Half of me believed that Benji was just dumb and insensitive sometimes, but the other half was less convinced. We pulled up in front of my house and I got out.

"Hey, don't be mad, Hilda. Wanna go to Wonderland Avenue tomorrow? The place where John Holmes and those drug dealers bludgeoned all those losers to death?"

"It was never confirmed that John Holmes was actually there," I said, avoiding his gaze. "The evidence against him is entirely circumstantial."

"Yeah, because porn stars are such model citizens. Come on. Don't make me beg."

I turned back and managed a grin. "How can I stay mad at you? You had me at 'bludgeoning'."

14

I CONTINUED TO VISIT HANK, but there was no way I was going to let Benji come along after his last performance. I would go to the apartment in Echo Park in the afternoon, after Benji and I had completed our expedition for the day.

As summer went by we visited the people and places that made up LA's ghoulish tapestry of despair. The bend in the road near Bakersfield where James Dean met his grisly end in a car he affectionately named Little Bastard. The apartment where Sal Mineo, who also starred in *Rebel Without a Cause*, was stabbed to death during a robbery gone wrong. We even did a dedicated Night Stalker tour, driving the same roads and freeways as Richard Ramirez had, right to the doors of his victims.

We hung around the bus station where Ramirez regularly met with his fence, eager to offload jewelry and other valuables he had stolen from his victims in exchange for cash to feed his dope habit. But that's not why Ramirez killed people. The dope was a way to curb his addiction to killing; it mellowed him out, kept him balanced. It didn't work very well. Richard Ramirez loved to kill. It fed his soul, a soul he believed belonged to Satan. He was convinced that his killing spree would earn him a place at Satan's throne in the afterlife.

When Ramirez was on trial, no one knew that his father suffered from such terrifying fits of rage that one day he beat himself in the face with a hammer while a cowering young Richard looked on from the corner. The jury didn't know that Richard's cousin came back from Vietnam and showed him photographs of Vietnamese women giving head at gunpoint. They didn't know that Richard's cousin shot his own wife in front of the young boy, that he aimed the gun right at her face and pulled the trigger. Even Richard's family didn't know about that until after he was in jail.

As Benji and I drove the quiet streets, neighborhoods once shrouded in terror, doors locked and windows barred, because of the Night Stalker, I thought about all the ways to make a man a killer. I tried to imagine what was going through Ramirez's mind as he peered through windows and pried off screen doors. Was killing really the natural order of the world, as so many serial killers believed? Had the rest of us all been duped by the idea of a civilized society, where killing people just wasn't neighborly? Was that why everyone screamed at one another on the freeway? Maybe a good kill was nature's way of restoring the balance. Maybe it wasn't natural for us to suppress our rage, to shrug off every insult and disguise our pain with smiles. Maybe a good kill was enough to set us straight. Maybe a good kill would make us all feel a hell of a lot better.

If Benji knew I was still visiting Hank, he didn't let on. After he dropped me off at home, I would walk inside, call a cab, and then walk back out to the porch to wait for it. Some days Hank and I didn't talk about much. Maybe we'd discuss the weather or the latest old movie he had watched on cable, or he'd regale me with a story from when he first arrived in Los Angeles, like the time he mowed Sinatra's lawn and accidentally cut the flowers with it. Most of the time we'd just sit, watching the television or staring into our drinks. It was as if my presence was enough, something to break up the day, a welcome relief from his solitude.

One late afternoon, when it was even hotter than usual, I suggested we sit outside on the balcony to catch some of the breeze that had started up as the sun was setting. To my surprise Hank agreed. I considered it a small victory: Hank had barely set foot outside his front door since the moment I met him. We went outside where there was an old sofa with the stuffing coming out and an overflowing ashtray; the concrete was black from where the butts had burned the ground. We watched the sun go down over the apartment building and listened to the sound of the washer and dryer churning downstairs. Hank sucked on a cigar, the end all slick and glistening. The silence was broken only when a police chopper made its way low across the sky, probably chasing a car or looking for someone on the run. The sound roared through the apartment building and was gone in an instant. I thought I saw Hank wince as the blades cut across the sky. He put the cigar back in his mouth and sighed.

"Another man running for his life," he muttered. "This place is a goddamn war zone. Just as many casualties here as there were in Germany or Vietnam or Iraq. And refugees."

"Sometimes I feel like I'm one of them," I said.

"A refugee?"

I shook my head. "Casualty."

"Ahhh, the casualties of the heart," he said, and I noted his sarcasm. "Young love."

"Nothing like that."

"No? What about that goddamn kid you brought over?"

"Benji? We're just friends."

Hank took a drink from his beer. "The boy is sick."

"What do you mean, sick?"

He took another drink as if steeling himself. "There's a hell of a lotta darkness inside him. It's swirling around, going in circles, with no way out."

"No way out, huh? That's very profound."

He took another drink. "No way out. Yet."

I picked up my tea and my hand was shaking. I knew exactly what Hank was talking about. He had seen something in Benji that most people missed or wrote off as arrogance or boyish bravado. Benji was a bending branch, ready to snap at any moment. I could see it as we drove around and when we stood outside a house where someone had died. There was an intensity about him that scared me. I put my tea down.

"I need to go to the bathroom," I said, although it was more that I didn't want to talk about Benji.

Hank put his bottle down. "Get me the wine from under the sink."

I went inside and peed quickly, not wanting to be in that bathroom any longer than necessary, not with the possibility that Bernie Bernall's ghost could make an unscheduled appearance. I went to the kitchen, found the bottle, and brought it out to Hank.

"Cheers," he said, taking it and unscrewing the cap. He took a mouthful and let the bottle rest on his leg. The sky was beginning to darken, the cool breeze settling in for a long stay.

"So tell me about war zones, Hank," I said. "You were in Norway during the war. What was it like?"

His face crumpled. "Aw, hell, I was so young. I don't remember a goddamn thing."

"But there were concentration camps in Norway, right?"

"Yeah, sure. I mean, there were concentration camps everywhere."

I looked at the mark on his arm. It was hard to keep my eyes off it. "Is your family Jewish?"

"No."

"Then what?"

"Then nothing. Just not Jewish."

"So you were a Nazi?" I said, trying to provoke him.

"No!"

"Hey, I don't care," I said, though I wasn't sure how I would've responded if he had said, Yeah, sure, I was a Nazi. I threw babies in ditches and put my bayonet through men's hearts, and here we are just having tea and wine on my balcony while the sun goes down. As right as Hank was about Benji, he didn't know that Benji also had *him* pegged. Hank was hiding something.

"What were the concentration camps in Norway called again? Bardufoss, wasn't that one?"

"How do you know so much about it?"

I didn't tell him that as soon as he mentioned he had grown up in Norway I'd done a little research on the Internet.

"Learned it at school," I said. "The History Channel. There's this big fight going on at the moment about whether to restore Auschwitz so people can keep visiting it or to let it fall down."

"Fall down," Hank said without hesitation.

"Really? You don't think that maybe it's important to keep it standing so people can go and see it? There's kids at my school who don't believe the Holocaust happened. If it's still standing, people can't deny what took place there."

"People will find ways to deny anything." Hank scowled, staring at the concrete, not looking at me. "Won't make a lick of difference if that building's still there or not. I say let it fall to the ground."

The sun disappeared into the horizon and the sky went dark. The wind grew colder and the street lamps illuminated in unison. Hank stretched.

"Tell me," he said, "what do your parents think of you spending so much time around here?"

I took a deep breath. "My parents died."

"They did?"

I nodded. "It was an accident. Um, a car accident."

"Oh." Hank was thoughtful for a moment. "I'm sorry to hear that."

"It's okay."

"Doesn't sound okay."

I took another deep breath. "Well, it happened about five years ago, so I'm really cool with it now."

"Oh. Well, that's good, then."

We sat in silence for a moment. "Hey, are you sure I can't take you anywhere?" I said finally, breaking the silence. "You spend all day cooped up in that stuffy apartment in the heat."

"Suits me fine."

"Hank, it's not healthy."

"I tell you what," he said, "you give me something worth going out for, and we'll go out."

"Ah! A challenge."

He stood up, opened the front door, and stepped inside. I waited a moment, enjoying the quiet of the night, then heard the sound of an old movie floating out on the breeze. Ginger Rogers and Fred Astaire were singing "Let's Call the Whole Thing Off." I peeked inside and saw Hank at his spot in front of the television, basking in the glow of its warmth as a tiny fan blew air across his face.

15

"Hey, Hilda. Come look at this."

I was sitting on the floor in Benji's room flicking through magazines and drinking lemonade his mom made for us. It was ninety degrees outside and too hot to be driving around, so we had decided to hang at Benji's for the day. You wouldn't know we were in the middle of a heat wave sitting in Benji's room. His house had air-conditioning and was chilled like an icebox. Goose bumps were forming on my flesh. I worried about Hank in his stuffy old apartment, with those thick, insulating curtains and only a crappy fan to keep the heat out. Old people died in weather like this, and their bodies weren't found for days. Not until the smell coming from their apartments became too strong to ignore. I decided I would make sure to visit Hank the next day to see if he was all right. Benji and his parents were heading up to Yosemite for a weekend of rafting and hiking. They'd invited me along but I had made up a story about Lynette having time off work (like that would ever happen) and we were going to have a "girls" weekend together. In truth I had some expeditions of my own planned.

Benji opened his closet and rustled around inside. A moment later he emerged from the darkness holding a small fishbowl. The bottom of the bowl was covered in sparkling pebbles, and in the center was a plastic castle with a hole through the drawbridge large enough for a fish to swim through. For a moment I couldn't see anything else, then a small flicker of movement caught my eye.

"Is there a fish in there?" I asked. "I can't see it."

"Yeah. Right there. His name's Sid Vicious, but I call him Sid Fishious."

Benji tapped the side of the bowl and again something moved. I looked closer and saw a goldfish. It was white.

"Mom put him in the cupboard when she was cleaning my room and we forgot about him. I found him yesterday when I was looking for my Buzzcocks T-shirt."

"I thought goldfish were, you know, gold," I said.

"He was. Without light they lose pigmentation. Cool, huh?"

"How long has he been in the cupboard for?"

"Dunno. Probably a couple of weeks." Benji tapped the glass again and examined the fish closely. I watched as he placed the bowl back in the closet, in the darkest part, and threw a dirty T-shirt over the top of it.

"What the hell are you doing?"

Benji took a small notepad from his cupboard, wrote something down with a chewed pencil, then threw the notepad beside the bowl. "I'm going to watch him die. Every day I chart the changes in his mood: whether he's listless, moving around a lot, or has changed color. Soon he'll be floating."

"You can't do that, Benji! That's horrible!"

"Too late. He's half dead already."

"He's just lost pigmentation. If you bring him out now, he might get better."

"He might, but this is much more interesting."

I looked into Benji's eyes and searched for a hint of madness, the tiniest glint of insanity. But there was nothing lurking in those pinprick pupils, just a chilling indifference. I remembered the cat in the Dumpster, the way Benji had thrown it over the rim like a sack of old potatoes, even though its death the previous day had reduced him to tears.

"The first step to becoming a serial killer is torturing animals," I said. "You don't want to turn out like Jeffrey Dahmer, do you?"

"I'm not torturing anything," Benji argued. "It's an experiment. A science experiment. It's perfectly valid to use animals as test subjects."

"Maybe if you're finding a cure for cancer. But not this."

Benji sat down, swiveling in his seat like an evil genius from a bad spy movie. "Let me ask you a question," he said slowly, as if addressing a child. "Do you use antibiotics?"

I groaned, which he ignored.

"Did you know," he continued, "that Nazi Germany was responsible for some of the greatest scientific breakthroughs mankind has ever known?"

"Like what? The sound a baby makes when it's thrown against a wall?"

"Mock me you may, Hilda, but the Holocaust was a period of great scientific discovery. The lack of medical regulations meant doctors could finally test on humans, real people, not rats or pigs or animals that have totally different biological makeups. The Nazis were the first to discover that smoking caused cancer."

"They also injected ink into people's eyeballs to see if they would change color."

"Hilda, are you telling me you wouldn't be interested in whether that could actually happen?"

"So what are you saying? That Sid Fishious is being killed for the good of goldfish everywhere? How is torturing your goldfish benefiting mankind?"

"I'm just saying, don't dismiss things outright because you don't understand them. Some of mankind's greatest discoveries were made by thinking outside the box."

Benji turned back to his computer, satisfied, and my eyes returned to the cupboard. I was sure Benji was just saying those things to shock me, because he loved to play devil's advocate. But it didn't change the fact that there was a goldfish in the cupboard, slowly dying. Looking back I saw a pattern, but at the time it was invisible to me. A dead cat had brought me and Benji together, and a dying goldfish would mark the beginning of the end. Benji's fish experiment was the first sign of a deeper problem. It was the point where I decided Benji was starting to lose it.

"I've gotta go," I said, standing up.

"But you just got here! *Faces of Death* just arrived from Amazon. Mom's making popcorn."

"I've got to help Lynette with a case. Do some research for her. You know how it is."

Benji wasn't convinced. "Sure I do," he said, sulking. "I know how it is."

"So have fun in Yosemite, okay?"

"Whatever."

I slunk out, leaving him to his computer and his magazines; Sid the fish still in the cupboard. Mrs. Connor stopped me in the hallway.

"Hello, dear," she said, smiling broadly. "Benji tells me you aren't coming to Yosemite with us."

"No, sorry, Mrs. Connor. Lynette wants a 'girls' weekend.' You know how it is."

"But surely she can make an exception in this case. We would so love to have you. Benji would be very happy if you came."

Yeah, well, Benji's too busy in his bedroom playing Mengele, I wanted to say, but instead I frowned as if I were disappointed.

"I know, but I've already said yes to Lynette. I don't want to let her down."

"Oh, okay, then." Mrs. Connor sighed, giving up. Her blond ponytail was pulled back so tight I thought her scalp might come off. "But if she changes her mind, you will let me know, won't you?"

"Of course. Thanks, Mrs. Connor," I said, and started off down the hall.

"Good-bye, Hilda," I heard her say, and I couldn't help catching a hint of sadness in her voice.

16

THE AD IN THE newspaper gave me an idea. For days I had been trying to figure out how to coax Hank out of his apartment. I had suggested going to the local pool, where we could dip our feet in the shallow end and drink beer.

"I can drink beer here," Hank had grunted, sweat trailing down his face.

"How about a walk down to the lake?" I offered. "We could sit in the shade and feed the ducks."

"I got enough trouble feeding myself!" he bellowed. "I ain't giving my bread to the goddamn ducks. Screw them."

I became obsessed with getting him outside. The heat was becoming intolerable and I didn't know how much longer I could stand it. I was also worried about Hank. At his age heat like this could kill, and when I arrived at his apartment I was always relieved to find him hot, sweaty, and cranky, sprawled in his chair in a bad mood rather than lying dead on the floor.

I began to think that maybe Benji was right, that Hank was hiding something in his past so terrible that to go outside would expose him. I scolded myself for buying into Benji's wild fantasies. I told myself Hank was just a lonely old man, cast aside by an uncaring and indifferent world. He had lost interest in life and was content with his wine and cigars and old movies from Blockbuster. There was no one to push him out of his complacency, no one to tell him there were better ways to spend your twilight years. But he had me now, and I wasn't going to let him live out the final years of his life in a sweatbox.

THE ADVERTISEMENT IN THE newspaper was exactly what I had been looking for. I pulled a pair of scissors from the kitchen drawer and cut around the edges. Lynette gave a startled yell as she stirred her coffee. It was one of those rare Saturday mornings when she was home, and not at the gym or some fund-raising benefit.

"How about you ask before you start cutting into the weekend paper?" she said, looking at me over the edge of her glasses. "There are two people living in this house, you know."

"So you keep reminding me."

She drank her coffee. "What are you going to do today?"

"Just hang out with Benji."

"Well, perhaps you should be spending less time with him."

"Why? Since when have you cared who I hang out with?"

"Since your attitude started to stink." She put her arms on the countertop and turned away, not looking at me. "I've tried so hard to make things comfortable for you, and half the time you act like you don't even want to be here. You're always racing off to Benji's place. Maybe you should just go and live with the Connors. That seems to be what you want."

"Don't speak for me. You don't know a thing about me."

"It's not like I haven't asked! Every day I ask how you are and you barely tell me anything. What the hell do you and Benji get up to anyway?"

To my surprise Lynette had tears in her eyes. I had never seen her cry before and wasn't even sure she had the capacity to. Even at my mother's funeral she had been stone-faced, coordinating the event as if it were a military operation. She asked the priest if she could "sample" the sandwiches the church provided before passing them on to guests. She even told off the grave diggers for leaving a spade near the headstone, claiming it was "unsightly." What was unsightly was my mother's body after the truck tore threw it. Who the hell cared about a fucking shovel? But to Lynette it was a symbol of disorder in her neatly organized world, just like I was. Like a trial she'd lost, the fact that Mom was gone sentenced Lynette to life with a teenager without parole. It was like a death sentence. I closed the newspaper and put the clipping in my pocket. Lynette came over and sat beside me, her face grave.

"We can't go on like this much longer."

"Don't worry. I'll finish school next year and be out of here."

"Don't say that." She put her hand on mine, where I let it rest, even though every nerve in my body wanted to push her away. "I'm not going to let this relationship deteriorate any further than it already has. We are going to resolve this situation and move forward."

I shrugged her off. "Give me a break, Lynette. I'm not a client."

She sat back, hurt filling her eyes, and I had to look away. "Does Benji speak to his mother like that?"

"Benji's mother lets him do what he wants. She leaves him alone."

"One minute I'm not paying attention, the next you want me to leave you alone. You are being totally irrational. If you want me to be interested, you need to give me consistent messages."

"If I *want* you to be interested?"

"I *am* interested."

"Really? Okay. You want to know what I do all day? Fine. Benji and I visit houses where people have been murdered. We take photos and try to imagine what it was like to be bludgeoned to death."

"Hilda—"

"And I'm having a relationship with an old wino in Echo Park. We'd have sex only I think he's too old to get it up."

Lynette looked at me like I was insane. "I think I need to take you to a doctor."

"Why? Because you feel obligated to look after me?"

"Obligated? You really think that's how I feel? Well, Hilda, you may feel I know nothing about your life, but it would appear you know just as little about me."

Lynette took her coffee and left the room. I felt terrible. Lynette tried so hard to connect with me, but every time she got too close, I pushed her away. I read the front page of the newspaper, trying to forget that Lynette was in her bedroom, probably seething after our confrontation. A female serial killer in Russia was claiming she was much more ambitious than other female killers, who were content to drown their own babies at home. "I want to be as famous as the men," she was quoted as saying. "I will continue to fight for equality."

A few minutes later Lynette emerged from her bedroom in gym shorts and a tight tee, her hair pulled back in a ponytail.

"I'm going to the gym," she announced, and I didn't say anything. I had my own places to retreat to.

"GUESS WHAT," I SAID when I arrived at Hank's later that evening. The sun was going down and I could tell he was surprised to see me so late.

"Didn't know you were coming," he grunted as he turned around and went back inside. He collapsed in his chair wearing nothing but a pair of boxers. I stepped in and closed the door behind me, barely containing my excitement.

"We're going out," I announced.

"No we ain't."

"Here."

I pulled the newspaper clipping from my pocket and thrust it in his hand. Reluctantly he started to read. When he'd finished he folded the clipping and passed it back to me, looking disgusted.

"That's sick," he said. "I don't wanna get involved in your sick death shit."

"What are you talking about? It's really popular. Loads of people go."

"Bullshit."

"It's true. It's kind of a hip thing to do."

"People go to the cemetery to watch movies?"

"Absolutely! Last summer Benji and I saw *The Shining*. It was a blast!"

"I ain't interested."

Hank put his feet on the table and stared at the football game playing on the television. I leaned over and switched it off.

"What the hell?" he yelled.

"It's *Sunset Boulevard*, Hank. With Gloria Swanson. Are you telling me you don't wanna see that on the big screen? Under the stars?"

I stood, opened the curtains, and pointed outside at the setting sun.

"Look, soon it will be totally dark. No one will see you."

"What the hell does that mean?"

"I'm just saying, there's no reason to be nervous."

"I told ya, I ain't nervous about going outside!"

"Then do it!"

"I will!"

Hank stormed into the bedroom and slammed the door. I heard drawers opening and cupboards slamming. A moment later the door swung open and there was Hank, dressed in a white shirt and old beige suit pants, a pair of leather shoes in his hand. He looked at me uncertainly.

"Well?" he asked.

"What?"

He gestured down. "Is this okay? Is this what people wear to movies at the cemetery these days?"

"You look great, Hank," I said, and I meant it. He grunted his appreciation.

"I gotta take a shit," he said, and disappeared into the bathroom. When he emerged his hair was slicked back and I could smell cologne.

"This is bullshit," he said, and headed for the door like a cannonball. "I can't believe you talked me into this."

"Wait—we need something."

"What?"

I raced into his bedroom and ripped the pillows from the bed. "To sit on," I explained. "Is it okay to use these?"

"Whatever."

I went to the fridge and grabbed a six-pack of beer. "Okay. We're ready."

"Fine. Let's get this over with."

Leaving the apartment was an ordeal. With every step Hank was looking over his shoulder. He didn't relax until we hailed a cab on Sunset, and as we pulled out from the curb he sank down into the backseat, looking as if he expected someone to open fire on us at any second. We left Echo Park and made our way toward Hollywood, watching the suburbs silently rolling past us, and I looked for any kind of expression of excitement on Hank's face, but saw only fear. I began to wonder whether this was a good idea after all.

17

HOLLYWOOD FOREVER WAS ONE of California's most exclusive cemeteries, a coveted resting place for the stars. Rudolph Valentino had a crypt there. Cecil B. DeMille. Tyrone Power. Even Dee Dee Ramone was interred in its lush green lawns, a strangely conventional resting place for a punk rocker. The waiting list was long and difficult to get on. It was a far cry from the tiny little cemetery in Topanga Canyon where my parents were buried, and where I would one day probably join them. Lying next to Dee Dee Ramone for eternity seemed like a more exciting option. You could be sure there would be a regular influx of teenagers to tip bottles of bourbon into the soil.

A few years ago they started showing movies at the cemetery during the summer, mostly Hollywood classics like *Singin' in the Rain* and cult films like *Rosemary's Baby*. When Hank and I arrived, people were already teeming through the gates with picnic baskets under their arms and trailing beanbags along behind them.

Sunset Boulevard was a popular movie, a perverse film noir that would appeal to anyone excited by the idea of watching a movie in a graveyard. Everyone was walking fast, clambering to get the best position on the lawn, and I grabbed Hank by the shoulder and pulled him along.

"Hurry up, Hank, we've got to get up front."

We walked past the headstones that lined the driveway. Unlike in most cemeteries where the graves were crowded and almost on top of one another, these were spaced far apart, with plenty of room to wander in between without worrying you were stepping on someone. Some of the mausoleums were the size of houses. We passed a sign that announced the chapel was now equipped for webcasts. Someone accidentally bumped into Hank and he jumped.

"Sorry, dude," the guy said, putting his hand on Hank's shoulder before walking off.

"Hank? Everything okay?" I asked.

He swallowed hard and nodded. As the people milled around I saw Hank shrink, pulling in his shoulders as if he were hoping his head would disappear. I took his hand like he was a lost kid and to my surprise he gripped it firmly. I pulled him along the lawn until we arrived at the space that had been designated for the screening. It was a large stretch of grass named the Fairbanks Lawn, due to its location next to the crypt of movie star Douglas Fairbanks. People had already laid out their blankets and were rifling through picnic baskets, pouring champagne, and opening beers.

"Here looks good," I said, and threw Hank's pillows on the ground. We sat down and watched as the people continued to arrive, placing beanbags and directors' chairs next to us, squashing us in. Hank was beginning to realize that no one was paying attention to him and actually started to enjoy himself. I handed him one of the beers I'd taken from the fridge and he almost smiled.

"Thank God," he said, twisting the top off. A woman nursing a baby walked past and smiled at us.

"Who the hell would bring a baby to something like this?" he said.

"Settle down, Hank. What's the big deal?"

"You shouldn't bring a baby to a cemetery."

"Why? The kid doesn't seem too bothered by it. It's not like it's old enough to understand what's going on."

Hank leaned back on the cushion. "I hate kids," he grumbled.

"But how great is this?" I said, looking around at the crowds as they settled in. "If any film was made to be watched at Hollywood Forever Cemetery, it's *Sunset Boulevard*. It's like the ultimate Hollywood horror film."

"Gloria Swanson sure was something in her day," he said. "Stunning."

"Were you ever in love, Hank?"

"Yeah. We nearly married, but she couldn't live with my goddamn demons." He looked at the grass thoughtfully. "Sometimes even I can't."

"There's still so much I don't know about you," I said.

"You know enough."

"I know that I have successfully managed to extract you from your house. I'm feeling pretty pleased with myself."

"Don't get too cocky. The only reason I don't leave my place is that there ain't no good reason to."

"Are you kidding me? Hank, we live in *Los Angeles*. This is the best city in the world. There's always something going on, and it's like something amazing happened on every single street corner. Everything has a story behind it."

"I've heard a lot of stories in my time," Hank said. "And not all good ones."

"Like what?"

Before he could answer, the projector started and the wall of the Cathedral Mausoleum became a screen. Everyone clapped and cheered and even Hank let out a laugh. "We're ready for our close-up, Mr. DeMille," someone yelled, and the crowd laughed and clapped again.

"Benji would've loved this," I said quietly, not sure if I was speaking to Hank or myself. This was exactly the sort of thing Benji and I would've done together. I had to admit that Benji and I were growing apart. Whenever I thought of him, all I could see was Sid the white goldfish swimming listlessly in his bowl, jammed in the back of the closet and waiting for death. I wondered what could possibly come next.

The score burst to life, and the night was filled with the sound of a wailing police siren. I crossed my legs and watched as the images flashed across the wall: a police car speeding down 1940s Sunset Boulevard, a gothic mansion hidden behind enormous gates, a man floating dead in a pool. There was nothing better than the movies.

Sitting in a cemetery in the dark of night should have been scary, but it wasn't. Surrounded by couples and families, bathed in the glow of light from the screen, it was almost comforting. Watching movies in a cemetery is a liberating experience. You almost feel like you are keeping the dead company. I imagined the ghosts of Douglas Fairbanks and Peter Lorre were pleased that we were there.

It seemed a fitting tribute. In a way, all these people sitting on the lawn were just like me. They all found comfort among the dead.

I'd seen the movie a few times already. An aging movie star refuses to believe her time as a famous actress has passed, and asks a struggling screenwriter to write her comeback project, a proposal that ends in betrayal and murder. Her house is a decaying mansion that looks like Dracula's Castle. The movie star herself is as terrifying as her surroundings, old and sinewy like a black widow spider. In the end she loses her mind. Unable to come to terms with her lost career, she descends into madness, becoming convinced that life is actually a movie. The film ends with the actress slinking toward the camera and the audience, beckoning us to join her. "Those wonderful people out there in the dark," she says. Yes. All us wonderful people in the dark. The film ended, and when the screen shut off, the lawn was plunged into darkness. I looked over at Hank and even in the shadows I could see he was crying.

We took a cab back to Hank's apartment. It was still strange to see him out in the night air, standing in his front yard, the wind gently blowing through his grayish blond hair. It was a beautiful sight. I handed him back his bed pillows.

"You sure you don't want me to help you with those?" I asked.

"I'm fine, I just gotta get in," he said, racing for the front door of his apartment. I yelled out the window of the cab.

"Hank!"

He turned around. "Yeah, what?"

"How 'bout next time *you* tell *me* where you wanna go?"

"Next time. Yeah, sure," he yelled back, and before I could say anything else he was flying up the stairs to his apartment as fast as someone his age could.

18

THE NEXT DAY I found myself standing on Benji's doorstep even though I knew he wasn't home. Benji and his parents were long gone up to Yosemite. Mrs. Connor had given me a spare key years ago, just in case Benji ever forgot his, as if we were glued at the hip. To be fair, that wasn't so far from the truth, but it was the enthusiasm with which she gave it to me that made the whole exchange a little awkward. I felt like she was trying to push us closer together and turn us into a couple and was secretly hoping that we would "play house." It was all a little creepy.

I took the key from my pocket, opened the door, and went over to the wall to punch in the alarm code. The house was deathly quiet. I crept through the kitchen with its spotless surfaces; a ray of sun broke through the closed blinds, exposing not a single particle of dust. I walked down the hallway, past all the happy portraits of Benji through the years, flanked by his parents. Freddy Prinze snuggled into my legs, happy to have the house all to himself, content with the automatic cat feeder that sat in the corner, exposing a fresh batch of food each day.

I pushed open Benji's door. For some reason I hesitated before stepping forward, as if expecting the room to be booby-trapped, or for bats to fly out as if abandoning a cave for the night sky. Mrs. Connor had made his bed before he left; the sheets were freshly laundered. Nothing looked out of the ordinary. The posters on the walls were the kind that you would find in any teenager's bedroom; the collection of objects in the cabinet were, to the unknowing eye, bric-a-brac collected from yard sales. But the reality was something much more disturbing. I opened the cabinet door and touched the piece of floor where RFK had supposedly fallen. I placed my hand flat on the piece and waited for something, anything—perhaps an electrical charge, a bolt of light, a dose of meaning. Nothing came. It was just a piece of floor.

I turned to the closet, the reason I was there. I hoped I wasn't too late. Slowly I opened the door, pushed aside all the perfectly pressed T-shirts on hangers, and felt my way through the darkness of the mess below. Finally I felt it; underneath a carelessly tossed robe was the unmistakable smoothness of glass. I picked up the robe, not wanting to look but knowing I would have to. All of a sudden an image of the cat came back to me: poor little Oscar, thrown in a Dumpster and left to bake in the summer heat.

I held my breath. There in the glass bowl was Benji's goldfish, but he wasn't lying motionless on his side, and he hadn't floated to the top. He was hiding in his little castle, not moving much, but enough to let me know he was alive. I put the robe back over the top and pulled the bowl out carefully. I would have to expose him to the light a little at a time: too much at once might send him into shock.

"Come on, Sid," I said. "We're running away."

I closed the closet door, left Benji's room, and set the alarm again before leaving.

19

THAT AFTERNOON WHEN I arrived at Hank's I was surprised to find the door wide open and the chair in front of the television empty. In the middle of the room stood a guy wearing a baseball cap, as unexpected as a mirage. I froze. On first glance I couldn't help noticing how young, tanned, and bizarrely out of place this guy looked in Hank's apartment. He was wearing a gray track tee with jeans that were fashionably too big for him, exposing the rim of his boxers beneath, and red Converse sneakers so bright they looked like they'd just been taken out of the box. He was gathering empty bottles from around the apartment, and as he bent down to scoop up another Bud Lite from the floor, he finally noticed me standing there. We stared at each other, his hands full of empty beer bottles, the liquid starting to drip down his arms. I cleared my throat.

"Who are you?" I said, trying to sound authoritative.

"Who am I?"

With his thick soft lips, large brown eyes, and rounded face, he reminded me of Jim Morrison. His baseball cap had the name of a movie studio emblazoned on the front, and a few tufts of long, unruly black curls escaped down the back and around his ears.

"Yeah. Who are you?" I demanded, not letting his good looks distract me. "Where's Hank?"

The guy shrugged. "He's, uh, not here."

"Hank!" I yelled, racing toward the closed bedroom door and swinging it open. Empty.

"I said he's not here," the guy repeated, throwing the bottles into a black recycling container I hadn't noticed before. I walked to the bathroom and opened the door. No one. There was water everywhere, as if someone had just stepped out of the shower and not bothered to put down the bath mat. That's when I saw a spot of blood on the edge of the bathtub. I'd seen enough photos of blood to know it was fresh. It hadn't dried yet.

"Where is he?" I demanded, storming back into the living room. "I saw blood in there. Tell me what's going on!"

"Whoa, take it easy," he said, holding up his hands as if shielding himself from attack. "Hank's in the hospital."

My lip started to tremble. "What happened?"

"He fell down in the shower. Hit his head. He's out of emergency so it's all cool. I'm just tidying up, then I'm grabbing some things for him."

"What hospital is he in?"

"Calm down. He's fine."

"Just tell me where he is!"

He picked up the recycling container and placed it under the kitchen sink. I was surprised at his familiarity with the place. He obviously knew his way around.

"I'm going over there now," he said, running his hands under the tap and wiping them dry with a towel. He waited. "Are you coming or not?"

We drove to the hospital in a rusty old convertible with torn leather seats, top down, CD player blasting some crappy dance music. It was midafternoon and the sun was at its hottest, leaving long, glistening waves of heat along the surface of the road, like in a dream.

"I'm Jake," he yelled over the music. "Jake Gilmore."

He tapped a cigarette from a packet and put it in his mouth before adding, "I've seen you before at Hank's place."

"Can you turn the music down, please?" I asked. My mind was racing and the last thing I needed was some inane dance track blaring in my ears.

"Sorry," he said, and turned the volume down. He took the cigarette out of his mouth and put it behind his ear. "What's your name?"

"Hilda."

"Hilda? Like the Saint?"

"I don't know. Is there a Saint Hilda?"

"Sure is. She was meant to be very wise, very knowledgeable."

"If I'm so knowledgeable, then how come I've never heard of you?"

He flashed me a large grin, and his teeth were the whitest I had ever seen, even whiter than Benji's. "Hank hasn't mentioned me?"

"No. He hasn't."

After all of Hank's paranoia, it was odd to walk into his apartment and find a complete stranger standing there, especially someone like Jake. He pulled a pair of aviator sunglasses from his pocket and put them on.

"Strange," he said. "It's interesting he hasn't said anything, I mean, considering the amount of time you spend with him."

"How would you know that?"

"I'm his neighbor. I live downstairs."

"You mean in the apartment under his?"

"Yeah, that's right. Man, who did you think I was?"

"I don't know. You could have been, like, a debt collector or something."

"Or the Feds?" he asked with a grin. "A long lost son, perhaps? Heir to the Anderson fortune?"

"I don't know. It's just strange that he's never mentioned you. I didn't know Hank had any other friends."

"Well, we aren't exactly *friends*. I just help him out with stuff occasionally, odd jobs and things like that."

"Why?"

Jake looked over at me. "Why? Because I'm his neighbor. That's what neighbors do."

"I don't know many guys your age who like hanging around with old guys like Hank."

"I don't know many teenage girls who do, either. I guess we're both kind of strange, huh?"

We? I hadn't been aware that I was part of a team, a veritable contingent tending to Hank's needs. I thought it was strictly a solo venture. Even Benji had been banished from the operation when three became a crowd.

We pulled up to the hospital and I followed Jake up to the ward where they had Hank under observation. He was in a room at the end of the corridor, sitting up in bed, a bandage around his head.

"Hank!" I said, bursting into the room and making the nurse jump. "What the hell did you do?"

When he saw me, his eyes grew wide. "Hey, Hilda!" he cried, and gave me a big, toothy grin. "How ya doin'?"

"I'm fine. What the hell happened to you?"

"Bernie! He pushed me over in the shower!"

Jake pushed forward. "What is he talking about?"

"No one pushed you, Hank. You probably fell."

"No, I didn't! Bernie pushed me!"

"Who's Bernie?" Jake asked.

"He's a guy who lived in Hank's apartment," I explained. "He was an actor."

"What's this actor got against Hank? Why would he come in and push him over?"

"He wouldn't. He's dead."

"He died in my bathroom!" Hank yelled as he tried to sit up. The nurse pushed him back down. "He killed himself in my bathroom!"

"An actor died in Hank's apartment?" Jake asked. "When?"

"It was decades ago," I explained.

"I'm very confused," Jake said.

"Nurse!" Hank yelled.

"No need to yell, Mr. Anderson. I'm right here."

"Gimme your ass," he said, reaching out. She slapped his hand away.

Jake laughed, then clasped a hand over his mouth when I glared at him. "What?" he said. "Come on. You've gotta admit that was kinda funny."

"I'm so sorry," I said, turning to the nurse. "He's probably just concussed."

"It's perfectly fine," she said, smiling through gritted teeth. "It's just the morphine talking."

"Cocktease," Hank muttered.

"Hank, do you know this guy?" I said, nodding toward Jake. "He was at your apartment."

"Hey, Hank," Jake said, holding the toiletry bag aloft. "Got your toothbrush."

"What'd you bring him for?" Hank yelled. "The kid's a goddamn pain in the ass."

"He gave me a ride."

"I'm his neighbor," Jake said, explaining to the nurse. "I live in the apartment under his."

"Are you the one who called the ambulance?" she asked.

"Sure am."

"That was really lovely of you to look out for an old man like that," she said, and she inched closer to Jake, stopping just short of batting her eyelashes.

"Oh, please," he said, all fake humility. "I did what any other decent person would do. If we didn't look out for each other, the world would be a very soulless place indeed."

"Soulless," the nurse repeated, nodding and contemplating. "Yes, it would."

"You've got to be kidding me," I muttered under my breath, and when I looked back at Hank I was relieved to see he had passed out, his snore filling the room like the sound of a jackhammer.

WE STAYED AT THE hospital until the doctor arrived. He told us that Hank would need to stay overnight so they could take X-rays. It appeared to just be a concussion, he explained, but they wanted to be sure.

"In your medical opinion," I asked, "should a man his age be living on his own? I mean, doesn't he need someone to look after him? Perhaps he needs to be in a home."

"He's not alone," Jake said.

"Are you family?" the doctor asked him.

"I'm his neighbor. I check in on him all the time. Hank's more than capable of looking after himself."

"You do?" I said, surprised. "I've never seen you."

"Actually, Mr. Anderson's had a few close calls recently," the doctor said, opening Hank's medical file and running through it with a pen. This wasn't the first time Hank had been admitted to the hospital. The previous year he'd been brought in unconscious and was diagnosed with alcohol poisoning. Prior to that he'd fallen down the concrete stairs outside his apartment, bruising his back and spraining an ankle. Still, I remembered Hank's words: *Bernie pushed me.* What role had I played in this? What crazy ideas had I put in his head?

I thanked the doctor and walked away, heading back down the corridor toward Hank's room. Jake's arm shot out.

"Whoa," he said, grabbing me. "Where are you going?"

I shrugged him off. "To see Hank."

"He's asleep. Nasty bump like that, he needs his rest. How about we go for a coffee?"

"Listen, I don't even know you."

"Hey, come on! What are you, some kind of punk Nancy Drew? Here, pull my face. This isn't a Scooby-Doo mask, and it's not gonna come off in your hands. I just want to buy you coffee."

"Okay." I sighed. I was tired, had no idea where I was, and didn't have the energy to try to figure things out. On top of everything else, I was feeling disappointed. Benji had said that I liked being the only person in Hank's life, that it made me feel special, and I guess that was true. Everything started to fall into place: Jake was the person who bought Hank's groceries for him and maybe even tidied his apartment. But why? What the hell would a guy like Jake want with an old man like Hank?

"Like I said, Hank's mentioned you before," Jake said as we walked from the ward. "But he hasn't told me much. I'd like to get to know the mysterious girl who's been spending so much time with my neighbor."

"Yeah? Well, I have some questions I want answered myself," I said, and somewhere in the hospital an alarm sounded and we watched doctors and nurses rushing from one room to the next.

20

WE DROVE DOWN ROBERTSON Boulevard in Beverly Hills, where all the famous people go to get photographed by the paparazzi. They loitered on the streets and spent ridiculous amounts of time looking in store windows, shielding their faces from the cameras and smiling coyly. Jake gave his car to a valet and we walked into a small coffee shop that was swarming with the young and rich of Beverly Hills. I immediately felt out of place. I pulled my Wayfarers from my bag and tried to act like I was too cool to care what I looked like, but I needn't have worried because no one gave me a second glance. They were all too concerned with themselves, with their appointment books and cell phones. Jake himself took a call on his cell as we walked in, and held up two fingers to the host, who seated us in the middle of the room. The windows were reserved for celebrities, where they could see and be seen. It all confirmed for me again that I liked them better dead.

"No, I can't have the rewrite with you tomorrow. I've had a

family emergency," Jake said, winking at me. "How about next week? Yeah, Monday should be fine. Should we meet at the studio? Okay, good buddy, take care."

He snapped the cell phone shut, took off his baseball cap, and let all his black curly hair come tumbling out, swishing it around like he was in a shampoo commercial. He picked up the menu and scanned it.

"You work in the film industry?" I asked, guessing from his phone conversation.

"Yes, I do," he said, almost beaming proudly. "I'm a screenwriter."

"Have you written anything I would know?"

"Probably not. At the moment I'm mainly a script doctor. Most people don't realize there's sometimes twenty or thirty writers on these big movies. Audiences complain about seeing five or six names credited on a screenplay, but they'd have a fit if they knew how many writers were really involved in the crap that's out there."

"So what does a script doctor actually do?"

"We fix things. We all have our areas of specialty. Dialog, fight scenes, car chases. Mine is sex."

"Excuse me?"

Jack smirked. "Sex scenes. Where they go in the movie, how they play out, the length, the amount of nudity involved."

"Are you serious? You mean, like, the hand on the misty window in *Titanic*?"

"Can't take credit for that one. But that was good work. Even I can admit that."

The waitress came over to take our order. "I'll have an egg-white omelette," Jake said, smiling up at her, "with mushrooms and spinach, and a fruit cup on the side. Gotta have my protein."

The waitress giggled. "For you, miss?"

"Just coffee."

"You don't want to eat?" Jake asked, sounding concerned.

"I'm not hungry."

"Hank's gonna be fine," he said, picking up on my unease. "You should really eat something."

"I can't."

"You'll have to excuse her," Jake said to the waitress. "We've had a very traumatic experience today. Our dad is in the hospital."

"Oh no," the waitress said.

"What?" I almost shrieked.

"He was hit by a bus. The one-oh-eight out of Echo Park."

"How horrible," the waitress said, putting her hand on Jake's shoulder. "Will he be okay?"

"He's in a coma. They expect him to make a full recovery, but until then my main priority is looking after my little sister here."

"You're so lovely to do that." The waitress beamed and actually patted me on the head like I was a puppy. "You poor little thing. I'm sure your dad will be okay."

"Why, thanks," I grumbled.

"You're lucky to have such a nice brother."

"Tell me about it."

"Listen," she said, leaning forward and speaking in a low voice. "I really shouldn't do this, but I'm going to comp your meals today. Don't worry about paying for anything."

Jake took her hand. "Why thank you so much, Ruby," he said,

looking at her name badge. "I'll have a side order of toast, too. Whole wheat. And my sister will have a fruit salad."

"You got it, sweetheart," she said, writing it on her pad and leaving.

"That wasn't funny," I said.

Jake laughed. "Come on, we got a free meal, didn't we? Anyway, enough of this small talk. Let's get serious. So, Hilda, what do you do?"

"I go to high school."

"High school, huh?"

"I've nearly finished. One more year to go."

"Right, so you're, like, uh, sixteen or something?"

"Seventeen."

"How old do you think I am?" he asked, a grin spreading across his face.

I shrugged. "I have no idea," I said, trying to sound disinterested. He leaned forward.

"I'm nineteen," he whispered, sounding proud.

"Nineteen?" I couldn't believe it. "Are you kidding me?"

"Well, I just turned twenty," he said, "but I was nineteen longer than I've been twenty, so as far as I'm concerned, I'm still a red-blooded American teenager."

"But, how are you—"

"So spectacularly successful at such a young age?"

I crossed my arms, unimpressed. "That's not how I was going to put it, but sure. I'll indulge you."

"Dropped out of high school," he said, relating his life strategy as philosophically as if he were Tony Robbins. "High school doesn't mean shit in this industry. I always knew what I wanted to do. So

I got a job writing ad copy for a studio, gave a few story treatments to the right people, and bam! Here I am."

"Writing sex scenes."

He beamed. "That's it, baby."

"Well, you look much older," I said a little cruelly.

"Not too much older, I hope," he said with some concern. "But yeah, it's helpful. But you'd be surprised. Most of the studios are run by kids barely out of diapers. Kids just out of college are deciding the fate of millions and millions of dollars and, more often than not, getting it wrong. It's scary."

"Yeah," I murmured, not really knowing what to say. I was still thrown by how someone barely a few years older than me could have accomplished so much already. Jake was so different from Benji, and from me. He seemed to have it all figured out already, when the only thing Benji and I knew for certain were the final resting places of the rich and famous. I played with my napkin, suddenly not feeling so confident.

"Do you live around here?" he asked.

"Encino."

"Wow. You're a long way from home."

I looked around the coffee shop, at all the Bulgari diamonds and Botox. "Tell me about it."

"So I understand you're part of some cult obsessed with death?"

I froze. "Did Hank say that?"

"Something like it."

"I don't belong to a cult. It's more like an informal online community."

"Obsessed with death."

I rolled my eyes. "How do you even know all of this?"

"So you're not a member of the Children of God?" he said, ignoring the question. "You're not trying to convert Hank into some weird Jonestown-type deal?"

"Of course not. I don't even believe in God."

"Interesting. So you told Hank his apartment was haunted?"

"No. I didn't say his apartment was haunted, I just told him someone died there."

"But now he obviously thinks it is. He thinks this actor guy, Bernie or whatever his name was, pushed him over."

"I didn't mean for him to get scared," I said, feeling guilty. "I didn't know he'd take it that way."

"Well, the dude's pretty messed up about it. Next thing he'll be calling for an exorcism or asking for the Ghostbusters."

"Like I said, I never told him the place was haunted. Are you saying this is all my fault?"

Jake sat back. "Far from it. I just want to get to know you. I get the feeling we'll be seeing each other around. We can't pretend we're strangers."

The waitress came back with our food. I picked at the fruit salad with a fork while Jake wolfed down his meal. A piece of egg got caught on the corner of his lip and made me feel a little sick. There was something off about Jake, something not quite right in the way he had appeared out of nowhere, an extra who seemed to have suddenly burst forth as a major player. The egg dropped from his lip back onto the plate and he scooped it up with a forkful of mushrooms. Something flashed in my mind: the first day Benji and I went to Hank's apartment, I saw a figure in the apartment below Hank's, hunched over a desk, music blaring.

"So this 'death' thing you're involved with—"

"It's not a 'thing.' I just like visiting places where people have died."

"Sounds kinda sick."

"It's no sicker that this," I said, looking around the restaurant at all the Beverly Hills housewives and their superskinny daughters. "Half these people are walking corpses as it is. Botox has killed their skin cells."

Jake laughed loudly, almost choking on his food. "You crack me up, Hilda. You're like Mae West, or Ethel Merman. One of those larger-than-life, wise-crackin' vaudeville types."

I didn't like the way he said my name, implying more familiarity than we had with each other. It felt too slick. "So I'm a joke?" I shot back.

Jake put his fork down. "Man, everything's an inquisition with you."

"You've got to be kidding me. You're the one asking a hundred questions like this is a *Playboy* interview."

"I am?" He looked down at his food and thought for a moment, and I could practically see the cogs turning in his head. "Sorry, I get a bit overexcited and don't realize I'm asking so many questions. I guess it's the writer in me."

"No, I'm sorry," I apologized, slumping into the table. It wasn't fair for me to be so hostile toward Jake. It wasn't his fault that Hank had never said anything about him. It wasn't his fault that I inexplicably didn't feel quite so special to Hank anymore. I picked up my coffee mug, stirring it absentmindedly. "I guess I'm just worried about Hank."

"He's a strong guy, Hilda. Stronger than you know. He can take care of himself."

I put the spoon down. "He doesn't have to take care of himself," I said through gritted teeth. "He has me."

"He's got me, too," Jake replied defensively. "You and me, we're quite the Good Samaritans, huh?"

Something about the way he said it made me think of the cat in the Dumpster. *You're such good kids*, the woman had said. "I'm not trying to be a Good Samaritan," I said. "Hank's my friend."

"I didn't say he wasn't. Why are you so defensive?"

I picked up my bag and stood. Jake wiped his face with his napkin and stood as well.

"Where are you going?"

"Home."

"Oh, come on, we're just having a conversation."

"Look, Jake, I'm really tired. Maybe we can talk some other time."

He wiped his fingers with his napkin. "At least let me drive you."

"I'll get a cab. Thanks."

I walked outside. He didn't come after me, and I hadn't expected him to. Out on Robertson Boulevard the sun was bright, too bright, and momentarily the photographers turned in my direction to see if I was anyone, saw that I wasn't, and skulked off toward another restaurant.

21

As the cab left Beverly Hills I felt terrible. Maybe I *had* been a bad influence on Hank. Maybe he'd been happier before I came along and pushed him to go out into a world he was scared of—for what reason I still had no idea. Jake was his neighbor and had obviously known him for much longer than I had. Did I really know what was good for Hank better than anyone else?

Benji was back from his vacation with his parents and ready to continue our expeditions, and to my surprise I was relieved. At least with Benji I knew who I was, where I stood in the pecking order of our relationship. There would be no surprises with Benji, or at least that's what I thought. Our next planned excursion was to the ritzy suburb of Brentwood, and the condo on Bundy Drive where Nicole Brown Simpson and Ron Goldman were stabbed to death. Benji picked me up outside my house and I could immediately tell he was agitated. His eyes were a little red, his movements jumpy. As we pulled out he hit the curb, sending one of the hubcaps flying onto my lawn.

"You think you might wanna get that?" I asked as we sped off.

"Later. We gotta get moving."

"Are you okay?"

He gripped the steering wheel tightly. "I don't know, it's just being around my parents for so long, puts me on a fucking knife's edge. All that time in the woods with them, and no escape. I felt so closed in I could've killed someone. But I'm back now, and we're back together, doing what we do best."

"Sure," I said, unconvinced. He was starting to freak me out with his skittishness.

"That's right," he continued. "Me and Hilda against the world. So what did you do while I was away? You must have been pretty bored without me, huh?"

"Totally," I said as convincingly as possible. "I just hung out at home, you know, surfed the Net."

"Did you go see that old guy again? Hank?"

"Maybe once," I lied. "Can't remember."

"Don't worry, Hilda. You can have other friends. I'm okay with it."

Benji started talking about the good parts of his vacation: jet-skiing on the lake, the day he took his new dirt bike out and went riding through the woods. I was only half listening. I watched as the beautiful Brentwood houses went by, with their lush green lawns and high gates. I wondered if one day Jake might write a screenplay that would sell for millions of dollars, and would some-day live in a house like that. Benji swerved onto Bundy Drive and the tires screeched.

"Chill out, cowboy," I said. "You're gonna kill somebody."

"Oh, I forgot to tell you. On the trip, Dad took me hunting

for the first time. It was awesome. We used handguns. It's so much more badass than hunting with a rifle. He even gave me my own gun as an early birthday present, even though I'm not legal yet. He totally trusts me with it."

"You don't need a gun. That's crazy."

"Is it? There are so many fucking psychos out there, Hilda. You can't trust anyone anymore. Especially in Los Angeles. This town breeds killers."

I was shocked but not exactly surprised that Benji's dad had given him a gun. Mr. Connor was a big gun nut and always went hunting on vacation while Benji and his mom stayed back at the cabin and did something innocuous like playing board games. But I didn't think he'd be stupid enough to give his son a gun. He probably thought it would make a "man" out of him, and it's not like Mrs. Connor could have said anything to stop him. "I can't believe you went hunting," I said, still reeling from the fact that Benji was now in possession of a firearm. "Hunting is so fucking barbaric, Benji."

"I sure did! Got some birds, a rabbit. One night I snuck into the woods while Mom and Dad were asleep and bagged an owl. Do you know how hard that is to do?"

"Benji, what the hell are you thinking? What right do you have to kill another creature?"

"As much right as anyone else. It's Darwinism, Hilda, survival of the fittest. Here—"

He reached across me to open the glove compartment, and to my absolute horror, the handgun his father had given him came tumbling out, falling into my lap. I thought at the very least Mr. Connor would have locked it up in his gun case at home, but here it was, lying in my lap, the muzzle pointed dangerously at my thigh. Benji scooped it up and cocked it like he was in an action movie.

"Christ, Benji! What the fuck are you doing?"

"Don't worry. It's not loaded."

"Why are you driving around with that fucking thing? If the cops see you, they'll shoot you on sight! It's broad daylight!"

"I don't care," he said, and waved it out the window like he was Dirty Harry. "Look out, motherfuckers!"

I grabbed his arm and pulled it back in.

"You're nuts, Benji, you know that? That's not a toy. What are you trying to do? Commit suicide by cop?"

Benji just laughed. He put the revolver back in the glove compartment and closed it. "Relax, Hilda. We can go shoot some shit later so you can see how well it handles. And we won't shoot any animals, seeing as how it makes you *so sad*."

Before I could answer we had passed the house on Bundy Drive. The condo where Nicole Simpson died was an unassuming beige color and obscured by a flowering garden. The new owner had renovated the front to make it less recognizable. "We've gotta go 'round the back," Benji said as we raced past. "That way we can see over the fence."

"Look, maybe we should just go home," I said, freaked out by the gun in the glove compartment, loaded or not. I wanted to be out of the car and as far away from Benji as possible. He looked at me with crazed eyes.

"God, just chill out, Hilda! You're so fucking weird these days."

We screeched around the back alleyway and when we pulled up there was a car already there. A tourist wearing a Disneyland T-shirt was standing in front of the back gate, her husband taking her photograph. As we pulled up they looked at us uneasily, the same guilty look I used to get when I first started death touring, that look of shame from being caught. Before I knew what was happening Benji had leaped out of the car and was charging toward them.

"What the hell are you doing?" he shouted, his voice filled with menace. "Huh? I said, what the hell do you think you're doing?"

"Oh, I'm sorry," the woman stammered, walking briskly toward her husband.

"You're sorry? What the hell do you think you're doing?"

"We were just taking a picture. We didn't mean to offend."

"Offend?"

The couple ran to their rented car, with Benji following fast. He thumped on the hood, slammed down two closed fists while the man struggled to put the keys in the ignition. I jumped out of the car.

"Benji, stop it!" I screamed, too scared to go any closer. "Just stop!"

"You should be ashamed of yourselves!" he yelled, kicking their tires. "Have some respect for the dead!"

Just as the woman began to scream, the car roared to life and her husband slammed his foot down on the accelerator. Benji laughed as they sped away from us, nearly crashing into another car as they pulled out into the busy intersection, tires screeching. Benji stood with his back to me, panting hard, watching them go.

"That wasn't funny," I said, my voice shaking. He turned around.

"Come on, Hilda, it was just a joke. Did you see the looks on their faces?"

I did. They were terrified. But it could have been worse. Benji could have taken his gun with him. "Benji, are you okay?" I asked softly. "You cool?"

"Fuck yeah, I'm cool!" he yelled again, wiping his hand across his nose. "Stop asking me that. I'm fucking great. Being alive is great, isn't it, Hilda? This is what it's about!"

I hovered near the car, hands in my pockets, not knowing what to do. I kept thinking about that revolver burning a hole in the glove compartment. Benji turned toward the condo's back gate.

"Well, come on," he barked. "Get my camera."

I took his camera from the front seat and slowly walked over, feeling like a hostage. He snatched it and jumped up, hoisting the camera high in the air and taking photos over the fence.

"Let's go around the front, too," he said. "Leave the car here. You can give me a boost."

We walked around the corner to the front of the condo. I tried to look casual even though my heart was pounding. When we thought no one was looking I helped Benji up onto the gate and held him in position while he took more photos.

"Your turn," he said after snapping off a few shots. He jumped back down and helped me onto the top of the gate, his hands tight around my waist. I cringed at the feeling of his hands on my body. I just wanted to get the hell out of there.

"You see the walkway?" Benji said. "That's where the bodies were found. The blood ran all the way under the gate and out onto the road."

He didn't have to tell me. I'd seen the pictures. Nicole Simpson had nearly been decapitated. She had stab wounds all over her body, her chest, her neck. So did Ron Goldman, some poor guy from the local restaurant who was returning a pair of glasses Nicole's mother had left there. Benji was right. The blood had run like a river through the paved tiles, pooling in the edges. So much blood.

"I want to get down now," I said, and Benji dropped me, then started to take photos of the mailbox. The air was still and the neighborhood quiet, and in the silence I could imagine what it was like for Ron and Nicole that evening. Did they see it coming? How long did they fight, and when they gave up, did they know the consequence would be death? I tried to focus on the facts but all I could think of was the terror, the fear, and the despair. It felt like it was coming off the gate and the surrounding walls. I thought of Nicole's dog howling beside her body, a cry that woke the neighbors. The courtyard was narrow and the pathway short. Such a small space to hold so much pain.

I looked at Benji as he took photos, wondering what was happening to him. Sometimes it seemed so easy for someone to become a killer, to do things you never thought they could possibly do.

"Poor Ron," Benji said as he snapped off another shot. "Wrong place at the wrong time, buddy."

"Yeah," I managed to say.

"Poor bastard dies because OJ couldn't stand his cokehead ex-wife anymore. Tell you what, if my wife ever acted like a hooker in front of my kids, I'd probably cut her up, too."

Benji stood with his camera slung over his shoulder like it was a rifle. He picked a leaf off a nearby tree and tore it into tiny pieces that floated to the ground.

"Ashes to ashes, dust to dust. You know what's sad, Hilda?"

I swallowed. "What, Benji?"

I thought I almost saw a tear in his eye. "No one in this town cares about anyone else. Nobody notices anything unless it has something to do with them. Like, I could take my gun and kill you right now, and I bet no one would notice your body for days. No one." He looked down at his feet. "It just makes me so sad, you know?"

21

BENJI DROPPED ME OFF at home, and I didn't invite him in. I was relieved to be out of his car, away from him and away from that gun. I picked his hubcap up off the front lawn and handed it to him, and he carelessly threw it into the backseat.

"You want to do some more Black Dahlia spots tomorrow?" he asked. "We could go downtown to her old apartment."

"I promised Lynette I'd help her out tomorrow with the yard work," I said, thinking fast. I needed time to digest what the hell had happened that afternoon. All I knew was I didn't want to be near Benji at the moment, not when he was acting like this. He tilted his head quizzically at me.

"Helping Lynette? Has she got the day off?"

Tomorrow was a Wednesday. Shit. "Yeah. She's taking the day off. So see you later?"

I caught something in his eye that let me know he knew what I was doing, that there was no "yard work" arranged. I was backing off, backing away from him. His face flashed recognition, but a moment later it was gone. I thought again about the gun.

"Fine," he said, sniffing loudly and wiping his nose with his finger. "Smell you later, I guess."

And then he took off.

As I walked up the path I heard the phone ringing inside the house. I scrambled for my keys and the ringing stopped, but as I put my key in the door, it started up again, shrill and insistent. I raced inside and picked up the phone.

"Hello?"

"Who's this?" the voice asked, and at first I didn't recognize it.

"This is Hilda. Who is this?"

"Hilda? It's Jake. Jake Gilmore. We met the other day. I'm Hank's neighbor."

"I remember."

"So I made an impression on you? Nice."

"What do you want?" I snapped, in no mood for his games. My encounter with Benji had left me exhausted, but what Jake said next immediately got my adrenaline running.

"I'm calling about Hank."

"Why? What's wrong?" I heard something crash in the background and Hank's voice, angry and distressed. He yelled something that I couldn't make out, and then there was another crash. "What was that?"

"He's tearing the place up," Jake said. "The neighbors are threatening to call the cops. I found some sedatives the hospital sent home with him but he refuses to take them. Can you just come over, please? Seriously, if they call the cops, his ass is getting hauled out of here, and I don't have money for bail, you dig?"

I heard something crash again in the background and an angry woman's voice yelling something I couldn't make out.

"How about you go inside and mind your own business?" Jake yelled back.

"Okay, I'm coming," I said, then I hung up and called a cab.

The cab ride felt like it took forever, and by the time I finally got there my fingernails were bitten down to the quick. I raced up the concrete stairs to Hank's place. Jake was outside the front door, arguing with an old woman who was shouting in another language. Jake had obviously given up trying to explain the situation to her because now he just stood there, arms folded like he was a body-guard, rolling his eyes.

"Lady, this is his daughter," he lied to the woman when he saw me, but it didn't matter because she wasn't listening. The other neighbors were standing in their doorways watching the madness with curiosity: a housewife in a bathrobe, a little boy in a diaper and Spider-Man T-shirt. "She's going to take care of everything. Isn't that right, Hilda?"

I walked past Jake and went straight into the apartment. The place was wrecked. The couch was toppled over and bottles lay broken on the floor. In the kitchen the cupboard doors were open, the contents strewn out across the linoleum. Hank was nowhere to be seen.

"Okay, everybody," I heard Jake yelling outside. "There is nothing to see here. Please return to your respective places of residence. We thank you for your understanding during this difficult time." He backed inside and closed the door.

"Where is he?" I asked, out of breath.

"In there." He pointed to the bathroom. "He's put something against the door. He's been in there an hour."

"Hank Anderson!" I yelled, giving the bathroom door a hard knock with my fist. "What the hell is going on in there?"

No answer.

"Hank?" I yelled again. "You're not doing yourself in, are you?"

Jake said, "Maybe we should kick the door down."

"Don't you touch my goddamn door!" Hank yelled back. "I told you to get out of here!"

"Open the door!" I yelled.

"No! They're trying to kill me!"

"Who's trying to kill you?"

"The doctors. Everybody. Everybody knows what I did. They want to poison me!"

"Hank, come out here. No one is trying to kill you."

"You all want me dead!"

"Hank, I'm your friend, and so is Jake. We're concerned about you."

"*He's* not. He's a spy. He wants me dead."

"That's ridiculous," Jake said through the door. "I was just bringing up some frozen quesadillas."

"Hank, Jake is not a spy," I said. "Do you think a spy would be caught dead wearing neon sneakers?"

"Hey! These sneakers cost me three hundred bucks!" Jake protested.

Hank opened the door a crack. "I'm not taking the pills," he said.

"Fine," I said. "Don't take them. If you want to keep feeling like shit, that's up to you. But you can't stay in the bathroom forever."

Slowly the door opened. Hank looked terrible. He hadn't

shaved and he smelled like he hadn't showered since returning from the hospital. He was wearing a ratty old blue dressing gown with holes in it. He blinked his eyes like an animal emerging from a long hibernation. He looked us both up and down, pulling his robe tightly around him. I looked into the bathroom behind him. The mirror was shattered, and glass was glistening across the floor and sink. A wastebasket lay on the floor, trash strewn everywhere. He'd used the wastebasket to break the mirror.

"Come on, Hank," I said. "Let's get you into bed."

He shuffled out into the living room, defeated. I turned to Jake.

"Give me a minute," I said, and before he could answer I walked into the bedroom with Hank, closing the door behind us.

Hank slid into bed, exhausted. I closed the blinds, turned off the lamps, and pulled the sheet up around him.

"That was a hell of a show you just gave us," I said, trying to sound strong. "You want to tell me what's going on?"

Hank rolled over like a petulant child, turning his back to me.

"You're lucky no one called the cops," I said. "It came damn close."

He grumbled into the wall. I looked around the room. There was nothing personal in it, no books or photos or pictures. Just the bare essentials: furniture, clothes on the floor, lamps.

"Hank, I know you're not crazy," I said.

"It would be better if I was," he muttered.

"Is this my fault? Maybe we shouldn't have gone out. You know, to the movie. I didn't know it would upset you."

"It's got nothing to do with you," he roared back, suddenly strong again. I heard footsteps outside.

"Hilda!" Jake yelled, knocking on the door. "You cool in there?"

"We're fine," I yelled back, but we weren't. Nothing was fine. I looked at Hank's back. I was suddenly overcome with the urge to embrace him, to lie down, wrap my arms around his body, and fall into a deep sleep. Instead I walked out of the bedroom and closed the door, figuring the best possible thing Hank could do now was sleep. Jake was standing in the middle of the living room, neon sneakers dazzling amid the chaos. We looked at each other.

"You know, those sneakers really are ridiculous," I said, and couldn't help giggling.

Jake looked down at his feet. "You really don't like them?" he said, sounding a little crushed. "I thought they were cool."

"Maybe in the eighties," I said. "But then again, what do I know? I'm just a dumb kid who goes to high school, remember?"

"Hey, don't be like that. I'm sorry. You actually did really great."

"I did?"

Jake started collecting bottles from the floor and throwing them under his arm. "Sure you did. Did you see anyone else out there taking control of the situation? You should be a hostage negotiator."

I went into the kitchen and found some plastic shopping bags along with a dustpan and broom. Together we tidied the room, sweeping up glass fragments and returning furniture to its rightful place.

"You don't have to do this," I said as we collected the trash from the bathroom and turned the wastebasket the right way up.

"Hell, I'd look for any reason not to have to go downstairs and work," he said. "The studio's riding my ass for these scenes and I'm as blocked as John Candy's colon."

"What a colorful image."

"After we finish cleaning up, do you think you might want to, I don't know, grab a coffee with me?"

I shook my head. "Look, I appreciate you making an effort, Jake, really I do. But I've had a really crappy day and I'm really tired. Anyway, coffee didn't work out too well for us last time."

"I know. We got off on the wrong foot, that's all. Come on. I owe you. My treat. I know if I don't get a break, *I'll* be the one going batshit crazy."

I dropped the garbage bag at my side. I was too keyed up to go home now, and anyway, there was part of me that didn't want to be anywhere Benji could find me at the moment, at least until he calmed down. "Okay," I relented. "But no more Beverly Hills coffee shops. I get to choose."

He smiled. "You get to choose," he agreed. "But I get to pay."

"No arguments there."

"Then let's get out of here," he said, opening the door for me. "This place has some bad juju."

22

WE DROVE DOWN SUNSET to the Coffee Bean & Tea Leaf, a low-key hangout for actors and bloggers with a fireplace outside that was always filled with cigarette butts. Jake ordered a long black for himself, and a large mocha Ice Blended with whipped cream and a chocolate brownie for me. As we sat by the fire in the dark I dipped the brownie in the whipped cream and licked it.

"Slow down," he said. "I don't know the Heimlich Maneuver, and I've had enough excitement for one day, thank you."

His phone started to ring. He looked at the screen to see who it was, then pressed the Ignore button.

"Girlfriend?" I asked, surprised to find my stomach had dipped a little.

"Nah. Just some crazy chick. She's an actress who thinks that by banging the screenwriter she's gonna get a part in the movie. Boy, does she have it ass backward."

"How long have you been together?"

He leaned forward and ran a finger through the cream in my

iced mocha, put it in his mouth, and sucked. "She's not my girl-friend," he said, finger still in his mouth. "I just don't have time for a girlfriend. I'm too busy—I've got my career, my crazy neighbor to take care of, his crazy goth girlfriend."

"I'm not a goth, and I believe I was the one who diffused the situation today, so I don't need taking care of, either."

"Anyway, I don't like actresses," he said dismissively. "They're soulless."

"That's a bit extreme," I said.

Jake wiped his finger on his jeans, which had fashionable holes in all the right places. "Here, give me your hand."

He leaned in close and took my fingers in his.

"You feel this?"

I felt the color rising in my cheeks and swiveled in my seat to see if anyone was watching. Jake's hands felt warm and soft, as if he'd never done a hard day's work in his life. My heart quick-ened.

"This," Jake said, delicately running his fingers along the back of my hand, "is more warmth than I ever experienced with that actress who just called, and we dated for six months."

I snatched my hand back, embarrassed.

"Hey, slow down," he said. "Chill out. You take things too seri-ously. These are the best years of our lives."

"So everyone keeps saying."

He took a sip of his coffee, ran a finger along his bottom lip. "So. What are you going to do when you leave school?"

I shrugged. "Don't know."

"Really? But you're graduating next year. How can you not know what you're gonna do?"

"Some of us don't have it all figured out like you do." I scowled.

"Well, what are your hobbies?"

"Dead celebrities, but I don't think there's much of a career in that. I don't know." I shrugged, overwhelmed by the immensity of the decision. "Maybe I could work in a bookstore or something."

"What do your parents want you to do? I'm sure they've got an opinion."

"My parents died," I said, bracing myself for the inevitable reaction such a statement usually brings, but to my absolute surprise Jack barely raised an eyebrow.

"Oh, that's right," he said, snapping his fingers as if suddenly remembering. "Car accident."

"How did you know that?" I said, taken aback to say the least. I was positive I hadn't told him this before, and was sure I would remember if I had.

"You told me," he said, not missing a beat. "When we had coffee in Beverly Hills."

I shook my head. "I don't think I did."

He shrugged. "Maybe Hank told me. Maybe I guessed. It figures, really."

"What does?"

"Hmm? Oh, just the fact that so many people die in car crashes. Do you ever think about the fact that we're all driving around in really big chunks of metal at ridiculous speeds? I'm surprised we don't crash into one another more."

I decided that Hank must have told Jake, as there was no other way he could have known. I was a little disappointed but decided to give Hank the benefit of the doubt. He hadn't been the same since hitting his head in the shower. He probably blurted it out before he had any idea what he was saying. He probably didn't even remember saying it. At least that's what I hoped.

"I agree," I said. "I'm never going to get my license, but then I might have to move to a city with better public transportation, like San Francisco."

"Because of the car accident? Come on, Hilda. Just because your parents crashed doesn't mean you will. Anyway, is that why you're into all this death stuff? Because your parents died?"

"No," I said, rolling my eyes. "Why is everyone an armchair psychologist?"

"But it's pretty obvious, don't you think? Normal girls aren't into the types of thing you are."

"Normal girls? That's right, normal girls are into bulimia and getting date raped. That's much healthier."

"You've gotta admit it's a strange hobby. Most people spend their lives avoiding the topic of death. It's not something most people like to be reminded about."

"Believe it or not, it's actually kind of fun. It used to be anyway."

"Used to be?"

I thought again of Benji. "Something wrong?" Jake asked.

"Sorry, I'm just worried about a friend."

"What's the problem?"

"I don't know exactly. He just seems . . . off. Like he's not there anymore. Hank thinks he's sick."

"Like a virus?"

I shook my head. "I don't think that's what he meant."

We finished our drinks in silence and watched the cars driving down Sunset. At the other tables, writers with open laptops chatted about screenplays and meetings, and I was once again struck by how insignificant Los Angeles could make you feel if you didn't work in the movies. There was a real us-and-them mentality. If you didn't work in the film industry, you were invisible. Unless you became a serial killer, then everyone suddenly sat up and took notice.

"There are a lot of people like me," I said, suddenly feeling like I wanted to explain to Jake why I did the things I did, why I wasn't the freak he thought I was. "There's a whole community of us. We're all interested in it for different reasons, I guess. I suppose I want to look darkness in the eye and not be afraid. I want to feel the resonance of history and all the bad things people have done and try to understand why. I want to stand inside the Colosseum, feel the vibrations of so much death and despair. I want to walk the corridors of Columbine High. I want to touch the walls of Auschwitz."

"Really?" Jake said, sounding amused.

"It sounds weird, huh?"

"Well, a little."

"It's just that, ever since my parents died, I feel like death has been with me, you know?"

"Why would you think that?"

"Because I was kind of there when it happened. But I got out. Now I've got this weird feeling, like something bad is going to happen to me."

"Not while I'm around," Jake said, puffing up his chest, and I couldn't help laughing.

"You know what, Jake? I think I'm starting to like you."

"Really?" he said, sounding a little surprised.

"Yeah. You're okay, Jake."

"Just okay?"

I nodded and smile. "*Barely* okay."

"At least I've got something to work with," he said, sounding pleased. "Hey, you know what you were saying about Auschwitz?

Have you ever thought about how many layers of skin and blood are on those walls? When people take those tours of the death camps, do they think about the fact that they're standing on mountains of skin cells and DNA?"

"That's gross. You sound like the one who needs help, not me."

"Sorry. I guess I have a habit of coming at things from a different angle. You know, attention to detail. Do you think disinfectant can remove traces of skin cells?"

"Perhaps. You'd think there'd be some kind of residue left."

"Maybe prisoners were forced to clean the areas where their cell mates had been killed. Like when they made them dig their own graves, and when the hole was dug they'd shoot them, and the body would fall straight in. Maybe I'll ask Hank."

"What do you mean, ask Hank?"

"Hank was in a concentration camp. He didn't tell you?"

A piece of brownie caught in my throat. "No," I said, coughing. "He didn't tell me. He told you?"

"Well, not exactly. I just kind of figured it out, then when I mentioned something to him, he didn't deny it, so I figured that was a yes. I mean, the mark on his arm, the fact that he's European. It all adds up, doesn't it? Don't you think that's why he's been going crazy lately, some kind of 'posttraumatic' thing?"

We were quiet for a moment. Jake chewed on the edge of his paper coffee cup, bit off a piece, and spat it back out into his hand.

"So did he say anything else to you?" I asked.

"About what?"

"Being in a concentration camp."

"Not really. I just said something like "Did you get that mark in a camp?" and he said "something like that." I guess if he hasn't talked to you about it, he doesn't want to talk to anyone."

This made me feel a little better. It was one thing for Jake to figure out Hank had been in a camp, but quite another for Hank to bare his soul to Jake about what had happened there.

"But I mean, can you blame him for not wanting to talk about it?" Jake said. "I probably wouldn't want to relive that shit, either."

"I guess not," I said, but I still felt hurt. I thought Hank and I knew each other well enough that he would talk to me about something like that.

"So are you going to ask him about it?" Jake said.

"I don't know," I said, feeling dejected. "Maybe."

"Listen," Jake said, changing the subject. "Do you think you might like to do this again with me? I was thinking of taking a day off tomorrow, and if I don't plan to do something, I'll just end up back at Starbucks working on my screenplay."

"You write at Starbucks? That's a bit of a cliché, isn't it?"

"It's the only social interaction I get nowadays, apart from meetings with the suits at the studio, who I'd rather avoid. I sometimes work from home, but I like the buzz of the coffee shop, the idea that we're all in there hammering away at our own little stories. It's a cool energy. Mind you, there's a hell of a bitch fight for the power sockets."

I thought for a moment. "How do you feel about taking a ride into the dark side of Los Angeles?"

Jake smirked. "Murder sites?"

"Who knows? Maybe you'll find a great idea for a screenplay."

He screwed up his empty coffee cup and threw it on the fire, where it melted in on itself and burst into flames.

"When you put it that way," he said, smiling. "I'll do anything for a good story."

"Cool. Well, I guess I better be getting back."

"Me too."

We stood. Jake threw his backpack over his shoulder and something came tumbling out, hitting the ground with a crack. He scooped down to pick it up but I beat him to it.

"What's this?" I asked, examining it, knowing very well what it was.

"That? Just a tape recorder," he said, snatching it out of my hand.

"What's it for?"

"Oh, for when I get ideas and I've left my notepad at home."

"Is that so? You ever recorded anyone on that secretly?" I teased.

Jake gave me a serious look. "I've been recording this entire conversation."

"You have not."

He broke into a broad smile. "Of course I haven't. That would be a gross invasion of privacy."

"Well, don't let Hank see you with that. He's so paranoid about everything he'll get the wrong idea."

"He sure would," Jake said, and stuffed the recorder back into his bag.

23

THE NEXT DAY JAKE arrived at my house in his rusty convertible. He opened the passenger door and I saw the seat was a mess, covered in papers, candy bar wrappers, and empty Coke bottles. I stood and waited.

"Oh shit, sorry." He stepped forward and threw everything onto the backseat.

"What is all that stuff?" I asked.

"What do you think it is? It's my work."

"Shouldn't you be more careful with it? One gust of wind will send all those papers flying out the window."

"Like in the movie *Wonder Boys*? That would be hilarious."

We drove down Ventura Boulevard, past restaurants, trendy boutiques, and gas stations. Jake lit a Marlboro Light and let his hand hang out the window as he blew smoke outside. He was wearing brown cords and a T-shirt that said BETTY FORD CLINIC, and looked effortlessly cool with his black curls blowing against his forehead, cigarette hanging from the side of his mouth like he was James Dean.

I looked down at my black cords and plain gray T-shirt and hoped that my look came off as effortless as his did. Some people were able to wear plain clothes and make them look ridiculously fashionable: James Dean did it with a tight white tee, Marlon Brando with denim jeans. But everything I put on felt too well thought out; the T-shirt wasn't creased enough, and my sneakers were hardly soiled. I figured the key to the look was not to care, but the problem was I did. I found myself caring too much what Jake thought of me. And Jake, tapping his fingers on the dashboard to Guns N' Roses' "Welcome to the Jungle," looked like he didn't care at all.

We turned right on Beverly Glen and headed up over the Hollywood Hills, then crossed Mulholland Drive and made our descent into the wilderness of the canyons. Any anxiety I had been feeling slowly started to drift away. The canyons had that effect on me; the thin, snaking roads lined with eucalyptus trees, the rustic charm of the houses. It was amazing that such a rural area existed barely five minutes from the bustle of the nightclubs and restaurants on Sunset Boulevard. It was an oasis in the city, a wilderness where people could disappear into the bush and scrub, a place where you could hide from the world. I loved the little cottages that dotted the hills; they had so much more character than the gaudy mansions of Beverly Hills. If I could live anywhere in the world it would be here, snug in the comfort of the canyons, surrounded by their secrets.

"So do you like school?" Jake asked, flicking ash out the window that immediately blew back on him.

"Do I like school?" I repeated.

"Yeah," he said, taking his hands off the steering wheel and driving with his knees as he brushed himself off. "School's cool, right?"

"Yes, Jake. It's, like, totally awesome."

"Hell, I loved school when I was there. I just decided it wasn't for me, you know? My parents were hippies who didn't believe in the 'state' and 'institutions.' I went to this special school in Malibu where you could do whatever you wanted. If you wanted to finger paint all day, you could do that. If you wanted to eat glue, you could do that, too. I did nothing but woodwork for the first eight years of school. I made some beautiful birdhouses."

"Birdhouses?"

"It's true. I couldn't read or write until I was fifteen."

"And now you're a screenwriter? How does that work?"

"Hilda, have you been to the movies lately? You don't have to be a great writer to make a career out of it. Anyway, it's not about how well you can write; it's all about *story*. I'm a born storyteller. Let me give you an example. Here's a story for you: A young girl is driving through the Hollywood Hills with a guy she barely knows, looking at murder sites. The canyons conceal things, make it real easy to pick someone off if you were so inclined, you know? He murders her and throws her body into the brush, where it's picked apart by coyotes. Then she becomes a ghost and haunts the canyons like the dead celebrities whose houses she came to explore. See how I did that? See how I did the irony thing at the end?"

"Yeah, well, the girl would've kicked him in the nuts before he had a chance to do anything."

He broke into a smile. "An ass-kicking heroine, huh? I like it. There's not enough positive role models for girls these days."

He took a long drag on his cigarette, then flicked the butt out the window and straight into a thick hedge where I half expected it to go up in flames.

"Left here," I said, sitting up and pointing. "That's it."

We almost missed the turnoff, a narrow lane called Easton Drive that we could barely fit the convertible through; the sides scraped against overhanging pine and oak tree branches. We passed cottages with wooden porches and small front gardens filled with firewood and swing sets. The front doors were wide open, and inside people talked and laughed in doorways. I could smell home-made cooking, like stews and freshly made bread, hearty foods full of starch and calories. One home even had a fire going, smoke rising dreamily from the chimney. The gardeners and maintenance workers paid us no attention. This was not a road you drove on unless you lived there, and the men in sun hats holding shears and pitchforks went about their business, arms deep in muck, pulling weeds out by the roots.

"So what is it exactly that we're looking for?" Jake asked.

"Ninety-eight sixty Easton Drive. It's the house where the movie producer Paul Bern lived with his wife, Jean Harlow. He died there from a gunshot wound. They never found out whether it was murder or suicide. When it happened, there was a rumor that he shot himself because he couldn't satisfy his wife."

"He couldn't satisfy Jean Harlow?"

"Apparently he was a closet homosexual," I said, straining to find the place. None of the houses on the road looked like the pictures I'd seen on the Internet. "Some people think he couldn't get it up. But there are other people who say he and Jean Harlow were madly in love. I don't think he killed himself. Turns out he had a crazy ex-wife who he hid in an apartment and never told Jean Harlow about. This crazy lady ends up escaping from the apartment, comes to this house to try and reconcile, and shoots Bern when he refuses to leave Harlow. She then runs off to San Francisco, gets on a ferry, and throws herself overboard so no one will ever know what really happened."

"But you think you do."

"Jake, would you kill yourself if you were married to Jean Harlow? They were in love."

"Does love mean never having to say you're impotent?"

"Jay Sebring lived in this house, too," I said, ignoring the last comment.

"The hairdresser? The one who was killed by the Manson Family?"

"His friends warned him the house was cursed. He was living there when he was murdered at Sharon Tate's house just around the corner."

We reached the end of the street. "Damn," I said. "Turn around. We might see it on the way back."

Jake squeezed the convertible around the tiny end of the cul-de-sac and we started to crawl back down the hill. "I don't see it," Jake said, looking around. "I think you imagined this demon house from hell."

"Wait, there it is."

Through the treetops behind the cottages was the jutting outline of a gothic-looking house. There was no entranceway and the number was not visible to the street. I couldn't see a way in: no driveway, no gate, not even a walking track. It was as if the house had its back to us. "Damn it," I said. "Everything in this town is hidden behind high fences. It sucks."

"Would you rather they have an open house for you? Make you some sandwiches?"

"I just think the public has a right to visit these places. These are historic landmarks. They shouldn't be hidden."

"How would you feel if you were murdered and some jerk with a camera came sniffing around wanting to be photographed next to your bloodstains?"

"I wouldn't care. The public has a right to know."

"The *public*? Gimme a break. Vampires more like."

I slumped back in my seat, annoyed. Beside me something suddenly moved. An old man in overalls stood beside the car, a rake in his wrinkled hand. He was wearing a sun hat and his face looked a thousand years old. He gave me a look of suspicion I hadn't seen since the rednecks in *Deliverance*.

"Oh, hi," I said to him. "You scared me."

"My apologies," he replied with a gravely voice, and I was relieved by his friendly tone. "Are you looking for the Bern house?"

"Yes," I said, sitting up. "Yes we are. Is that all we can see of it?"

"I'm afraid so," he said. "Many people come 'round here looking for it, and always go away disappointed. I grew up on this street. I was a little boy when that movie producer died."

"No shit," Jake said.

"I don't remember much," the man said, leaning on his rake. "Just a lot of cars, commotion, people. It was just one of those things. I was really young. Like I said, I don't remember much."

It was the first time I'd actually spoken to someone at one of these murder spots, the first time I'd had a conversation with someone who was there when the event actually took place. I was excited but I also felt guilty. Once an angry woman had thrown tomatoes at Benji's car as we sat outside her house taking photos. Later on I looked at pictures of the case on the Internet and found out that the woman who'd thrown tomatoes at us was the mother of the person who'd died there. Even then I hadn't felt bad. If she didn't like it, she could move, I thought. Her son belonged to the world now, whether she liked it or not.

"When they see how narrow the road is, that usually puts them off," the old man continued. "I figure, if you're that interested in what happened up here, where's the harm? It's all history."

"Did you ever see Jean Harlow?" I asked.

"If I did I was too young to remember. Sorry."

"Thanks for that, man," Jake said, putting the car in gear. "Sorry to have troubled you."

"What gives, Jake?" I said as quietly as I could so the old man wouldn't hear. "I've got more questions."

"No more questions," he said, and we started to roll down the hill, the man waving at us as we went off. We turned back onto Benedict Canyon and headed up the hill toward the San Fernando Valley.

"Jake, I wanted to ask that guy more questions. He was there when it happened!"

"Hilda, enough of this death crap. Look out the window. It's a beautiful day, the sun is shining, the smog is, well, not as smoggy as usual. Let's do something fun. I think I know a place you'll like."

IN THE VALLEY, OFF a main highway and behind the Sepulveda Dam, was a beautifully landscaped Japanese garden, complete with artificial brooks, overhanging blossom trees, and waterfalls. It took me completely by surprise: I'd never heard of it, and if someone had told me such a breathtaking sanctuary existed in the middle of dirty, gray Van Nuys, I wouldn't have believed it. Jake made a dollar donation for us both and we wandered inside. The garden was quiet and serene. An ibis drank from the lake. The traffic from the freeway was only a hum, a distant buzzing in my ear. "This is amazing," I said. "Who would think you could find this in the middle of Los Angeles?"

"I like to come here to get some peace and quiet," Jake said. "To think about things. Recenter. I get my best ideas out here. Some days I meditate, go searching deep within for creative answers, let my subconscious dive for ideas."

"Oh, give me a break," I said. "You sound like a self-help manual."

"Why are you laughing? I take my job very seriously. Writing is a quest for truth."

"Sure it is," I said, still poking fun, but from the look on his face I could see he was hurt. "I just couldn't picture you meditating, that's all. It doesn't seem like you."

"Well, I guess there are still a lot of things you don't know about me. Transcendental Meditation is amazing. David Lynch does it."

An elderly couple walked along the path toward us, arm in arm, smiling as they passed. Jake and I walked side by side, a whole world between us. But I had the feeling that chasm was slowly starting to fill. We arrived at a hard steel bench overlooking the lake and Jake sat down. The footpath beneath our feet broke into smaller sections of rock, straight lines giving way to a pattern of circles that covered the ground.

"Are you sure you don't want to sit over there, out of the sun?" I pointed toward an arbor at the end of a log bridge. The bench was small, and we would have to sit close together.

Jake shook his head. "Sit here," he said, patting the space next to him. "Trust me. I won't bite."

I sat. Jake pointed to the ground, to the broken pieces of rock.

"This is called the Directional Stone," he said. "The way the path is broken up is a metaphor for life. It shows that your destiny is not predetermined. You don't have to do everything that is expected of you. There are other paths to take."

I carved the outline of the path with my foot, tracing the edge. "Is that what you did?" I asked. "Chose another path?"

"Not really," he said quietly, in an unexpected moment of self-reflection. "I mean, do I look any different from anyone else in this town, Hilda? I sold out like all the rest."

I didn't say anything, not because I felt sorry for Jake but because I'd heard it all before. Everyone in Los Angeles worked their asses off to get rich, then spent the rest of their lives complaining about it. Most held off the self-loathing by giving some of their wealth to charity or doing something "artistic," like taking up pottery classes. Most just couldn't handle the responsibility that came with the big studio job or the home-based clothing line. I guess they thought that once they got to the top, all the hard work would be over, when really most of the work was maintaining what you already had. "Money is just a beast," I heard Dad say to Mom when the bills piled high and we barely had enough for a bag of lentils. "Once you've got it, you have to keep feeding it, and if you don't it will devour you." Jake was just another tiger eating his own tail.

"My mom used to bring me here when I was a kid," he said.

"Well, she'd wander off and 'recenter' herself and leave me to feed the fish."

"It's really nice, Jake. Peaceful. There aren't many places where you can find peace in this town."

We watched the ibis make its way across the rock pool, long legs extending carefully on the wet stones.

"If only—" I started to say, then stopped.

"What? What is it?"

I traced my finger along the edge of the bench. "I just wanted to ask that man more questions about growing up on that street, seeing the things he did. He's a piece of living history."

"I've got to admit, as freaky as your interests are, they make for some kick-ass stories. How's this for an idea? Young boy witnesses murder, comes back to the place where it happened as a caretaker when he's an adult, and sets out to solve the crime."

"Everything's just a script idea to you, isn't it?"

"What do you mean, alienated girl who befriends old man and discovers meaning in life through her obsession with death?"

"That's great. I don't think I've ever had my entire existence distilled into a movie pitch before."

"Be thankful. I just saved you tons of money on psychotherapy."

"You're very strange, Jake. I'm not sure how to take you sometimes."

"Most chicks feel that way at first. You'll come around."

"Can I ask you a question?"

Jake put his sunglasses on top of his head and leaned in a little closer. "Sounds ominous."

"I'm just curious—why are you so involved with Hank's life?"

"Why are you?"

"I'm trying to help him."

"And I'm not?"

"Don't take this the wrong way, but you don't strike me as the philanthropic type."

"You're very quick to judge, Hilda. Can't a guy have a beer with his neighbor every now and then?"

"I guess, but tidying the place for him? Buying him groceries? There's not a lot of guys your age who'd do that. Well, any age, period."

"Maybe you should take a look in the mirror before you start asking questions. Maybe you're asking the wrong person."

"How very Buddhist of you."

He didn't say anything. When the silence became too much I slapped the bench.

"So what now?" I asked. "Disneyland? Shall we put our hands in the cement at Grauman's? All this peace and quiet is freaking me out."

"Actually, I should probably head off," Jake said, looking at his watch. "I've got a lot of work to catch up on."

"That's okay. I have stuff to do, too," I said, trying to hide my disappointment. I realized I was beginning to enjoy Jake's company. It was strange to be around someone with drive and ambition, someone who thought about more than the best way to chisel a piece of marble off Johnny Ramone's cenotaph.

Jake gave me a thin smile. "I'm halfway through a rewrite."

"Of course," I said, standing. "Hollywood calls. Don't let me keep you from it."

24

W E DEPARTED THE JAPANESE Garden, leaving the birds and the
fish to their beautiful sanctuary. Jake dropped me off in front
of my house. Some of the kids on bikes stopped to stare at his dirty,
run-down convertible, ugly and dangerous in a suburb filled with
station wagons.

"You have a nice house," Jake said as I got out of the car. "Very
cozy-looking. Homey."

"More like suffocating."

Jake threw his head back and laughed. "Oh, the angst of youth.
"No one understands! No one!'"

"What about all your 'writerly' angst, huh? 'The words, the
words, they do not come!' You have to sit and chant by a lake just
to get ideas."

"Speaking of which, the muse is calling. Gotta fly."

He put the car in gear and was just about to pull away when I
ran back to him.

"Jake!" I called. The car screeched to a halt and he leaned out. "What?"

I hesitated, not sure exactly what it was I wanted to say. "My parents were hippies, too," I said.

"Sorry?"

I stammered, "You were saying your parents were hippies. Mine were, too."

He smiled, and this time there was no hint of a smirk. There was warmth in it. "I guess we have more in common than we first thought," he said.

"I guess so."

"I'd like to hear more about them," he said. "That is, if you're up to talking about it. Maybe you should come over after one of your visits with Hank."

"I didn't think you'd feel comfortable letting me into your place with all my 'death vibes.'"

He grinned. "I'm not that superstitious."

"You'd be surprised. A lot of people are. I saw an interview with the LA County Coroner on A&E. He said most people were too scared to even shake his hand, in case they suddenly keeled over, like death was contagious or something."

"Believe me, I'm sure if you walked into my apartment the plants wouldn't die and blood wouldn't start pouring from the toilet."

"Who knows? Maybe someone famous died in your apartment once, too. In Los Angeles you have a one-in-three chance of moving into a place where a celebrity used to live."

"You sure do have a lot of useless information in your head."

"I guess so," I said. I was quite happy for it to be that way;

useless trivia meant there wasn't enough room for other thoughts. Darker thoughts. "Well, I'll see ya."

I started to walk away, hoping he might call out to me, but I heard the engine roar as he sped off. I felt a strange sensation in my stomach, like milk curdling. Now that Jake was gone I felt the dark clouds of my thoughts forming again, as if on cue. When I was with him everything felt lighter. As I walked across the lawn I struggled to keep the demons from pulling me back down. I imagined them clawing their way through the crisp summer grass, tearing away at the soil and the weeds and tugging at my ankle. When I was with Jake the demons disappeared, and death seemed to recede just a little. I wanted it to stay that way.

As I walked toward the balcony I heard Lynette's rickety patio chair swinging behind the eucalyptus tree. The air was still and for a moment I wondered if Lynette had come home early and curled up on the patio with her latest casebook or one of those crappy police procedural novels she loved. But her car wasn't in the driveway. As I came closer, the squealing of the chair stopped, and I took the steps one at a time, peering slowly around the corner.

"Benji."

"Hello, Hilda."

He looked a mess. His cargoes were covered in mud and he stank of sweat. I could see it dripping down his temples.

"What have you been doing?" I asked, not really wanting to know the answer. "You look like shit."

"You're the one who should be looking like this. I thought you and Lynette were doing yard work today?"

"Oh, we were going to, but a case came up and she had to go," I said. "So—"

"So who was that guy?"

I played dumb. "What guy?"

Benji shook his head as if clearing away whatever was rattling around inside. "The guy in the fucking convertible."

"He works with Lynette," I lied, although I wasn't sure why I didn't just tell him the truth. Like Benji had said, I was allowed to have other friends, wasn't I? "I took her some lunch and he dropped me off at home. Are you spying on me, Benji?"

He stood and walked toward me, and I took a step back. He broke into a broad grin and put his arm around me. "That's what I love about you, Hilda," he said, rubbing my shoulder. "So feisty. I've never met a chick with so much moxie."

It was like being in a bear's grip. I squirmed. What was it they said about bears? It was best to play dead and let them roll you around a bit. They'd eventually lose interest.

"That's just because you never meet any chicks," I said. Benji softened his grip and laughed, and I carefully pulled away like it was the most natural thing in the world.

"That's exactly what I'm talking about," he said. "Come on. I've got something awesome to show you."

He dragged me down the street toward his car.

"Benji, I'm really tired. Can't we do this tomorrow?"

"No, Hilda! We cannot do this tomorrow. You're going to love it. I promise you."

25

A MOMENT LATER WE WERE in Benji's car and speeding downtown into parts of Los Angeles most people refused to go. We drove past the gates of Chinatown, the slums of Koreatown, the junkies of Skid Row. I locked my door.

"Where are we going?" I asked.

"This is the best part of the city," Benji replied. "This is where the real gritty living happens. I love it."

Benji was right, but there wasn't much to love. Downtown Los Angeles was the nerve center of bureaucracy and civil administration, the engine room for the city. During the day this part of town administered to our waterworks and power stations, processed our criminals, and made our laws. Then at night it became a ghost town, and one by one the homeless people shuffled out of their cardboard boxes like zombies in a Romero film, taking over the streets. I looked at Benji's clothes. His knees had grass stains and his boots were covered in mud, which hardened and dropped to the floor in big clumps. Benji didn't seem to notice.

"Why the hell are you covered in dirt?" I asked.

He looked down at his muddied cargoes. "I've been hanging out with these guys I met in a chat room. Hilda, you've got to meet them. They're just like us, into the same things. This one guy Ted, he's awesome. He's into the sickest shit."

Coming from Benji that was saying something. I was, however, relieved that Benji had found some other friends. Only a few weeks ago the idea would have filled me with anxiety, but now I was happy there was someone else to share the burden of Benji's neuroses. "You still didn't tell me why you're all dirty," I said.

"Oh, that. Today we dug up a grave."

I was sure I hadn't heard that right. "Did you just say what I think you said?"

He gave me a grin that put me on the edge of my seat. "Hilda, it was amazing. It was a fresh one, just filled in this morning, at the far end of the cemetery where no one could see us. We dug it up, had a look inside, then filled it in again. Man, you should have seen this guy. He looked so *fresh*, but he was, like, *so not there anymore*."

I didn't say anything. Benji was crossing boundaries I had never dreamed of traversing. It was one thing to look at photographs on the Internet, but digging up graves and gawking at dead bodies was quite another.

"You just have to meet these guys, Hilda," he said with an enthusiasm that bordered on mania. "You'll love them."

We continued driving downtown, past Boyle Heights, City Hall, the LAC+USC Medical Center. I wondered how Hank was doing.

"Look," Benji said. "There it is."

He pointed at a nondescript government building, one story, painted white. "That's the coroner's office," I said.

"Sure is," he replied, and before I knew it Benji had cut across traffic and turned into the parking lot.

"You brought me to the coroner's office? Why the hell would I want to come here, Benji? Of all places!"

"Jesus, Hilda. Do you ever stop? Just trust me. You are going to get a kick out of this."

I followed him into a small reception area that was bare except for a few scattered plastic chairs and a vending machine. The walls were fake oak paneling and the floor hard concrete. A large woman sat in a corner chair, her back to us. Two young girls sat on either side of her, holding her hands. The woman rubbed at her eyes with bunched-up tissues, some of them dropping on her feet and onto the floor. One of the girls looked up, her eyes filled with tears. Benji strolled up to the tiny reception window and smiled at the lady seated behind it.

"Good afternoon, ma'am," he announced loudly. "We are looking for the gift shop."

The women sitting in the corner looked up at us, disbelieving.

"No problem," the receptionist said, much to my surprise. She took two visitor passes from a drawer and slid them beneath the glass.

"Go to the next building," she instructed. "Knock on the door in reception and they'll let you in. Then take the elevator to the first level. Room two-oh-eight. It's at the end of the corridor."

"Many thanks." Benji smiled, as if he had just received directions to the gorilla enclosure at the zoo. I lowered my head as we walked past the woman in the corner with her family, their hands interlocked in quiet solidarity.

"Are you high?" I said as we walked out the door. "What the fuck are you doing?"

"Chill out." He handed me a visitor badge and stuck his own to his jacket. It took him a moment to find a spot that wasn't covered in dirt. "This is all totally legit."

"Did you see that family, Benji? Do you know why they were there? They were identifying a body! I want to go home."

He stopped walking. "But don't you want to see the gift shop?"

I paused. I couldn't believe a place like this would have a gift shop, but the receptionist had confirmed its existence. At the very least I was intrigued.

"Okay," I relented. "But it's the gift shop and nothing else. This isn't a fun park."

We walked into the next building to find the reception area deserted. Benji knocked on a wood-paneled door and waited. A portly woman wearing glasses and a suit opened the door and eyed our visitor passes.

"Can I help you?" she asked me.

"We're looking for room two-oh-eight," I said.

"You mean the gift shop?"

"I guess so."

The woman ushered us into a sparse corridor lined with offices and pointed toward the elevator. "Second floor," she said. "Turn right."

"Thank you so much," Benji said.

"Do you have to be so goddamn happy?" I snapped. "How about a little quiet respect?"

"Quiet respect? Hilda, I'm going shopping!"

Two men wearing stiff white shirts entered the elevator carrying folders and clipboards, barely glancing at us. "There's a twenty-two slug in the hallway," one of them said. "We have to move him now. It's messy."

"After I check out this stabbing in three-fourteen," the other man said, looking down at his papers. I looked at Benji and he winked at me, rubbing his hands in excitement.

At the end of the corridor on the second floor was a converted office with a tiny sign that read SKELETONS IN THE CLOSET. We walked in and found a small room decked out in merchandise branded with the LA County Coroner name: baseball caps, T-shirts, bags, even mouse pads decorated with the outline of a dead body and plastic skulls for holding pencils. A pleasant-looking woman with frizzy hair sat behind a desk that doubled as a counter. She smiled at us as we walked in.

"I can't believe this," I said, picking up a key chain in the shape of a toe tag. "This is by far the strangest thing I have seen in this town, and that's saying something."

"This shit is cool," Benji said, putting a cap on his head. "I look like I'm from *CSI*."

"We used to sell jackets as well," the woman said to us. "They looked like official jackets, with 'coroner' written on the back. We had to pull them when people started turning up at crime scenes in them, pretending to work for us."

"No shit," Benji said.

"They had no idea what they were doing and usually ended up trampling all over the evidence."

"Cool."

Benji bought two baseball caps and a T-shirt. "You want anything?" he asked. There was a time when I would have leaped at the chance to buy this stuff, but today everything seemed wrong. I shook my head.

"It goes to a good cause," the woman said, sensing my uncertainty. "All the money goes to educating kids about drunk driving.

We bring them in here on tours, make them look at the bodies of crash victims. It's very effective."

"I'm sure it is," I said, "but I'm fine. Thank you."

Benji looked at me, shrugged, and handed over his credit card. As soon as he had paid, I left the room and started to make my way back to the elevator. The building was old and sterile, and I couldn't help thinking of how many dead bodies we were surrounded by, hidden behind locked doors and dumped in passageways. This place was different from the streets and houses we visited, where the famous and infamous had met their demise. There was no mythology here, no feeling that you had stumbled upon a sacred place, imbued with history and story and legend. There was only the smell of formaldehyde and the tedious bureaucracy of the processing and disposal of remains. Here bodies weren't sacred; they were paperwork. I felt Benji's hand around my arm as I walked toward the elevator, pulling me in the opposite direction.

"What is it?" I snapped, eager to leave.

"Not that way," he said, and motioned to the other end of the corridor. "Let's have a look around."

"We're going to get into trouble."

"No we won't. Just act like you're meant to be here. I want to do some exploring." Then he was off down the corridor, and I had no choice but to reluctantly trail behind, cursing that I had once again allowed myself to be taken in by one of Benji's misguided adventures. He raced toward the end of the hall and rounded a corner. I chased after him, holding my breath, unsure of what we would find.

"Let's go back," I said, and Benji let out a yell.

"Holy shit!"

At the end of the darkly lit corridor was a gurney. There was no one around, everything was quiet, and it looked like someone had parked it there momentarily and forgotten about it. I saw the unmistakable form of a body covered by a soiled white sheet, its feet pointed toward us.

"That's it, Benji," I said, my hands covering my face. "We're going." But he was already bounding down the corridor toward the gurney, and before I knew it he was right beside the body. Without hesitation he yanked the sheet back. The body of a young man stared at the ceiling with open eyes. He had black wispy hair and looked no older than a teenager. His skin had started to turn blue. Benji pointed to a small clean hole above his heart.

"He was shot," he said. "See the bullet wound?"

I shrank against the wall.

"What are you doing all the way over there?" he said. "Come on. It's not going to do anything to you. It's a corpse."

I stayed where I was but slowly craned my neck forward. "This isn't right," I said, and it came out as a whisper. "We've gone too far."

"What do you mean? The elevator is just around the corner. We can find our way back."

I looked at the boy's eyes, open and dry, the reflection of the harsh fluorescents burning his retinas. I half expected them to suddenly move, to look at me and ask what I was doing. I wanted to lean forward and close them, give him peace, but I was scared. We had interfered too much already.

"Put the sheet back, Benji," I said, but he wasn't listening. He was long gone, enraptured. Voices echoed down a nearby corridor and somewhere a door slammed closed. I grabbed Benji's arm.

"Benji! Put it back!"

He looked at me. "But isn't this what you wanted to see?" he asked, confused. "Isn't this what you've been looking for?"

"Take me home," I said. "I want to go home."

"Jesus, calm down, we'll go."

Benji took the end of the sheet in both hands and drew it slowly over the boy's face, taking his time, watching the fabric settle into the grooves of his features.

"Let's get out of here," I said.

We found our way back to reception. The woman with glasses smiled and opened the door for us.

"Thanks for all your support," she said, and raised her coffee mug to us. "Have a good day."

"Don't mention it," Benji yelled back as I dragged him outside. We got to the car and Benji wrestled his arm free from my grip.

"What is wrong with you?" he said. "You used to love this shit. All of a sudden you're too good for it! What happened to you this summer to make you so prissy?"

I could barely control my anger. "*Prissy*? Benji, there were people in there who had just been told that their kid was dead! That their husband was dead! That's not some old mansion or apartment, or some hotel room. It's a morgue. Death is happening in there *right now*. Those people were in pain, in horrible pain, and you couldn't care less."

"Why should I care?" he yelled. "It's just death. Most natural thing in the world, remember?"

"You wouldn't know anything about it, Benji. You've never lost anyone."

"Oh, for God's sake," he roared. "Poor Hilda. Her parents are dead. It's not fair. She can't be happy because she's an *orphan*. Just get over it."

"Get over it? But, Benji, isn't that why you like hanging around me so much? The novelty of being around someone who nearly died? I know that's the only reason you were ever friends with me, so *you* get over it. You're the one who gets such a kick out of all this. But it's my life, Benji. It actually happened to me. You're just a fucking tourist."

Benji made a face like he'd just eaten a handful of peppers. He walked to his car, got in, and drove off, leaving me standing alone in the garage. I walked back into the coroner's office, past the crying women and the eerily cheerful receptionists. I used a pay phone to call a cab. I took a seat, turned my back to them, and waited for my ride, and after a while I put my fingers in my ears to drown out the sound of crying.

26

I NEVER MEANT TO HAVE sex with Benji. It wasn't intentional. I didn't plan for it and I didn't plan on doing it again. It just happened. And I wish I could say that my first time felt right and natural and pure, but it didn't. I can't even say that it was traumatic or painful. The best word for it was *pleasant*, or perhaps something more benign, like *nice*. We came together and we came apart and it was just *nice*. In a way I was relieved to have it over with, that milestone in my life checked off and filed away in as efficient a manner as possible, and to be honest I couldn't see what the big deal was. But I always got the feeling Benji felt differently. I think it might have meant much more to him than I could imagine.

It happened last summer. We were sitting in his bedroom late one night. Benji was on the bed and I was on the floor. *Groundhog Day* was on the television. Mrs. Connor was somewhere in the house but you wouldn't have known it; I swear that woman always wore slippers just so she wouldn't be a disturbance to others.

Ironically, I'd seen *Groundhog Day* before, at least a dozen times. It was the kind of film you could slip into like an old nightgown, a faithful, trusty companion you knew would deliver the goods every time without fail. *Groundhog Day* would never let you down. The gentle softness of its repetition was soothing and reassuring.

Bill Murray wrapped his arms around Andie MacDowell's body and suddenly Benji's hands were on my shoulders, massaging, kneading, both apprehensive and eager at the same time. The longer I let it go on, the harder his grip became, until the constant rubbing friction on my shoulders felt like it would set my skin on fire. Benji had never touched me before, not even to brush past me. I sat, frozen, completely surprised and unsure of my next move. I kept watching the television. Benji continued rubbing my shoulders.

"What are you doing?" I asked, not turning around.

"You seem tense," he said in a matter-of-fact tone. I could tell he was trying to sound confident, but his next sentence came out as a croak. "Does that feel good?"

It didn't feel bad, but it wasn't great, either. There was no spark, no butterflies in my stomach, just a vague, uncomfortable awkwardness.

"Yeah, it does. Thanks," I managed to say, still watching the television. I moved my shoulders slightly to adjust Benji's pressure, but didn't pull away. Bill and Andie were in a full embrace now, love was all around, and I felt myself being seduced, by the movie and the actors and everything they told me love should be and the love that was being offered to me now. I felt Benji's breath on my neck, smelling of the half-eaten bowl of popcorn that sat next to him on the bed. Slowly his mouth came down, and I tilted my head up to meet him, and we kissed, teeth clunking, and I found myself trapped in his embrace, twisted like a pretzel. In a single moment hundreds of questions crashed through my mind and were just as easily discarded. A romantic song swelled from the movie that had been forgotten in front of us and I thought, Is this how it's going to happen? And before I knew what was happening, it did.

Benji pulled my T-shirt over my head and I raised my hands up to let him. His hands went down to my breasts and he squeezed them like they were melons at a supermarket. He turned me around and I let him, let him bring me up to face him, and I kept my eyes closed because I wasn't sure I wanted to look at him. I felt him kiss my lips, the top one and then the bottom one, and then my neck, his hands running down my back. I felt his hands on my scar, the scar that ran down my front, the scar from where the seat belt had pulled me back so tight it almost cut me in two. He lingered on it, running his fingers up and down the crusted skin, and finally I pulled his hand off.

I let him bring me up onto the bed. The popcorn was kicked to the floor. I lay flat on my back, undid my jeans, and pulled them down, happy to have my gaze concentrated on the button and the fly and the challenge of working my tight Levi's down over my hips. Benji was already in his boxers (how that happened so fast I'll never know) and his chest was flat and hairless. He pulled down my underpants and kept kissing me, stuck a clumsy finger between my legs. I looked up at the posters on his walls, at Fall Out Boy and Green Day, anywhere but his face. After some rummaging around in his boxers he was finally inside, and it lasted only a second because a moment later I felt stickiness all over my legs, and Benji rolled off and was lying next to me, panting.

"Sorry," he said, looking at the ceiling and running a hand through his hair. I bent over and pulled my underpants back on.

"It's fine," I said, even though I wasn't sure which bit he was apologizing for. I joined my hands on my stomach and lay there, unsure what to do next. The Sonny & Cher song "I Got You Babe" started to play from the movie and I had the sudden urge to throw the television out the window.

We lay there like that for a few minutes, backs to the bed, staring at the ceiling, our hands crossed on our stomachs. Then Benji turned and wrapped his arms around me, and I stiffened, and once again his breath was on my neck.

"I love you," he whispered, then kissed my cheek, and I didn't say anything. I guess we both fell asleep, and when I woke up Benji was gone. I pulled on my jeans and walked out into the kitchen. Mrs. Connor was making eggs in a frying pan and the smell made me feel sick. Benji was sitting on a stool at the marble counter, eating a bowl of Cheerios, a cocky look on his face.

"Hey, Mrs. Connor," I said, and when she turned to me her smile was so wide it looked like someone had slashed it with a knife.

"Hilda," she cried, putting the spatula down and walking toward me. Before I could say a word her arms were around me, squeezing tightly. I started to squirm a bit and she released her grip, but not before putting her hands on my cheeks and looking me square in the eyes. "Are you hungry? Do you want breakfast?"

"Um, sure," I said, and she hugged me again, and over her shoulder Benji was practically glowing.

"You want some Cheerios?" he asked, jumping down off the bar stool and racing over to the cupboard. It wasn't like Benji at all to be so accomodating, so I meekly agreed to a bowl of Cheerios, even though my stomach was churning with guilt. As we sat there side by side, eating cereal at the kitchen counter while Mrs. Connor tried to make herself inconspicuous in the corner, I was overwhelmed with the feeling that I had made a huge mistake.

Over the next few days Benji tried to bring up what had happened, but each time I quickly changed the subject. We drove to Forest Lawn Cemetery to see the grave of Freddie Prinze, and as we stood looking over the headstone Benji tried to thread his fingers through mine, and I let my fingers go slack, my hand falling to my side. After that he drove me home, not saying a word, and when he dropped me off outside my house he slammed the door and sped off, swerving out of control and almost hitting a kid on a bike. I let him have his space, not sure if we would ever be friends again, and a week later he called me as if nothing had happened, excited by the news that a famous rock star had OD'd at a hotel downtown, and eager to get down there in time to see the body being wheeled out.

Although we never spoke of it again, what happened that day hung between us, like the dead cat swinging in the garbage bag, but more putrid, more fetid. It was the stench of dishonesty. Benji gave me something that day, and I chose to accept it, but I didn't really mean it. That was wrong. I had betrayed Benji, and it wouldn't be the last time. I liked to think I had no choice. Now I wasn't so sure.

27

THAT NIGHT I LAY on my bed, trying to get the episode at the morgue out of my head. I tried to destract myself by reading *American Psycho*, one of my favorite books, but all I could think about was that boy's cold, unblinking eyes as he lay alone on that gurney, and Benji's excitement at our morbid discovery. Benji was out of control, and I had no idea where it was going to end. I felt guilty, as if my friendship with Hank, a friendship I had refused to share with Benji, had kick-started Benji's decline. I really had abandoned him, but there was nothing I could do now. Now I was scared of him, of what he was capable of. There was a soft knock at the door and I put the book down.

Lynette opened the door a crack and peered in. "Hilda?" Her voice sounded tense. I looked up.

"What's wrong?" I asked.

"There's someone here to see you."

Mrs. Connor was standing on the doorstep, neat and tidy in a pink cardigan and pearls, her face somber. I looked for Benji, but thankfully he wasn't with her.

"Hi, Mrs. Connor," I said, and she gave me a small smile, as if it took all her strength to form it.

"Hello, Hilda. How are you?"

She said it with such concern in her voice I thought it was a trick question. "I'm good," I assured her. "Really good. Just reading, hanging out. You know."

She nodded slightly but didn't say anything, just stood there in the middle of the porch fingering her pearls, her blond hair plastered down and severe.

"Do you have a minute, dear?" she asked, looking at the porch swing.

"Sure."

We sat down. For a moment I saw Lynette through the window, looking out at us, but when I turned to look again she was gone.

I put my foot up on the swing and pushed it slightly so we began to rock back and forth. I waited for Mrs. Connor to say something, but she just stared at Lynette's geraniums hanging from the ceiling in a little wicker basket.

"They're beautiful," she said, still looking at the flowers. I began to chew on my thumb.

"Is everything okay, Mrs. Connor?" I asked. I'd never seen her look so pained, and for once I wished she'd flash me one of her robotic smiles, a reassurance that all was right with the world. She looked down at the ground.

"When you have children, you never quite know how they're going to turn out," she said. "Of course you hope for the best, try to give them everything they need to grow, make sure they feel loved and nurtured. Make sure they feel like they are important. You can control only so much. You can't control whether your child becomes, well, a beautiful flower, or something else. Something else."

"Like what?" My mouth went dry.

"Something else, Hilda. Like a weed. Or a parasite."

"Mrs. Connor, don't say that."

Her eyes started to well. "It's true. You can have all the best intentions in the world, but intentions don't mean shit."

I flinched when she cursed. It was like seeing a Stepford Wife malfunction. I half expected her eyes to start spinning and her head to come flying off, exposing the wires beneath.

"Maybe it's my fault," she continued, sounding stronger, as if taking the blame for Benji absolved him, protected him. "I always worried about him. You know, most parents worry that their child will become sick, or be crippled in a horrible accident, but I never thought about those things. I worried that my son would be different, too different to ever be accepted. I worried he would be wrong."

"Wrong?"

Her eyes widened. "Everyone loves to blame the parents, to point their fingers and say it's their fault, they are to blame. No one ever thinks how hard it is for the parents. Those boys that killed all those children at their own school, did anyone give a thought to how horrible it was for their mother and father? The fact that their child had become everything they feared? What do you do when your child becomes a monster?"

My stomach dropped. "Has something happened, Mrs. Connor? Is Benji okay?"

Something in her eyes snapped. "Oh, Benji's fine," she said, panic rising in her voice. "He gets up, he showers, he eats, he goes out with those *people*. Everything *seems* fine, but I know, Hilda. A mother knows. Something is very wrong with my boy. He's like a tightly wound spring, coiled, and soon, I don't know. Something is going to give. Soon."

She grabbed my hand, her hard, French-manicured nails digging into me sharply. "Mrs. Connor, you're hurting me," I said, and tried to twist my wrist away, but she held on tighter, fixed me with a deathly stare.

"Hilda, you are the last chance for my boy. Help him."

"I can't!" I cried. "I don't know what to do!"

"Be a friend to him," she said, and her grip tightened again. She looked at me like a woman possessed, a mother fighting for the life of her child. "You're his only chance. His only chance at being normal. Please, Hilda, help us."

"Is everything okay?"

Lynette was standing in the doorway, her hands on her hips. Mrs. Connor let go of my arm, smoothed down her skirt.

"Everything is just fine," she said, the robot having returned once more. "Hilda and I were just chatting about when she might pop by again." She leaned across, stroked a lock of my hair, and placed it behind my ear. "It's so long since we've seen Hilda, and we miss her. Benji misses her."

"Yes, well, Hilda's been helping me with my work," Lynette said, sensing something wasn't right. "She's been very busy. And school starts again soon. I'd like her to get ahead on her studies. I'm sure Benji's doing likewise."

"Yes," Mrs. Connor said quietly, and her voice sounded a hundred miles away. "Next year's a very important year for them. Soon they'll both be out and on their own. They grow fast, don't they?"

Lynette moved inside the door. "Hilda, don't be much longer. I need you to finish your chores."

"Sure," I said, quickly standing while I was free from Mrs. Connor's clawlike grip. She looked so small and pathetic sitting there on the porch, her clothes perfectly creased, her insides breaking.

"Mrs. Connor," I said. "Benji will be okay. Don't worry."

"Uh-huh," she said, but I didn't think she was listening. She suddenly stood, patted her hair down, and before I could say anything else, had hurried off down the path.

28

H ANK AND I WERE watching *Rear Window* the night Jake turned up at the front door, cup in hand, making an unconvincing plea for coffee.

"I'm doing an all-nighter," he said, pushing past me. "Need the caffeine. Hey, Hank. How's the head?"

Hank grunted at him.

"Good to hear."

"Coffee's on the counter," I said, pointing toward the kitchen, but I needn't have bothered. Jake was already in there, opening the cupboards, peering inside the fridge, taking food out of a can.

"Help yourself, Jake," I said.

He bent over, then reappeared from under the sink, a cookie in his mouth.

"What are you looking for?"

"Whatever you've got. I didn't have time to get to the store today. I'm working on something great, Hilda. Something important."

"Would you shut up?" Hank growled. He picked up the remote control and turned up the volume on the television.

"Whatcha watching?" Jake trotted back into the living room, the cookie still hanging from his mouth, the cup, now full of coffee granules, in his hand. "*Rear Window*? I love this movie. Hitchcock is a genius. This movie is about cinema in its purest form."

"And nosy neighbors," Hank huffed.

"That's right, Hank—voyeurism," Jake replied, undeterred. He sat down on the sofa, put the cup on the table, and chewed noisily.

"That's my seat, Jake," I said.

"I mean, the interest Jimmy Stewart has in his neighbors lives," Jake continued. "The morbid curiosity he takes in their day-to-day existence. All those skeletons in their closets. I mean, this film could be about us!"

Jake laughed, cookie crumbs spilling onto his lap. I could see Hank glaring at him. I perched myself between them on the side of the sofa.

"I'm not hidin' nothin'!" Hank said.

"Oh, come on, Hank, everyone's hiding something. That's what makes people so damn interesting."

Hank shifted nervously in his seat, crossed his arms, and kept his eyes on the television. Grace Kelly moved across the screen like a ghost, serene in a floor-length ball gown, face coming into focus slowly, like an angel's.

Jake took a cigarette and tapped it on the back of his hand. "Why do people do that?" I asked.

"To tell you the truth, I don't really know. Something about moving all the tobacco toward the filter. Bogart did it in the movies."

"Dumbass kid. You don't know anything!" Hank burst out.

I rolled my eyes at Jake to let him know I had no idea what had Hank so riled up, tried to make light of it. Jake just smirked. I assumed Hank was cranky because Jake was interrupting his enjoyment of *Rear Window*, a film he must have seen at least a dozen times.

"If everyone is hiding something, what are you hiding, Jake?" I asked.

"My genius. I am yet to unleash my creative brilliance on the world."

"I'm about to unleash my foot up your ass!" Hank roared, picking up a walking cane that had been sitting by his chair since his return from the hospital. As he swung it toward Jake I realized this was the first time I'd seen him use it.

"Hey, careful," Jake said, leaning back out of the way and laughing. "You'll take an eye out with that thing."

"I don't know who the hell you are, or what you want," Hank roared. "Are you spying on me? Is that it? Are you a reporter?"

"Hank," I said, stepping in between the two of them as they stood nose to nose, Hank's hand gripping the cane, ready to swing.

"I don't like this kid," he growled, still looking Jake dead in the eye. Jake didn't flinch.

"Come on, Hank, you and I are friends," Jake said calmly. "We're just having a friendly conversation."

"I don't trust you."

"Hank, this is Jake," I said carefully, thinking he had gone mad. "He lives downstairs, remember?"

"I know who he is, damn it. Don't condescend to me!"

Hank moved fast, faster than I would have expected at his age, and threw the cane up into the air, leveling it across Jake's throat. I gasped and threw my hands to my mouth, but Jake just stood there, a grin inching across his face.

"Come on, Hank, we're all friends here," he said. Hank stepped forward, pushing his face into Jake's, and Jake winced as if he couldn't stand the smell of Hank's breath on his cheek.

"Don't think I don't know what you're doing down there," he said. "I see you peering around corners and putting your face where it doesn't belong. Waiting for *her*."

Hank nodded in my direction, a small line of spit forming across his lips.

"Hank, what has gotten into you?" I said. "Jake came to the hospital with you and kept the cops away when you were tearing the place up. He bought you groceries, tidied up around the place. He's been nothing but a good neighbor to you."

"I don't need a good neighbor," he snarled. "I need to be left in peace. Don't be fooled, Hilda. There are no do-gooders in this world."

At this Jake actually laughed. "That's right, old man," he said, pushing the cane away from his throat. "Everyone has an agenda, an angle to play. But I'm clean, good buddy. You don't have to worry about me."

"Oh? You wanna tell me, then, exactly what it is you're workin' on down there?"

"He writes about sex," I chimed in. It was only after I'd said it that I realized how ridiculous it sounded. "I mean, sex scenes, for movies. Scenes that other people have written that have to be better. He fixes them."

"Hilda, thank you for your support, but I've got this," Jake said.

"Have you?"

Hank turned to me and must have seen the look of distress on my face, because when he saw me he slowly started to lower the cane until it was almost by his side. On the TV, Jimmy Stewart grappled with the movie's hulking villain from his wheelchair, as uneven a match as the one I was seeing right in front of me. Hank's sudden anger confused me, but so did Jake's cool, aloof detachment. It was as if he was actually enjoying himself.

"You ask a lot of questions," Hank snarled. "Too many."

"Listen, Hank, there's nothing but goodwill here," Jake said, and put his hands on Hank's shoulders as if to embrace him. Hank was a statue.

"Now," Jake continued, "how about we sit down and watch the rest of the film?"

"I've already seen it," Hank mumbled, sounding depleted.

"So then you know how it ends?"

"Yeah, I know how it ends. The guy learns to keep his nose out of his neighbor's business."

"Maybe you should go, Jake," I said. "Hank's really tired. I'll walk you out."

Jake bent down and picked up the cup of coffee granules from the table. "Don't want to forget these," he said, and walked out the door without giving Hank a second glance.

Hank sat back in his seat, looking exhausted, and I closed the screen door behind us. Outside the night air was cool and refreshing. I released my breath as if I'd been holding it for years.

"Jake, I'm so sorry about that," I said. "I have no idea what that was about. You know what he's been like. He's all over the place."

"He's just being protective," Jake said, lighting a cigarette, "and territorial. Doesn't want another man pissing in his corners. It's a guy thing."

"But all those things he said, he doesn't mean them."

"Like I said, he's just protecting his property," Jake said, expelling smoke from the corner of his mouth. I didn't like the sound of that. Was Jake jealous?

"That's not a very nice thing to say," I said.

"Sorry, that was out of line," he said. "I'm just having a shitty day, having trouble with work, and now this. Hank's a hard guy to get close to. I thought I'd made some kind of connection with him, but now, I don't know."

"I don't know what's wrong with him. I feel like he's getting worse. Like everything's getting worse."

"Everything?"

I thought of Mrs. Connor, her arms stretched out to me, eyes pleading like those of a mother on a charity pamphlet. *Help my boy.*

"I feel like everything's sliding out of control," I admitted. "Do you ever feel like that? Like everything is wound so tight that something's gotta give?"

"I like chaos," he replied, stepping onto the balcony ledge and leaning over like it was a set of monkey bars. "Chaos is underrated."

"Careful. That railing doesn't look strong."

"Are you concerned about me, Hilda?" he said, letting go of the railing and lifting his arms in the air like he was on the bow of the *Titanic*. "Look at me! I'm flying, Hilda! I'm flying!"

"Shhhh, quiet!" I grabbed his arm and pulled him back.

"Seriously, Hilda, Hank's just getting old. He's probably got a touch of dementia, you know. You get to that age, you start saying all sorts of crazy things. I can't wait till I'm that old. Even if I've got all my faculties I'm still gonna call everyone an asshole, 'cause I know I'll get away with it. I'm gonna push in line wherever I like and eat candy till I puke."

"I'm glad you can see the light side of it. Doesn't seem like much fun to me."

"What other choice you got? Go out in a blaze of glory like James Dean?"

"It'd be better than what Hank's going through," I said. Jake moved closer and put his arm around me.

"He'll be fine. He's got you."

"He said you ask too many questions," I said, trying my best to ignore his arm around my shoulder, feeling the heat rising in my cheeks. "What do you ask him?"

Jake let go. "Just stuff. Like, What kind of groceries do you need today? You got enough toilet paper? Stuff like that."

"Is that all?"

"No. I asked him if he was the second gunman on the grassy knoll. Christ, Hilda, it's hard enough dealing with him; I don't need you going crazy on me as well."

"Sorry. It's just strange that he would say that."

"As opposed to all the other stuff that comes out of his mouth?"

He had a point. But still, there was so much I didn't know about his relationship with Hank. It was as if Jake had appeared from nowhere, and Hank didn't seem to like him very much. It was strange that someone who had done so much for Hank would be so distrusted by him. There had to be more to it.

"You know, I was thinking of taking the day off tomorrow," Jake said, "letting my head reboot. You interested in hanging out?"

"Sure," I said. I'd decided that I wanted to show him there was more to me than my death obsession. "How about we do something normal, like go to a movie? We could see the new Adam Sandler film."

"I never see a movie in its opening weekend. You know why? There is no way I'm buying into the commercial interests of the studios, that's why. I am not giving any studio the satisfaction of taking my money in those first few crucial days. This whole industry is all about the first few days of a movie's opening. Not the lasting appeal of the story, or the reviews even. It's all about the dollar. And I'm not gonna play ball."

"Okay. No movie."

"How about a picnic?" he said, looking intently at his sneakers, like they might suddenly wander off without him.

"A picnic?"

"You know, a picnic. With a blanket and food and all that crap."

My eyes lit up. "I know just the place."

"So can I pick you up?"

"Sure. Eleven?"

He pointed his finger at me like it was a gun and clicked his tongue as if pulling the trigger. "I will be there."

I went back inside. Hank was sitting back in his chair, staring at me. I busied myself with putting the dinner dishes away. *Rear Window* had long finished and the television was turned to the news. A helicopter hovered high above a vanload of Mexicans who were pouring out the back doors and scurrying for the hills.

"You trust people too goddamn easily," Hank said, his voice grave. I slammed the dishes down in the sink, chipping a plate.

"For God's sake, Hank, *just stop*!" I cried. Hank's eyes widened, and I have to admit I was a little stunned myself. It was as if the hot, seemingly endless weeks of enduring his fits of paranoia and melancholy had suddenly broken me.

"I mean, just listen to yourself. Listen to what you're saying."

"The young are so easily taken advantage of. You, Hilda, are susceptible to the evils of the world. You open your heart because you want it filled, but not like that. Don't fill your heart with his kind."

"And who is my kind, Hank? You? I'm seventeen and my best friend is a senior citizen. And it's not charming like in a Woody Allen movie. I'm not Mariel fucking Hemingway, you know! Shit, now *I* sound like the crazy one. Listen, not everyone is out to get you, Hank. What can I say to make you feel better about Jake? He's done nothing at all to deserve this."

"Why do you care so much what I think?"

"Because he lives right below you and we all have to see one another, so we might as well get along."

I turned on the tap and started fiercely rubbing the plates with a cloth. I wasn't being totally honest with Hank. I wanted him to approve of Jake the same way I would have wanted my father to. I wanted his blessing. But if he was slowly going mad, what did it matter? But that was the problem. I didn't believe he was going mad. I didn't believe it for a second.

"Have I ever told you the story of Lenore Shoshan?" he asked.

"No, you haven't told me the story of Lenore Shoshan," I replied, impatient. I scrubbed the dishes a little harder. "Was she some starlet you banged in the fifties?"

"She was a girl I knew when I was very young, when I was a boy. She was in the camp with me."

I stopped scrubbing. "The camp?"

He nodded. I dropped the plate back in the water and wiped my hands on my jeans.

"She was a girl in the camp with you? The concentration camp?"

He nodded. "I didn't know her that well. She weren't too popular."

I sat down. "Tell me."

"She was scared. She would say aloud the things none of us wanted to give voice to, things none of us wanted to contemplate. At night she screamed for her mother. Sometimes we would punch her arm to make her stop. If the guards had heard her screaming they would have come in, and who knows what they would have done. Probably killed her, and a few others just for the hell of it. We hated that she showed fear when the rest of us tried so hard to stay strong. We hated that she would dance like a clown for extra food from the guards, then scoff it down while they laughed at her. We all wanted nothing more than to get out, get back to our families, but we never dared to say it. She would speak about it all the time, the fact that she wanted to get the hell out of there."

"Poor Lenore."

"Yeah, poor Lenore." He chuckled. "And poor us for having to put up with that shit. As if we didn't have enough to deal with. One day, one of the other kids, a real little shit—his name was Saul, I think—he told Lenore that he overheard one of the guards saying they were going to turn off the electric fences that night. That they needed to turn them off to let them recharge, or some bullshit. Filled her head with a whole lotta crap about how he reckoned someone could get through the fence if only it wasn't electrified, that she could squeeze underneath the wire, make it out, get back to her parents."

I held my breath. "What happened?"

"She fried. Or was shot. All we know is one minute she was there, the next she ain't. And you know what? None of us gave a damn. Hell, we were all relieved we didn't have to listen to her yapping anymore. So what I'm saying is that people come to you acting like they're gonna save you. And they're not. Sometimes they just wanna see you fry."

Without thinking I reached out, took his hand, and held it tightly. His eyes were gray and sad, his rage spent. "Hank, I'm so sorry you had to live through that," I said softly. "I am so sorry you had to experience those things. But that was a long time ago. Now you have people who care about you. Jake cares about you. I care about you. All the bad things that happened in the past, they are gone. Finished. You're safe now. You don't have to keep looking over your shoulder."

Hank grinned, a thin, mean grin that sent chills through me. I thought of Lenore Shoshan, hanging from the fence like a piece of burnt meat, skin singed, and pushed the thought from my head.

"That Jake," he said, "he asks too many questions. About the war. About what happened there. I don't trust him."

"You think he's a spy?" I laughed. "He's just being friendly. It's called showing an interest. You're just not used to it."

"You don't ask me questions. That's why I tell you. I'll tell you more, if you let me."

"You can tell me anything, Hank."

He took my hand, patted it. "All in good time, Hilda. When you need to know, I will tell you. Do you want to know?"

"Yes," I said, my voice trembling. "I want to know."

He grinned again. "You better be sure."

29

THE NEXT MORNING, AS I rifled through Lynette's closet looking for something to wear to my picnic with Jake, I suddenly felt a little nauseous. I opened shoe boxes and pushed aside coat hangers and still the feeling persisted, not entirely unpleasant, but uncomfortable enough for me to notice. I pulled a green floral housedress from its hanger, the sleeves short and billowy, and as I measured it against my body I heard footsteps behind me.

"That's vintage," Lynette said from the doorway.

I turned around, the dress still against me. Lynette looked exhausted. She'd just arrived home from the office, the night's work hanging heavily beneath her eyes. She threw her keys on the table, lay out on the bed, and sighed loudly.

"Sorry," I said, embarrassed I'd been caught in her bedroom.

"No no, it's fine," she said, sitting up. "You're welcome to borrow anything you like. I got that dress at a market stall on Venice Beach when I was a teenager. It cost me five dollars. I've never had a tear in it."

"It's beautiful."

She touched the hem of the dress affectionately. "I used to imagine who had owned it before me. I liked to think it had belonged to some Hollywood starlet. More likely it belonged to some suburban housewife who wore it to church. I love vintage clothes. They already have a story to them, and you get to add to that story. It's funny you chose that one."

"Why?"

"Because your mom really liked it. She used to borrow it without asking. Drove me mad."

I threw the dress on over my head, surprised that my aunt Lynette ever owned anything my mom would want to wear. Already I felt closer to my mother, like I could feel her presence through the fabric. I looked in Lynette's full-length mirror, disappointed.

"The pink kind of ruins the effect," I said, looking at the color in my hair, now starting to fade.

"I like your pink hair," Lynette said.

I laughed. "You do not!"

"I do. It's very you. Strong, rebellious, distinct."

I didn't say anything, embarrassed by the compliment, one of very few I had ever received from Lynette. I smoothed the dress down, slipped my feet into my sandals, and lay down on the bed next to my aunt.

"Where are you off to today?" Lynette asked, closing her eyes. "Surely you haven't gone to all this trouble for Benji."

"I don't really see Benji anymore," I said, and saying the words aloud immediately made me feel guilty. I could feel the desperation in Lynette to say something terrible, to leap in the air and whoop for joy that her niece was no longer friends with the strangest boy in the neighborhood, but she resisted.

"So where are you going, then?"

"On a picnic with a friend."

"A male friend?"

Normally this kind of comment would have irritated me. Instead, I found myself wanting to tell Lynette all about it.

"His name is Jake," I said.

"Jake, huh?" She tried to contain her excitement. "What's he like?"

"He's, uh, interesting, I guess. I feel like I've got a bit of a stomachache, though."

"You're probably just excited. It's just nerves. Butterflies in your tummy."

"Yeah, right," I said sarcastically, but maybe it was true. I couldn't remember the last time I was truly excited about anything. I was excited before I went to gravesites and places where people had died, but this was different. I felt giddy, euphoric. Most of all I felt stronger than I had in a long time.

I looked at Lynette. Her eyes were closed, and I could tell she was already drifting off to sleep. I removed her shoes and socks, and rolled her over. She groaned.

"Have a good sleep," I said, and she opened her eyes to slits.

"Hilda?" she mumbled.

"Yes?"

"I'm sorry I'm not around more. After this next case, I'll take some time off. After I have some sleep."

"Okay. After you have some sleep."

She closed her eyes and began to breath deeply. I turned off the light and tiptoed out, careful to close the door quietly. I took one last look in the bathroom mirror, ran a brush through my ratty pink hair, gave up, and made my way out the door.

30

JAKE PICKED ME UP in his convertible, which I was pleasantly surprised to see he'd cleaned especially for the day. A picnic basket sat in the backseat, a bottle of red wine next to it. He handed me a cheap satellite navigation box and I set a course for the Indian Dunes Park, an old dirt-bike trail in Valencia near the Six Flags Magic Mountain theme park. The sat nav told us it would take twenty-nine minutes to get there.

"There are plenty of places to go for a picnic around here," Jake said as we drove past a local lake. "You sure with the price of gas you want to go all the way to Valencia?"

"There's something out there I want to show you," I said. "Don't worry. You'll love it."

We drove down the highway, top down, and I couldn't help putting my hands up as the wind blew through my hair. The air was clear and as we drove past the mountains and valleys I was struck by how blue the sky was out here compared to in the city.

Sitting in Jake's convertible, driving down the San Diego Freeway, I felt cleaner than I had in years. I hung over the side of the car, letting my arms float on the breeze, and when I sat back I could feel Jake looking at me, and for the first time I wasn't embarrassed. I turned to smile at him but he looked away, focusing his attention on the sat nav, concentrating on the trail it was blazing for us.

"You don't have to look at it all the time," I said, laughing. "It tells you where you are. That's the point."

"I know. I'm just worried because we've been driving for a while and all that's out here is fields and fast food joints."

"That's where we're going. A field. Well, a kind of park. I just hope we don't have to climb any fences."

"Hilda, this isn't one of your weirdo cultish places, is it?" he said. "Let me guess. There's a hole in the ground out here where Charles Manson hid from the cops."

"Not quite. It's an old bike trail," I explained. "But it's been used in heaps of movies. You'll love it. They filmed a lot of Vietnam sequences out here, because there's a swamp and some palm trees. Ever see a movie called *The Exterminator*?"

"Ages ago. It sucked."

"Well, they shot all the Vietnam scenes from that movie here. They shot some of *The Rocketeer* here, too."

"You're not convincing me."

"Just wait until we get there."

We drove on until the GPS led us off the freeway along a dusty road, toward the mountains. We went past the turnoff for Six Flags Magic Mountain, past the families in their four-wheel drives full of screaming, excited kids, and I wondered if they had any idea of the tragedy that had occurred less than a mile away. On the horizon

I could see the outline of the roller coasters, and for a moment I wanted to be one of them: just a normal kid on a normal date, but I knew in my heart I wasn't that person. For a moment it made me sad, but as we drove away from the theme park, I started to get excited about the excursion that lay ahead. We drove on down the highway, toward the mountains, the houses that dotted the road giving way to lush green pastures and rolling hills like in a picture book. In the distance I could see a security fence, but it didn't worry me. It looked quite low, and I'd gotten myself through more difficult situations before.

"Pull over here," I said, and Jake maneuvered the car off the highway and into the gravel driveway.

"So what now?" Jake asked as we pulled to a stop in front of the fence, which I could see now was about twice my height.

"This is it," I said.

"This? How the hell are we going to get in?" he asked, surveying the gate, next to which was a waist-high electric fence that ran the perimeter of the park. "I hate to break it to you, but I don't have any bolt cutters on me."

I pulled the picnic basket and bottle of wine from the backseat.

"We jump the fence," I said.

"What?"

"Come on, Jake, live a little. I'll go first. Hold this."

I passed him the wine and before he had time to protest I was out of the car and making my way toward the fence. I threw the picnic basket over and it landed with a dull thud on the other side.

"Thanks a lot," Jake moaned. "It took me all morning to make those sandwiches."

"*You* made sandwiches? Now I do feel special."

"Are we really doing this?" he whined.

Just as I was about to hoist myself up onto the fence I remembered whose clothes I was wearing. I didn't want to tear Lynette's dress, didn't know how I would explain it to her. She knew I got up to some crazy things, but I'm sure jumping fences wasn't at the front of her mind. Without a second thought I pulled the dress up over my head and handed it to Jake. He took it in his hands and looked away.

"What the hell? Are we going skinny-dipping?" he said, one hand over his eyes.

"I don't want to tear my dress."

"You're crazy. You know that, don't you?"

I grabbed onto the fence and hoisted myself up, a little surprised at myself. Being around Jake had inspired some kind of confidence in me I never knew I had. I wanted to be more like him, fearless, not caring what anyone else thought. I figured jumping over a fence in just my bra and underpants was one small step in that direction. It took only one quick lunge and I was over on the other side, dropping to the ground next to our picnic basket. I stood up and dusted myself off. In the fall I had scraped my knee, and I brushed the dirt off to see a small trickle of blood making its way down my leg.

"Are you okay?" Jake asked, the wine in one hand, my dress in the other, eyes averted.

"It's just a scrape. Throw my dress over."

"I don't know if I want to." He grinned.

I smiled. "Just throw it over, please."

"How about I do this."

There was a gap of about a foot beneath the fence through which Jake passed me both my dress and the wine.

"What's that?" Jake asked, pointing at my side.

"Just a scar."

Jake made an "ouch" face. "Pretty big scar. Were you a cage fighter?"

I pulled the dress back over my head, relieved the material was concealing my body once more. In my eagerness to be seen as care-free I'd forgotten that my scar would be exposed, the only physical evidence of my parents' death.

"It's, uh, from an accident," I said, not sure how much I wanted to divulge. Jake didn't press me any further.

"Well, you can barely notice it," he said, and I laughed, the surprised look on his face betraying what he was saying.

"You really think I could be a cage fighter?" I joked, trying to lighten the situation.

"Oh yeah!" Jake exclaimed, happily taking the bait. "Hell, I'm scared of ya!"

"You are not," I teased.

"Well, maybe not, but I'm not too sure about this fence," he said, pacing behind the wire like a wild cat, looking for a way through.

"Come on, Jake," I yelled. "You wanna explore the jungles of Vietnam, or you want to eat tuna fish sandwiches in the car?"

Jake looked at the ground, took a step back, then leaped at the fence with such ferocity I was worried it was going to fall over. I clapped my hands on my face.

"That's it!" I yelled, impersonating a drill sergeant. "Come on, soldier. How bad do you want it?"

"I want it." He puffed as he reached the top.

"I can't hear you, soldier."

"I WANT IT!"

Holding his hands triumphantly in the air, Jake took an almighty leap from the very top of the fence and landed straight on his ass. As I helped him up I noticed he had torn the back of his pants.

"Looks like you've got a casualty there, soldier," I said, putting my finger in the rip. He jumped back.

"Shit. These are Dolce and Gabbana!"

"Serves you right for wearing designer jeans to a picnic. Soldier, there are no catwalks in the jungles of Vietnam."

"So we're here. I still don't see what the big deal is."

"Follow me."

I took his hand and led him along the dirt path toward the mountains and the thick of the jungle. He kept looking around, as if he thought we were going to be set upon by guards at any moment.

"Are you sure this is safe? There might be security dogs, or worse. I've already ripped my pants; I don't want my ass to get bitten off."

"It's perfectly fine. There's nothing here to protect, and who would be crazy enough to break into an old bike park?"

"You would."

We approached the edge of a steep ditch that sloped downward toward a small swamp and more marshland. We were now surrounded by rolling green hills and towering palm trees, totally secluded from the nearby highway. I placed the picnic basket down and opened it. Jake had packed a blanket, and I pulled it out and laid it across the dry earth.

"Perfect position," I said as I looked out over the expanse of Indian Dunes Park. I sat down and Jake followed, still brushing dirt off his pants and shoes.

"I guess it does look a little like Vietnam," he said, looking around.

A group of birds flocked overhead and there was no sound but the rustling of the trees and the distant ocean. I screwed the top off the wine and took a mouthful from the bottle. I passed it to Jake and he did the same.

"It's so peaceful out here," I said. "So isolated. I love it."

"You come out here often?"

"Just once, with Benji. Did you ever see *Twilight Zone*?"

"The TV show?"

"No, the movie."

Jake snapped his fingers. "I remember. John Lithgow played a guy who thought there was a gremlin attacking the plane he was on, and no one believed him. And Dan Aykroyd ripped his face off to show he was really a monster."

"And he says, 'You wanna see something really scary?'"

"That's right! That film scared the shit out of me when I was a kid."

"Do you remember the helicopter accident?"

"Vaguely. Didn't someone die while they were filming?"

I looked out across the now dry marshland, the place where it had happened. "They were shooting a helicopter scene at night that was set in the jungle in Vietnam. Vic Morrow, this old actor who thought the film was going to be his big comeback, was carrying two little kids across the river down there when a helicopter crashed right on top of them. Vic and one kid were decapitated.

The other kid was crushed under the helicopter. The director was brought up on manslaughter charges but in the end everybody walked free. And it happened down there."

"Shit," Jake said, sounding a little stunned.

"Yeah. The poor special-effects guys were the first to rush into the water to try and help the actors. They found Vic's head and torso floating next to the kids."

"Wow. That's really messed up."

"Hey, Vic wanted a comeback. This way, he'll be remembered forever."

"Great, as the man who was decapitated for starring in a shitty movie."

"Doesn't matter," I said. "He'll still be remembered. You think people would have remembered him for being the guy who starred in the *Twilight Zone* movie? Hell no. But the guy who had his head cut off during filming? That's a dude worth remembering."

"You really think that's preferable?"

"Of course."

"Sounds pretty warped to me."

I paused. "You wanna know why I'm so obsessed with dead celebrities?"

"I would love to know," Jake said, taking a mouthful of red wine. He passed me the bottle and I just held it in my hands. The rich smell of the wine reminded me of Hank.

"It's like, when I think about celebrities who have died, it makes me less scared of death, you know? If amazing people like John Lennon and John Belushi and Sharon Tate have all died, then it can't be that bad right?"

"It's a little early to be thinking of death, isn't it?"

"I don't think so. You can die at any time. Look at what happened to my parents."

"I'm sorry," Jake said.

I shrugged. "Don't be sorry. People die all the time."

"But that doesn't make it any easier on you. It may happen all the time, but when it happens to you, it's not a statistic. It's your life. But your life doesn't have to be all about what happened to your parents. It doesn't all have to be about death."

I stood and walked toward the edge of the cliff. I looked out over the palm trees, the sand dunes, and the forest. It was strange to think that such a beautiful place had been the site of such calamity, chaos, and pain. I thought of the movie crew dropping their cameras and running for the hills. I thought of the parents of the two little children who were killed. They were probably so excited their kids had a part in a movie.

"I should have died that day, too," I said.

"What?" Jake said softly.

"The day my parents died. I should have died, too. But I didn't. Now death follows me every day. I feel it in my skin."

"You were in the car?"

I nodded. "We were driving home from my aunt Lynette's house. Dad had had a few drinks and Mom kept telling him to slow down. In hindsight I think he'd been smoking some of the wacky stuff, too. He said he needed it to deal with my aunt Lynette. He ran into the back of a truck that stopped too suddenly in front of us. The front of our car went straight under the truck, stopping after the front seats. My parents were, well, decapitated is the best way to put it. Just like Vic Morrow. I sat trapped in the backseat, seat belt cutting across my chest, looking at them for what seemed like an eternity. I couldn't see their faces. All I could see was the backs of their heads, crushed against the seats."

"They died like Jayne Mansfield," Jake said.

"Yeah. Just like Jayne Mansfield. So I figure, if Jayne died like that, then it must be okay, right? It's not so bad."

"Hilda." Jake had turned pale.

"I'm not telling you this to upset you," I said, "or to show off or try to shock you. I'm telling you this because I want you to understand who I am."

"I know who you are," he said, and slid his hand behind my neck, pulling me closer. I shivered. "You're someone who looked after an old man when no one else gave a shit."

"I wish that were true," I said, trying to fight back tears. "But Benji and me, we only went to Hank's house to see where someone had died."

"But it's more than that now. You know that."

"No. Hank just wanted to live the rest of his life in peace and I kept poking at him, and made him go out. And he got hurt, and now he's miserable."

"Hank's always going to be miserable. People find excuses to be victims. If it wasn't the fact that he was in a concentration camp, it would have been something else."

"That's not fair."

"Life's not fair, but you have to deal with it. I could've used the fact that my parents were doped-up hippies as an excuse to drop out of everything, but I didn't. That's not me. I want to make my own way in the world. I want the things I own to be mine. I want to write stories that inspire and move people, and make movies that matter. I want to be part of something. Think about it, Hilda. We can do anything we want. We're alive, aren't we?"

I couldn't disagree with that. We were alive, and we were still here. We had a responsibility to the dead to keep on living, no matter how painful. Jake squeezed my hand.

"I think your parents would be proud of you."

I looked away, over the horizon and the blue expanse of sky that led to the ocean and beyond. "Some days I wonder if my parents knew it was going to happen."

"How could they possibly have known that? It was an accident."

"I know, but you hear stories about how people just get this feeling that it's their time to go. Like there was this guy I read about in the newspaper who was totally healthy, worked out every day, went to his job at the office, then one day people started to notice this change in him. He started calling all the people he'd lost contact with, all his friends and family who hadn't heard from him in ages, just to say hello and that he loved them. He started to smile more. He was nicer to his colleagues. He went out of his way to make people feel good, got them cups of coffee, all this stuff that was totally out of character. Two days later he died of a brain aneurysm."

"That's easy to explain," Jake said, putting his hands behind his head. "The dude clocked himself out."

"No, he didn't. They couldn't find any evidence of suicide."

"Well, then he probably knew he had the aneurysm all along."

"But how do you explain the change in his behavior two days before it happened?"

Jake smirked. "Maybe he was getting laid."

"No. Somehow he knew. I don't know if it was, like, a change in his molecular structure, something on a biological level that made his cells get ready. Maybe it was something spiritual. Maybe the universe gets you ready."

I chewed at my finger absentmindedly. "Don't chew your nails," Jake said. "There's plenty of food here, why you gotta be eatin' your hands all the time?"

"Steven Spielberg chews his fingernails," I said.

"And after you've won your first Oscar I'll be a little more lenient on you. In the meantime those stubby little nubs are just grossin' me out."

I took my hand out of my mouth, wiped it on my leg, and curled my fingers around Jake's.

"Ewww," he said, but didn't try to take his hand away. Any thought I had of my parents disappeared as I tightened my grip on Jake. Together we looked at the dunes, the curves in the dirt from its days as a bike park. I tightened my grip on his hand, worried that if I let go he would inexplicably be pulled into the abyss, taken from me, and he seemed to understand because he squeezed my hand back.

"Say, isn't this meant to be a picnic?" I reminded him, breaking the silence.

"Of course," Jake said, letting me go. He dived into the picnic basket and retrieved two sandwiches.

"Tuna fish or egg salad?" he offered.

"Which are you having?" I asked.

"Tuna fish. Egg gives me gas."

"Well, that's, uh, good to know."

We ate our sandwiches, drank the bottle of wine, and brushed the ants off as they marched up our legs. Jake lay on his back in the dirt and closed his eyes, and I watched his chest slowly moving up and down, his heart beating, life intact. A life connected with mine in a way I never thought possible again. I lay down next to him and buried my face in his black curls, and he held me close.

"This is actually a pretty place," Jake said. "I could think of worse places to die."

31

W E FINISHED LUNCH AND drove back to Distant Memories, stopping on the way to pick up groceries for Hank. I started to walk up toward his apartment, but Jake lightly grabbed my arm and pulled me back.

"Hey, come in here for a second," he said, tugging me toward his front door. "I want to show you something."

As he took his keys from his pocket, my heart raced. I started to get nervous and couldn't help blabbering on as we stepped inside.

"Did you know there's a city near San Francisco built right on a fault line?" I said. "You're not even allowed to go into the town hall because it's slowly breaking in half."

"What's that got to do with anything?" he asked, closing the door behind us.

"Well, why wouldn't you just not build anything on that spot? They're onto their third town hall because they keep falling down. It doesn't make sense. Why not just pave it over and put a fence around it?"

"Are you actually asking me?"

"Yeah. Doesn't that seem crazy to you?"

"I don't know. Seems pretty indicative of people to me. They don't want nature telling them where they can and can't build. They'll build where they want, and damn the consequences."

"Even if it means they could all die if the building fell on them?"

"That's people for you."

I looked around. Jake's apartment was not what I'd been expecting at all, and if I hadn't known the same exact apartment was directly above our heads, I would have never believed Hank and Jake lived in the same building. Jake's apartment wasn't a dingy old dive with cracks in the plaster and stains on the carpet. It was painted a soft salmon color, and the walls were lined with framed original movie posters: *Chinatown*, *Shampoo*, *Blade Runner*. The carpet had been pulled up to expose gleaming floorboards beneath; a fluffy mohair rug cushioned a polished black leather sofa. In the corner, facing the window, was an antique wooden desk, Jake's laptop sitting patiently on its surface, waiting for his return. Next to the laptop was an unopened pack of Marlboro Lights, a lighter, and a clean ashtray.

"Wow," I said, stepping forward and surveying the room. "This is nothing like your car."

"My car's where I let the inner pig out," he said, hanging his keys on a hook by the door. "Everyone needs a place where they can be chaotic, but your home should be a place of peace. Sanctuary. The chaos of the world must stay outside."

"It's fantastic."

I wandered over to a large bookshelf near the kitchen and started running my fingers along the spines. There were books about screenwriting, of course, but also other unexpected treasures: Steinbeck, Salinger, Orwell. I pulled out a novel by Maya Angelou.

"Oprah's Book Club selection?" I shrieked, reading the cover. Jake rushed over and took the book from my hands, slotted it back into the shelf.

"Give me a break," he said, fidgeting. "I don't really have people over. I'm not used to having my stuff touched."

"I'm sorry," I said, pulling a DVD from the same shelf. "Everything's just so shiny and sophisticated. I keep expecting you to flip a switch and have an Austin Powers–style bed spring out from the wall. Oh no."

I picked up a photo from the shelf: Jake with his arms around a nice-looking old lady wearing a knitted sweater, smiling, her hair wild and untamed. "Is that your mom?"

"Okay, you've snooped enough," he said, snatching the photo away. "Go and sit on the sofa, where you won't cause trouble."

I did as I was told, sinking into the soft leather of the couch. Jake retrieved his laptop from the desk and sat beside me.

"I want to read you something," he said. "It's something new I'm working on. I want to know what you think."

"What is it, a screenplay?"

His dropped his head, looking shy. "I'm not sure what it is yet. I guess you'd call it prose at this stage."

"Oh, prose! Okay, Shakespeare, lay it on me."

"You're not going to laugh?"

"Is it meant to be funny?"

"Hilda, quit joking around. If you're just gonna joke, I'm not reading it."

"I'm serious." I composed myself, folded my hands in my lap. "Proceed."

Jake appeared uncertain; he opened his mouth, then closed it again, then opened the laptop. I'd never seen him look so vulnerable. Jake cleared his throat and began to read.

"She doesn't know what it is that makes her who she is," he said. "And he didn't know what it was about her that tore into him, capturing him like a fish on a hook. When she walked, she carried the darkness of the world on her shoulders, but all he saw was the light inside, the ceaseless, boundless light of life and all its possibilities. The possibilities he never imagined he would have for himself. He didn't know if she knew that's what he saw, what she gave to him. He didn't know how to tell her he'd waited all his life for her, missed her every day even though they'd never met. Ached for her when he didn't even know her name. Ached still. Hung on to that possibility like a life raft, because it was all he had keeping him afloat. Her, a life raft, bobbing toward him in a cold sea, a promise of rescue."

He stopped reading and looked up.

"That's really impressive, Jake," I said, embarrassed and scrambling for words. "The girls must go weak at the knees."

"Hilda—"

"We should take this stuff up to Hank's," I said, looking down at the groceries by the door. "That milk will be getting warm."

Jake moved closer, then thought better of it. I could see his disappointment, but there were things I didn't know how to tell him, either. How I was scared to let him in, and that I didn't want to love him, because one day we would have to say good-bye, if not today then in weeks, or years, decades from now, when the clock stopped and took one of us from the other. After losing my parents I couldn't bear it. I would rather be alone.

"I've gotta take a piss," he said, dejected, and went to the bathroom. He closed the door and I opened his laptop and started surfing through the files on his desktop, wanting to see again what he had just read to me, that beautiful gesture I couldn't return. There were multiple versions of the same file, drafts of something called ICE MAIDEN SCENE that was probably a sex scene he was working on for a film. I opened it and scanned the page: I was right, just some terrible sex scene taking place on a research station in Antarctica of all places. I closed the document. Then another file caught my eye, shoved right down in the corner of the desktop where I might have missed it. The file was called THE_LIFE_UP-STAIRS. I looked toward the bathroom door, waited for the sound of the toilet flushing, but nothing came. I opened the file.

EXT. NIGHT. RUN-DOWN APARTMENT BLOCK. DOWNTOWN LOS ANGELES.

HENRY, a crusty old man, answers the door to a young girl, LUCY, a middle-class goth slumming it far from home.

I heard the toilet flush, the sound of a tap running, Jake whistling. I skimmed the next line.

HENRY
What took you so long? I'm an old man, I ain't got all the time in the world.

LUCY holds up a bag of videotapes, old movies.

LUCY
Yes we do.

The bathroom door opened and I slammed the laptop shut and slid it onto the sofa next to me. Jake walked out, pulling up his fly.

"You ready to go?" he asked. "Give the old bastard a visit?"

"Sure," I said, and forced a smile. I didn't want to feel the way I was suddenly feeling. I grappled with my panic, pushed it all the way down to my feet where I hoped I could stamp it out. "Let's go."

We left the apartment and I walked behind Jake, not letting him see my face, the confusion I could feel turning my cheeks scarlet. When we arrived outside the apartment, everything was deathly quiet. Immediately I knew something was wrong.

"The TV's not on," I said as we approached the door.

"Maybe he's taking a nap," Jake said. He knocked on the door and waited. When no one answered he took a spare key from under the mat and opened the door. All the curtains were drawn and the room was dark. As always there were empty beer bottles on the floor and dishes piled high in the sink. There was no sign of Hank.

"Hank!" I yelled, pushing in front of Jake. I dropped the groceries on the ground. "Where are you?"

"Hank!" Jake repeated, yelling louder. "Are you here?"

I opened the door to the bathroom. The window was open, the shower curtain rustling in the breeze. On the counter was a can of shaving cream, but no sign of Hank. I was about to turn and investigate the bedroom when Jake let out a yell that made my blood run ice cold.

"Jesus!" he screamed.

I raced into the bedroom. Jake was standing in the corner staring at the bed, his hands covering his mouth. Hank was on the bed, naked except for a thin sheen of red that ran the length of both his arms. I followed the trail to a straight razor that lay beside his hand. His eyes were closed, his breathing shallow. I dropped to the bed beside him. Jake paced in the corner, moaning.

"Hank? Can you hear me?" I said, trying to stay calm. Hank let out a soft groan. I turned to Jake. "Call nine-one-one."

"Oh shit. What's happening, Hilda?"

"For God's sake, Jake! Do it!"

I looked down at Hank's wrists as Jake fumbled with the telephone. The cuts looked deep, deliberate, the blood running down his sinewy arms. I ripped off a piece of bedsheet and tore it in half, then wrapped his wrists as tightly as I could. The fabric quickly became soaked. I could hear Jake talking to the 911 operator in the next room.

"He's in his eighties. I think he tried to commit suicide. Blood type? Um, I have no idea. Is that something I should know? Oh, God."

I leaned in close to Hank's ear. "Hank," I whispered. "You still with us?" He groaned again. I put my hand on his chest, felt his stomach rise and fall with each shallow breath. "Hank," I whispered again. "What have you done?"

Jake burst back into the room. "He's still breathing," he said into the phone. "We've wrapped sheets around his wrists."

Hank's lips started to move. I put my ear up to his mouth, tried to catch his words, but they were too faint. In the distance I heard sirens, and Jake started to yell again, but all I could do was focus on Hank's breathing and the gentle beating of his heart beneath my hand.

32

WE FOLLOWED THE AMBULANCE in Jake's car. At the hospital a nurse with a tight, old-fashioned bun asked us questions.

"It says here Mr. Anderson has had some 'falls' in the past," she said, going over his chart. "Do you think in hindsight these may have actually been early suicide attempts?"

"How the hell should we know?" Jake snapped. "The dude's an alcoholic. Alcoholics fall over all the time."

"So you're sure nothing like this has happened before?"

"What difference does it make? What exactly are you getting at?"

"It's important for us to confirm this was a suicide attempt. Past attempts can help us establish a pattern."

"Of course it was a suicide attempt. He slashed his fucking wrists."

"Sir—"

"You tell me this," Jake fumed, "how many old men do you get in here who have slashed their wrists? Huh? How fucking common is that?"

"He was in a concentration camp," I said to the nurse. Jake threw up his hands.

"Great, Hilda—what a way to complicate the situation. Well done."

"I'm just saying! He has a history of trauma; he's been depressed, paranoid. He hardly goes outside. It's like he's frightened of the world."

"They don't need to know this, Hilda! That's his private business!"

"What do you care?" I yelled back. "Why are you even here? You don't give a shit about him. Or me. You just want him back at home so you can keep using him."

"I think maybe you two should take this outside," the nurse said, putting her hand lightly on Jake's shoulder. He shook her hand off, almost violently, and she stepped back with a hurt look on her face.

"Why are you saying that?" he said to me. "Why are you being so difficult all of a sudden?"

"Oh, I'm being difficult?"

"Yeah," he said, his eyes hardening. "You're not being straight with me, and I don't appreciate it."

"*I'm* not being straight with *you*? Oh, that's funny. That's *really* funny. You're a piece of work, Jake, you know that?"

"Okay," the nurse said, trying to wrest control of the situation. "I really think you need to go outside."

Jake ignored her. "What the hell's that supposed to mean? Hilda, how can you say I don't care? Just who do you think I am?"

"I guess I don't know."

"I'm getting security," the nurse said, tottering off.

"I think she's right, Jake," I said. "I think you should just leave."

Jake's face crumpled in a way I had never seen before, a way I had believed he was incapable of. Standing in front of me, his eyes downcast, it was as if for the first time I was actually seeing him. He looked stripped bare.

"Did I do something?" he said. "Because I don't understand what's going on."

"I saw your script, Jake. On your laptop. *The Life Upstairs*?"

I watched as the realization dawned that he'd been found out, and his face crumpled. "Oh shit. Hilda, that's nothing. I'm not even working on it anymore."

"Is that all we are to you? Is that all *I* am to you? A story?"

"Oh, man," he spluttered, punching himself in the forehead with a closed fist. "I've fucked this up. I always fuck things up. Look, in the beginning, yeah, I thought it would make a cool story. I heard you guys on the balcony—"

"You were spying on us?" I couldn't believe it. All the pieces started to come together. "That's why you were his friend. That's why he said you were asking too many questions. How long have you been writing his story, Jake? Without him knowing?"

Jake took a step forward and I held up my hand.

"Don't come near me."

"I don't understand why you're so angry! You're just as bad."

"What the hell is that supposed to mean?"

"It means where do you get off judging me? You feed off that old man like a vampire. You think you and I are so different? We're the same, Hilda: we take what we need from people. There's nothing wrong with that."

"I am not like you. I will never be like you."

His expression turned mean. "Wise up, Hilda. You know I'm right. You're nothing but a bloodsucker, feeding off everyone's misery. You think saving some old guy will bring your parents back? Make everything right again? Gee, wouldn't that be a nice little character arc. But let me tell you something. Life doesn't work that way. It doesn't tie up in a neat little Hollywood-certified bow."

Behind him the nurse was returning, a security guard by her side. Jake followed my gaze and turned around.

"You know what?" he said. "I don't need this."

"Sir," the guard said, standing beside him. "I believe this nurse asked you to leave."

"Don't worry. I'm gone. I am so out of here."

He brushed past me and stomped down the hallway. "Jake!" I called out. He turned.

"What?"

I steeled myself. "Your writing sucks anyway."

He took his sunglasses out of his pocket and put them on, then kept walking.

"So long, Hilda," he said, and I watched him walk down the corridor. I wanted to chase after him, tell him we had been doing so well—couldn't we go back to before he betrayed me? But I couldn't. I thought of all the conversations Hank and I had had on the balcony and in his living room, couldn't erase from my mind the image of Jake listening from his apartment below. The tape recorder that fell from his bag. All the things he knew that I had never told him, that he'd never given me the chance to. I watched as the hospital doors closed behind him, and then I walked away.

33

POKED MY HEAD INSIDE Hank's room and was struck by the sound of the machines that were keeping him alive, a quiet but insistent whirring, the sound of momentum. It was always good to hear sounds in a hospital room. Silence was a sign of trouble.

Hank was lying in the bed with both wrists bandaged. Someone had given him a sponge bath so he actually looked pretty good, if not a little tired. His gray hair had dried into soft tufts and his beard looked like cotton wool. As I hovered near the door he turned to look at me.

"Am I still here?" he asked.

"Yeah."

"Shit."

I walked in and pulled up a chair beside his bed.

"Of all the goddamn luck. I had an out-of-body experience. I was flying high over this bed, looking down at myself. When I tried to fly away, someone told me I wasn't allowed to go yet."

"That was me." I smiled.

He grinned. "I thought it was strange that an angel would call me a selfish bastard. Can you get me some water? I feel like I've swallowed a thousand razor blades."

I poured him a glass and handed it to him. As he raised his hand he winced from the pain.

"So, cutting your wrists, huh?" I said. "It's a bit emo, isn't it?"

"Emo?"

"It's normally teenage girls who cut themselves. If you wanted to go that badly, surely you could have done it in a more manly way. You could have held up a liquor store and waited for the cops to gun you down."

Hank swallowed the water and tried to put the empty glass on the side table; he screwed up his face as he knocked his wrist against the side of the bed.

"Hey, I'll get that," I said, taking the glass from him. "Just lie down."

"I don't need any help."

"They say suicide is a cry for help. People who try to commit suicide, most of them don't really want to die."

"I do."

"Why, Hank? What's the story with you? Sometimes I think I have you all figured out, then you do something like this."

"It's none of your business," he grumbled. "Can't a man get some peace in here?"

"Did I do something wrong?"

"No, goddamnit. This ain't got nothin' to do with you!"

"But is there something more I should be doing? Are there things that you want to talk about?"

"I'm sick of talking," he said, sitting up. "I was fine until you two came along. I just want to be left alone."

"Well, you won't have to worry about Jake coming around anymore."

Hank arched an eyebrow. "Whaddaya mean? Did you two have a lovers' tiff or somethin'?"

"Something like that. You were right about him, though, I guess. I shouldn't have trusted him."

"Yeah, well, don't write him off yet. He may be an untrustworthy little bastard, but he likes you."

"I thought you hated him?"

"I do! Goddamn little son of a bitch, always hanging around, gives me the creeps. But like I said, he likes you, and soon, all the rest of that shit won't matter."

"I just don't get it, Hank. You've lived through so much, why kill yourself now? It's not like you're gonna be with us much longer, if you know what I mean. Wouldn't you prefer to clock out in your sleep? It's a hell of a lot nicer than bleeding out."

He grasped my hand, squeezing my fingers together until it hurt. "I can't live with it anymore," he said. "I can't live with what happened."

"I understand. You lived through a horrible time—"

"No, you don't understand. I did a terrible thing, Hilda. A terrible, terrible thing."

"Hank, don't blame yourself for what happened to Lenore," I said, remembering his story about the girl who perished in the camp. "You were young. It wasn't your fault."

"Not Lenore. Something else. Something unspeakable."

Somewhere in the hospital an alarm rang and I heard the frantic rush of footsteps. A few nurses raced past the door but Hank seemed not to notice the commotion.

"You're getting crazy eyes, Hank," I joked. "If you're not careful they'll think you have rabies and put you down."

He didn't smile. "My heart hurts. I need your help, Hilda."

"Hank, if I shut off your machine, I'm going down for twenty years, and even though life feels pretty shit right now, I'd rather not spend it in jail."

"Not now. Later. It's too risky now."

"Hank—"

The nurse appeared in the doorway, flustered, a pile of paperwork in her hands. "Oh, you're awake," she said. "Why didn't anyone tell me you were awake?"

"I wasn't aware it was the job of the visitors to keep the hospital informed on how the patient is doing," I said.

She smiled grimly. "In any case, visiting hours are over."

I bent over and whispered in Hank's ear. "What do you want me to do?"

"Wait," he replied, breathless, his voice like a clockwork toy winding down. "It needs to be done right."

"But I don't want to do it."

"Miss," the nurse said, tapping her clipboard impatiently with a pen. "I've asked you once."

"Fine, fine, I'm going," I said, sounding annoyed, but in reality I was grateful to her for giving me an excuse to leave.

"I'll be back, Hank," I said.

"Don't come back here. I'm gettin' out of this shithole as soon as I can."

I stood outside in the cold night air and looked around for

Jake. I waited to hear his voice, see him walking toward me, rushing to tell me he was wrong, he was sorry for what he had done, he needed me. But he wasn't there. Maybe he was right. Maybe I was looking for some stupid Hollywood ending, a happiness that didn't really exist. I saw a payphone on the wall and rustled in my pocket for some change. A man in a wheelchair smoked a cigarette by the hospital doors, staring up into the night sky. His face was pale, his eyes hollow pits. I picked up the phone and was about to dial when he spoke.

"You see that?" he said, pointing at the sky. I looked around.

"Who, me?"

He laughed. "Yes, you. Look at the stars."

I looked up. The sky was a vast expanse of darkness dotted with lights. "Am I looking for something in particular?" I asked.

The man didn't say anything for a moment, then, as if speaking in a trance, he recited something to me that I was sure he had spoken before, at another time to another person, but the same thing nevertheless.

"It's not just a sky; it's heaven," he said. "One day we will all be returned to heaven. And in heaven we will be turned into stars. And we will be brighter than anything down here."

"You enjoying the morphine there, good buddy?" I said, but he acted like he hadn't heard. I turned away and dialed.

"Hello?" Lynette said, and for a moment I couldn't say anything. It felt as if something was caught in my throat, and as I pushed it out I realized it was a sob.

"Lynette," I managed to say.

"Hilda? What's the matter? Where are you?"

"The hospital."

"Hospital? Oh my God, what's wrong? Are you okay?"

I drew back a breath. "Can you come and get me, please?"

I heard the jangle of keys. "I'm on my way."

I hung up the phone and looked back toward the man in the wheelchair, but he was gone. I looked back up at the stars.

34

LYNETTE TOOK ME FOR ice cream at Mel's Drive-in in West Hollywood. When I was younger it was my favorite place to go. A fifties-style diner featured in the movie *American Graffiti*, Mel's served traditional American food like hamburgers, hot dogs, and French fries. Best of all, Mel's was open all night, and I had many fond memories of late-night excursions for banana splits and ice-cream floats. In the early days we never had anything to eat in the house, as Lynette was used to grabbing food at work and didn't think to bring any home. She would try everything she could to make me happy, even if it meant plying me with as many sweets as I wanted. When she saw me at the hospital, looking like a zombie and rubbing tears from my face, I guess she resorted to what she knew best. And as I pulled up a counter seat and ordered a double-malt milkshake, I'll be damned if I didn't feel a hell of a lot better.

Lynette picked at some chili fries as I downed the milkshake with three quick gulps through the straw. "Mmmmm," I said, slamming the glass on the counter. "That's the ticket. Better than crack."

"You want another one?"

"Hell yeah."

Lynette ordered me another milkshake and I started to eat her fries. "Help yourself," she muttered.

"Don't mind if I do."

We sat and ate and watched people come and go. A waitress sailed by on roller skates. "Feels like old times," Lynette said. "Remember when we used to come here at least three times a week?"

"That was because you had no idea what to do with me."

Lynette laughed. "I still don't."

"Oh, come on," I said, stuffing her fries into my mouth. "I'm not that bad, am I?"

"Not bad at all. You're great."

We said nothing for a moment. I shoveled more fries into my mouth.

"So what's going on, Hilda?"

I stared into the center of my thick shake glass. The milk had condensed around the side.

"I feel like everyone leaves me," I said. "Or I end up having to leave them."

"I haven't left you."

"But you want to, right? I mean, I've been a real bitch."

"Bah," she said like it was no big deal. "We've both given each other a hard time."

I heard her cell phone ringing in her pocket. She scooped it out and pressed the silence button.

"I'll take it later," she said.

"It's okay, take it. It could be some innocent man sitting on death row, and for all we know you're his last phone call."

"He can wait."

I continued to shovel fries into my mouth, ravenous.

"We don't really talk much, do we?" Lynette said.

"I guess we don't."

"We never did really. Your dad didn't like me 'interfering.'"

"You were pretty hard on him."

Lynette gave me a surprised look. "How do you know?"

"Come on, Lynette. I heard you two argue all the time."

I swirled a French fry in ketchup, made little patterns with the salty tip. "I remember Mom. She liked wearing caftans."

"She sure did," Lynette said, laughing. "Your grandmother did, too. The whole family was a bunch of hippies. I guess I was always the black sheep."

To my surprise Lynette looked dejected. I'd always pictured her as strong and stubborn, not someone who would care what anyone else thought. She took her hand away from mine, started flicking through the selections on the jukebox on the table. No one in the restaurant had put a song on for at least five minutes, and I could tell the silence was making everyone uneasy. Lynette opened her purse and took out two quarters.

"You want to choose a song?" she asked, tapping the coins on the table.

This was something else we had done when I was a kid. One song each. There was something about a jukebox that made making a selection something special. Anyone could just keep jamming coins in, making the music vomit out with little attention paid to what was being chosen. To be allowed only one song out of all those hundreds made the whole enterprise worthwhile, gave it some gravity. After making a selection, I loved to watch the faces of the diners around me, see whether they agreed with my purchase or not. Some lady might screw her nose up in annoyance, but a biker might start tapping his foot under the table, making me feel like I'd found a kindred spirit. Out of all the people who had come to this diner, I had found someone like me. I gave one of the coins back to Lynette.

"You first."

Lynette put the coin in the slot and I heard it rattle down to the bottom of the machine. Her beautiful manicured fingers pushed two buttons together, and the sound of Elvis singing "Hound Dog" erupted through the diner speakers.

"A bit obvious," I said. "Everyone likes Elvis."

"Nothing wrong with a crowd-pleaser," she said. "Sometimes it's perfectly okay to be like everyone else."

I pushed my empty milkshake glass aside. I was still starving. I wanted burgers and fries and pancakes and whatever else was on offer. I wanted to eat until I was so sick I couldn't possibly think of anything else other than the discomfort in my stomach. Eating burgers seemed normal. Sitting in a diner was normal. It was more normal than being in a hospital, holding your friend's hand while he told you he had some big, terrible secret, like a dumb scene from the soap opera *General Hospital*. I didn't want to know what terrible sins Hank thought he was hiding. Part of me wished he would die before he could ever tell me.

"Hilda, I know living with me has been hard. I know I'm very different from your mom and dad, maybe a bit too serious, too forceful."

"Nah, you're cool," I said, eager to wipe the hurt from her eyes. I'd never thought about how hard it might be for Lynette to live with *me*.

"I don't know what was going on back there at the hospital," she continued. "You don't have to tell me if you don't want to, and I'm not going to force it out of you. We don't really work that way. It's something I've kind of prided myself on, letting you make decisions on your own. Just know that if you need my help, I'm there. Don't be too proud to ask for it."

"Okay, Aunt Lynette. Thanks."

"And if you need anyone arrested, just let me know. I can get it done. I know people."

I laughed. At that moment I wanted to tell her everything about Hank and Jake, the places I visited every day, and what I thought Hank planned on asking me to do. I wanted to tell her about Benji, how he had changed. But something stopped me. Deep down I knew that if I told her what had gone on at the hospital, I might never get to hear what Hank had to say and never have the chance to help him do what he needed to do, no matter how much it scared me. I picked up the remaining quarter from the table just as Elvis finished. "My turn," I said, and put the coin in the slot. I pushed two buttons I knew by heart and waited. The familiar sound of the circuslike keyboard started and Lynette smiled.

"'California Girls.' Talk about being predictable!"

"Everybody loves 'California Girls,'" I said. "Like you said, sometimes it's perfectly okay to be like everybody else."

35

WHEN I GOT HOME, all I wanted to do was sleep: crawl into bed, throw the covers over my head, and never come out. Jake hadn't called. At that point I hoped Jake and Hank never contacted me again, that they would disappear from my life just as quickly as they had arrived. If Hank wanted to die, he would have to do it without me. I'd rather forget I ever knew him than live through losing him, losing anyone, ever again.

I tossed and turned under the covers. I couldn't sleep. I turned on the television; there was nothing but infomercials and music videos full of hos dancing in front of gangsters. I turned off the TV and put on my headphones, but even the haunting, pitch-perfect voice of Karen Carpenter couldn't soothe me. I had that old death itch. I wanted to hide in corpses, find comfort in the dead. I jumped online, went to all the usual sites, but nothing was helping. Even newly posted pics of Princess Diana's car crash weren't enough to get me excited. Seeing that tuft of beautiful blond hair sticking out of the crushed Mercedes-Benz just made me feel even sadder. I started to wonder what was wrong with me.

I checked my email. There was a message from Benji; the subject line read GOLDFISH. I looked at Sid, now renamed Dee Dee after my favorite Ramone, swimming happily in circles in his new fish bowl from Petco, his scales glistening a healthy orange. I tapped on the glass and he turned his little fish head to look at me: it looked like he was smiling, but it could have just been my imagination. I considered just deleting the email, pretending I never got it. But there was something inside me that couldn't write Benji off quite yet, and now that my relationships with Hank and Jake were disintegrating, it kind of felt good to see Benji's name in my inbox. I took a deep breath and opened the email.

Yo,

So how's it going? Sorry it's been a while but I've been really busy—me and the guys have been on so many road trips I'm hardly home anymore. It's crazy. Tomorrow we're going to the shooting range. I'm getting good but not as good as Dan. He's got a semiautomatic (don't ask me how he got it) like the one Eric Harris had. Its sick ass.

Anyways, I just wanted to know if you know what happened to my goldfish? I looked for it today in the closet and it was gone. Mom said she didn't do anything with it so I thought you might know. Anyways, no big deal. Its just weird you know? I was getting some good data.

There's going to be a party soon and if you want you can come. I think you'll be pretty surprised by where it is.

It will be the coolest party you have ever been to. So come if you want.

                                                                    B.

"What do you think, Dee Dee?" I asked my goldfish. "You wanna go to a party?"

His mouth formed an O and I don't know if it was because I was just really tired, but I swear it looked like he was saying, No, no, no, and little bubbles started to pop to the surface. I rubbed my eyes and looked at the clock. It was 2 a.m., and I hadn't felt this alone in a very long time. "You love me, don't you, Dee Dee?" I asked. Of course he did. He had to; I'd saved his life. Is that what it took to get someone to love you? I turned off the computer, got into bed, and decided to think about it all in the morning, because tomorrow, as they say, would be another day.

36

THE MORNING BROUGHT NO answers. I took a cab to Westwood cemetery to see Marilyn Monroe's grave. It was a small cemetery, discreet, hidden behind the skyscrapers of downtown Wilshire. Truman Capote was buried there. Dean Martin. Natalie Wood. Jack Lemmon. Rodney Dangerfield had a headstone that read THERE GOES THE NEIGHBORHOOD. But Marilyn was the biggest star, the one we all came to see. Her crypt was toward the back and you could see it from a distance, the bright colors of a hundred roses, pictures, and teddy bears left every day by adoring fans. Already I could see there were people there, a large group of tourists, cameras raised, packed lunches carried in bus-tour backpacks. I approached warily. Marilyn's crypt in the wall was covered in bright red lipstick kisses. People had scribbled their names on it, left her messages, prayed at her feet. A woman in the crowd turned to her friend.

"Did you know Marilyn was a size *sixteen*?" she squawked.

"Sixteen? My goodness. She would never have gotten work today."

"Not a chance in hell. She was a *very big girl*."

I wanted to scream, tell them to leave her alone. What more did they want from her? Marilyn was hounded all her life, and now, even in death, she was given no peace. Some people believed Marilyn had been murdered by the Kennedys or the CIA, but I didn't believe that. Marilyn just wanted to die. Sometimes when people want to die, there is nothing that can be done, no way to stop them. And wasn't it their right to die if they wished? Who were we to tell others they had to live?

I turned away from them. Graveyards weren't for dead people; they were for us—reassurance that we wouldn't be forgotten when we were gone, that something would remain. I took a cab back to Encino.

37

WHEN I GOT HOME Lynette wasn't there, and I was happy to have the house to myself. I walked into my room, thinking I might keep reading *American Psycho*, knowing I didn't have the stomach for it anymore. Regardless, I picked the book up from where it was sitting on the bed and was once again struck by the barrenness of my own bedroom. It still pretty much looked like a guest room, with its bare walls and sparse decor. I decided it really was time for me to start making the space my own, because who knew? Perhaps I would still be there in a few years' time now that moving in with Benji was most likely not in the cards. I could extend my artifacts collection into a space larger than a single shelf, maybe a glass cabinet similar to Benji's, and I could maybe convince Lynette to let me put up framed posters from my favorite movies on the walls: *Harold and Maude*, *Mulholland Drive*, *Animal House*. I immediately thought of Jake and wondered what he was doing now, and I found myself thinking about all the years I had lived without knowing him; I wondered what he had been doing all that time.

It was then that I saw the photograph pinned to my corkboard, a photograph that hadn't been there when I left for the cemetery early that morning, a photograph I had never before seen in my life. It was an old-fashioned Polaroid of a young woman with long, auburn hair parted down the middle, a baby in her arms. My first reaction was that it was my mother. The baby, wrapped in a soft blue blanket, looked up at the woman in wonder, showed a hint of a smile. I knew who the baby was. The baby was me. I had that blanket all my life, had it in the backseat with me when our car ran into that truck. I carried it all the way to the hospital and wouldn't let the nurse take it from me no matter how gently she pulled on it.

That's when I realized who the woman in the photograph really was. It was Lynette, of course. The woman who had told my mother off for letting me watch *Porky's* when I was six, who had walked past me nearly every day for the last five years and barely brushed against me. Here she was, staring down at me with a large smile on her face, teeth showing, hand wrapped tightly around the blanket, keeping me safe. I wished that I had been shown this photo before, then I wondered why it should make such a difference. But it did. The fact that Lynette had pinned it there herself told me all I needed to know. Lynette and I would be okay, perhaps better than okay. I took the photo off the board, placed it on my desk, and decided I would buy a frame for it in the morning. It would be the first picture I would hang on my wall. It was small, but it was a good start.

I heard something at my bedroom window, the sound of tree branches snapping. I pulled up the blinds, expecting to find a possum or the neighbor's cat, and jumped back when I saw someone standing outside in the dark, peering in.

"Jesus!" I screamed.

"It's just me!" Jake yelled through the glass, tapping on it. "Can I come in?"

"Use the front door, you moron!" I yelled, my heart pounding in my ears. "What the hell is wrong with you?"

"I thought this would be romantic."

"It's not romantic," I said, opening the window. "It makes you a stalker. It gets you shot by the cops. What are you doing here?"

"Can I talk to you?" he said, producing a piece of paper. "I wrote something down—"

"Oh God, what is wrong with you? I'm not interested in hearing another one of your stupid little monologues."

"Come on, Hilda," he pleaded, struggling to push the tree branches out of the way and losing his balance. He had stubble on his face and his eyes were red as if he hadn't been sleeping, or worse.

"Around the front," I said, closing the window. He finally tripped and stumbled on a tree branch, and I heard him fall to the ground and curse.

I turned the porch light on and stormed out the front door. A few moments later Jake appeared from the side of the house, a leaf sticking out of his hair.

"What do you want?"

He once again pulled the piece of paper from his pocket and started to unfold it.

"No paper!" I said. "Just talk."

"But I don't know how!" he whined, sounding like a little kid.

"You're gonna have to learn, Jake. Normal people have conversations."

"I don't know what to say to you. Listen, I'm sorry. I wish I could make you understand, this is just what I do. I do it in cafes, on the street. I hear people talk and I write it down and I make stories out of it. And Hank's story was just so amazing, I was working on it before you even came along. One day he was struggling getting his groceries up the stairs, and I went to help him, and I saw the number on his wrist and immediately I knew I had a great story, a story that had to be written. Then you came along, and you made the story better. It got better when you got there."

"Hank was right about you. You *were* spying on him. Asking him questions. That why he's been so scared. Because of you. You and all your questions, making him think someone was out to get him. He's just an old man! Why can't you leave him alone?"

"That has nothing to do with me. He was crazy a long time before I came into the picture. Just ask some of his neighbors."

"Oh great, so you're asking other people about him? No wonder he's so paranoid."

"Do you ever think that maybe there's another explanation, Hilda? Do you ever think that maybe there are some things that Hank isn't being entirely truthful about?"

"Like what?"

"Don't be coy. There's more loopholes in his story than in a Star Trek movie. And you know what? I think he tries to tell you. I think he wants to tell you, but you don't want to hear."

I wrapped my cardigan tight around my shoulders and pushed Jake in the stomach as I enunciated each word.

"Don't tell me about what I know."

"Hilda, stop it. Stop pushing me."

"You stop pushing me!" I said, shoving him so hard he nearly fell over onto the grass. "I don't even know what you want!"

"I want you to feel about me the way you do about him!" he said, and I stopped. "Why the hell do you care so much about a crusty old fart anyway?"

"Because he gave me a tile!" I yelled. "And it made me feel like he really understood me, more than anyone else ever had. Until I met you."

I started to cry. Jake stepped toward me and wrapped his arms around me, and for a moment I fell into him.

"I just can't live like this," I cried into his shoulder.

"Like what?" he whispered, his hand on my hair.

"With all this death."

"I'm alive, Hilda. I'm alive."

I pushed him away. "No you're not," I said, and all I could think was that he was dead, we were all dead, and that's why it was a dumb idea to ever get close to people.

"Hilda—"

"Hey!" A voice yelled from the sidewalk: Lynette, home from work, her arms filled with casebooks. "What's going on?"

She looked at me, saw my tears, and a hard look settled into her features.

"Hey, buddy," she said to Jake. "Take a hike."

"Look, I'm just trying to—"

"I said, take a hike!"

I'm not sure at what point Lynette pulled her assistant DA badge from her bag, but all of a sudden it was in her hand, being flashed in front of Jake's face.

"You know what this is, son?" she said.

Jake sighed. "No, what is it?"

"It's a DA's badge."

"Really?"

"Well, assistant DA. Point is, I could arrest you on the spot. Now, I told you to take a hike. She doesn't want you here."

"Hilda—"

"No, you don't," Lynette said. "She doesn't want you here. Not now anyway. If you've got something to sort out, now is not the time. Do you understand?"

He sighed. "Fine. I'll go."

Jake held out his hand to Lynette as I stood silently on the front porch, the tears drying on my face.

"I'm Jake, by the way," he said. "Nice to meet you."

Lynette hesitated for a moment, then shook his hand. "Assistant DA Lynette Hannigan. Good to meet you, too. Now move along."

"Okay."

Jake slunk back to his convertible. Lynette came and put her arm around me, and together we watched him drive away. I put my head on her shoulder.

"Who was that?" she asked, stroking my hair.

"That was Jake."

"Cute."

I laughed, wiped my nose with my sleeve.

"Well, you gotta admit, he's a hell of a lot better looking than Benji."

"That's mean," I said, but couldn't help grinning.

"You want some ice cream?"

I sniffled. "Okay."

We walked back inside.

"You know what?" I said. "That thing you did with your badge? That was actually pretty cool this time."

"Next time I'll pull a gun," she said. "But only if you want me to."

38

THE PARTY SOUNDED TASTELESS even by Benji's standards. The invitation was a flash animation showing a bloated and passed-out John Belushi with a large hypodermic needle in his arm. *Come and party with the ghost of Belushi,* it read. *B.Y.O. beer. Speedballs optional.*

Benji had rented bungalow 3 at the Chateau Marmont on the Sunset Strip. Bungalow 3 was the room where John Belushi OD'd after a five-day drug binge, shattering the dreams of an entire generation overnight. Now Benji and his creepy friends would be trashing the place where he died, eating from his fridge, and doing God knows what else. The invitation billed it as a memorial event, but I knew there was nothing sacred about this little soiree. I was also pretty sure that the Chateau wouldn't have rented bungalow 3 to Benji had they known what he was using it for. Still, the hotel was notoriously difficult to get into unless you were an A-list star, and I had always wanted to see inside bungalow 3. Deep down I also wanted to see Benji. I was desperate for something familiar. Maybe the break had done us good, and when we saw each other we would pick up where we left off and everything would be as it once was. I also felt lonely. As a cab took me down the Sunset Strip, I thought about how much everything had changed. Once Benji and I had explored this town together. One night we had loitered outside the Viper Room, too young to actually get in, trying to imagine what it was like the night River Phoenix died on the pavement outside. Benji had come armed with a mallet and pike, determined to hammer out the part of the pavement where River collapsed and take a piece home for his collection. The moment Benji crouched down, tools at the ready, a cop car slowed to a crawl beside us. I told the cops Benji was mentally ill and thought there was buried treasure beneath the streets of Los Angeles. I promised to take him home and make sure he took his medication.

Another night we tried to sneak into On the Rox, the private room above the Roxy nightclub, where Belushi spent his final hours on earth before leaving for the Chateau. There was no bribing the doorman, who was well-versed in prohibiting entry to the many wannabes and hangers-on who plagued the Sunset Strip. Benji tried to convince him we were the kids of a major studio head, a claim we thought the doorman couldn't really dispute. But when he asked which one and Benji blurted out Michael Eisner, our distinct lack of Jewish features was enough to tip him off. It was hard to get away with anything in Los Angeles. Even the doormen at nightclubs read the trades.

Once this town had been *ours*. Now, like so many other things in my life, I had lost Benji, too. As the cab pulled up to the Chateau Marmont, that huge, towering castle on the hill, I hoped I might find something in my relationship with Benji to salvage. I paid the driver, and before I could reach over for the door handle, someone had opened it for me. The bellboy tipped his cap, and a crowd of photographers surged forward, acting on instinct; then I emerged and they went away just as quickly.

"Are you a guest?" the bellboy asked. "Do you have any bags?"

"I'm here for a party," I said, sure I would be turned away on the spot. I was wearing a black slip dress and a pair of Lynette's high heels, two sizes too big. "It's in bungalow three."

"Of course," the bellboy said. "Follow me."

Bungalow 3 had a private entranceway that couldn't be accessed from the hotel foyer. As I followed the bellboy up the lane that ran along the side of the hotel, I could already hear the music. A single street lamp illuminated the entrance to the bungalow, a gate familiar to me from the many photographs I'd seen on the Internet. I had seen footage of Belushi being carried through this gate under a white sheet. I waited for the shivers of excitement that usually came whenever I stood at a site like this; I felt nothing but the wind on my bare shoulders. The bellboy tipped his cap again. I gave him a few dollars and he scampered off into the night. I pushed the gate open and went inside.

The bungalows at the Chateau Marmont are more like little homes than hotel suites. I walked the few feet to the front door; the music was so loud I could barely hear my own footsteps on the concrete path. I knocked, and a moment later the door swung open as if someone had been waiting behind it. Benji stood there in a black suit and sunglasses, a black fedora on his head, Budweiser in hand. We looked at each other for a moment, saying nothing, then a broad smile broke out across his face.

"Hilda!" he yelled too loudly, and I could tell he was drunk. "Where you been?"

"Nice suit," I said.

"I'm a Blues Brother! Isn't this great?"

He stepped forward, awkward, and threw his arm around my shoulder. I walked in. The main room of the bungalow was a large lounge area with a kitchenette, and I was surprised to find it wasn't all that fancy inside; in fact, it looked like they hadn't updated the decor since the seventies. Inside, people I didn't know lounged on the red couches and milled around behind the kitchen counter, and as I walked in, nobody paid me much attention. The furniture was all old-fashioned in a hip kind of way, and sliding glass doors led to what can best be described as a backyard, a self-contained garden area where people were sitting on old garden chairs, smoking. Some of the people were dressed like Benji, while others were wearing togas, an obvious homage to *Animal House*. John Lee Hooker, Belushi's favorite blues artist, was playing on the stereo, and old episodes of *Saturday Night Live* were playing on an enormous flat-screen television, the most modern item in the place. I watched the screen. Belushi was prancing around in a giant bumblebee costume. Story goes that he hated that costume, and whenever the producers asked him to wear it, he could barely hide his disgust, even when on the air. You could almost see the boredom in his eyes. With his hands on his fuzzy yellow-and-black belly, antennae flying above his head, he looked like a man who had given up hope.

"Who the hell are all these people?" I asked Benji.

"They're just people, you know? I met most of them online."

Yeah, just people more than willing to take advantage of his hospitality. "How did you get this place?"

"Oh, you see Bruce over there?" He pointed to an enormous, brooding figure in the corner of the kitchen, clutching a bottle of bourbon close to his chest. "He works for some rock star. I met him at a séance. He got the room for us."

"A séance?"

"You should have been there, Hilda. You would have loved it. We talked to Sinatra!"

"Oh yeah?" I said, disbelieving. "Why the hell would Sinatra want to talk to you guys?"

"Because we made a sacrifice to him."

"A sacrifice? Not more goldfish, Benji, please."

Benji made the sign of the cross over his heart and smirked. "No more goldfish. That I can promise you. Can I get you a drink or something?"

"Anything."

He ran to the kitchen and threw open the refrigerator door. Séances? I didn't want to ask any further about the sacrifice part. It appeared to me Benji had sacrificed more than he knew to these new friends of his. I looked around the room. A woman wearing fishnet tights and a leotard scowled at me from the kitchen counter, her cigarette dropping ash on the floor. A guy in the living room pulled his toga up, and I caught a glimpse of pink, wobbling flesh before everyone started applauding. Benji came back with a beer and handed it to me.

"Who the hell is that?" I said, pointing toward the guy in the toga who was now waving his junk in everyone's faces. The girls screamed.

"That's Sammy. He's the coolest." Benji laughed and clapped his hands. "Way to go, Sammy!"

I felt the room closing in on me. I put the unopened beer on the counter. "Are you all right?" Benji asked. "You don't look good. Are you sick?"

"No, I'm just tired. Can I sit down somewhere?"

"Let's go over here."

Benji led me to an empty couch and I took a seat. "I'm just gonna get another beer," he said. "Don't go anywhere. Just stay right there."

"I'm fine. Go."

Benji went back into the kitchen and started talking to the woman in the leotard. A girl wearing a sarong came and sat down beside me. Her hair was long and blond and her hands were decked out in amber rings. "Cool party, huh?" she said. I put my hand to my head.

"Sorta. I guess. Sorry, I've actually got a headache."

"So you feel it, too?"

"Feel what?"

She lifted her arms in the air as if she were going to float off. "The energy in the air, the vibe of the place. Can't you just feel him here? He's here with us."

"Who?"

"Belushi. He totally wants us to party with him. That's what he was all about—energy, life, living it to the fullest. Rockin' out."

I stared at her. "I don't think I caught your name."

"It's Amelia. Like the Joni Mitchell song."

"Right, okay. Amelia? I'm sorry to disagree with you, but Belushi wasn't about life and energy and all that positive crap you're talking about. Belushi was an *addict*. Just another sad, pathetic actor wandering the streets of Hollywood, looking for all the attention he could get. There was nothing positive about what happened to Belushi. He died thousands of miles from his home, thousands of miles from his wife, in a hotel room with a hooker. Tell me what's so positive about that."

"I don't understand. Don't you like John Belushi?"

"God! Are you even listening to me? John Belushi was a genius, a supremely talented person who fucked up his life with drugs and alcohol. He may have been a genius, but in the end he was just sad and pathetic. He was just another piece of roadkill on the Hollywood highway."

"But he was pretty funny, wasn't he?" she said, looking confused. "He was a funny guy, right?"

"Yes, Amelia." I sighed. "He was *hilarious*."

"I like *The Blues Brothers*. That was a funny movie."

"Yes, *The Blues Brothers* was *hilarious*. By the way, that Joni Mitchell song, 'Amelia'? It was about Amelia Earhart."

"Cool. Who's Amelia Earhart?"

"Exactly," I said, and stood. "If you'll excuse me for a moment."

I walked across the room and down the hallway, looking for a bathroom. I passed the first bedroom on the right, not the one Belushi died in but a smaller one that was being used as the party's cloakroom. Jackets were thrown on the bed and the ground, and a fresh pool of vomit festered perilously close to a trench coat. I turned away, saw the closed door at the end of the hallway, the door to Belushi's bedroom, and instead of going toward it I quickly turned right into the bathroom, closed the door, and locked it.

I turned on the tap and threw water over my face. My eye makeup started to run. "Shit!" I mumbled, grabbing a tissue from next to the sink and trying ineffectively to dab away the black lines that were now running down my face. What was wrong with me? I was at a party at the Chateau Marmont, Hollywood's most legendary hotel, in bungalow 3 no less. Led Zeppelin rode their motorbikes through the foyer. James Dean climbed through a window to audition for *Rebel Without a Cause*. Jim Morrison nearly killed himself dangling from a drain pipe. Why couldn't I enjoy myself?

I turned off the tap and rubbed the black from my face, rubbing most of my makeup away at the same time. I took a deep breath and stepped outside. The party was in full swing. People were standing in the hallway, talking quietly in each other's ears, drinking, kissing. I turned toward Belushi's bedroom. The door was still closed, but behind it I could hear the sound of laughter. I turned the handle and pushed the door, and it creaked open slowly.

On the bed were three guys wearing suits, ties undone, and black sunglasses. One of them rolled over on the bed in quick, jerky movements while the other guys laughed.

"Look at me! I'm Belushi!" he said as he writhed on the bedsheets. He kicked and shook and made heaving noises. "Help me! I'm dying! Don't leave me here! Don't leave me here to die!"

They all started laughing. One of them noticed me standing in the door way, held out a compact mirror, and offered me a rolled-up bill.

"Want some coke?" he asked. I could see the powder sitting on the end of his nose.

"No thanks, I'm on the wagon," I said, and he shrugged before doing a line while his friends watched.

I closed the door again, suddenly feeling really sick, as if

someone had punched me in the stomach. It was my body trying to tell me I didn't belong there, that I needed to get out, get
away. Death was all around me. I stumbled down the hallway and
tried to make my way through the partygoers who were dancing
to "Louie Louie" in the living room, just like in *Animal House*. I
reached the front door and managed to pull it open, when Benji
came rushing over.

"Hey, what's going on?" he said, slamming the door closed and
standing in front of it. "Where are you going?"

"I'm sorry, Benji. I'm leaving."

I tried to push past him but he grabbed my arm and twisted it.
"Hey!" I almost screamed. "Get your hands off me!"

"Okay, I'm sorry" he said quietly, letting go. "Don't get so crazy.
Can't you just stay?"

"This is *not* my kind of scene, Benji. These people are dicks."

"Don't you want to see the bedroom? Hilda—it's where Belushi
died!"

"I've seen enough. These people don't even care about John
Belushi. They're just a bunch of poseurs."

"Oh, so you're the only one here who's not? That's so fucking
typical of you, Hilda. Always acting like you're so much better than
anyone else. Always acting like you're better than me."

"I'm going home," I said, trying to push past him.

"Look, I'm really sorry," he pleaded, his face softening. "It's
just that, everything between us is different now, you know? How
about you take a walk with me? We need to talk. We haven't talked
in ages."

I looked at Benji and saw something in him that seemed familiar, like the person I used to know, before everything started to

change. God, how I wanted my old life back. Everything seemed simpler before Hank and Jake. "We should talk," I agreed. "Let's go outside."

He smiled, relieved, and took my arm again, gently this time. He led me out the front door and through another gate to the pool area, leaving the party far behind. The pool was deserted. I sat on one of the cabanas and took my heels off, glad to stretch my feet. Benji stood in front of me, swaying a little, a beer bottle in his hand. Away from the party I started to feel a little better. I breathed in the air, savored it in my lungs, savored being alive. I fixed my old friend with a serious look.

"Benji, those people do not care about you. They are not your friends."

"Oh, and you are?"

"What's that supposed to mean? Of course I'm your friend!"

"Then where have you been?"

I looked at my feet. A blister was starting to form on my toe. "I just needed a break. Time to myself. I'm worried about you. You've been acting weird."

"*I've* been acting weird? You're the one who's changed, Hilda! I'm the same person I always was! I mean, fuck, we're at Belushi's bungalow, and you don't even care."

"I just don't think this shit is healthy anymore," I said. "I mean, look at us. All we ever do is talk about death. I mean, look what it's done to you."

He froze. "What do you mean, what it's done to *me*?" he sneered.

"Benji, come on. It used to just be visiting cemeteries and jumping over fences, but now, *digging up graves*? Going to the coroner's office and acting like it's *all a big joke*?" I stammered. "It's gone too far. You're hurting people now."

"It was always you and me, Hilda! Us against the world! *You left me*."

Benji's tie had come undone and now hung limply over his chest, a thin hangman's noose waiting for a neck. His eyes were wide and red. In the distance I could hear the sound of the party, a cacophony of sleazy blues music and laughter. Benji just looked at me. The light of a nearby room reflected off the pool's surface and glinted in his eyes. There was nothing in them. Benji's eyes were all inky blackness, and I'd seen that look before. That day so many years ago when Benji had handed the cat over to its owner, emotionless. At first he had been sad, even wept for the poor animal as it lay dying in the road, but once he got his hands on the corpse, something changed, something that had led us to Sid the goldfish, then the LA County Morgue, then here. There was nothing behind those eyes.

Benji was right. Once we had been a team, like Bonnie and Clyde, Sid and Nancy, Kurt and Courtney. I understood why he was angry, but there was nothing that could be done. I had changed. I wanted so desperately to be far away from all of this, all the madness and death. I had my whole life to live and I didn't want to spend it in darkness any longer. I stood, picked up my shoes.

"Enjoy the party," I said, and began to walk away.

"Hilda."

"No, Benji. No more. I don't think I can be your friend. Not now. So just leave me alone, okay? Let's just take a break."

That's when I saw it. Something shiny and long in Benji's hand, but it wasn't a beer bottle. It was *too* shiny; the light from the lamp-posts caught the object and reflected off it, like a mirror.

"Benji? What are you doing? What's that?"

Benji put the object lengthwise in his mouth, held it between his teeth. He unbuttoned his shirt, pulled it off, and stood beside the pool naked from the waist up. His body wasn't as I'd remembered. It was as if he'd been in training: his arms looked stronger, showed the tiniest hint of muscle. He dropped his shirt beside him, took the object out of his mouth, and once again held it in his hand, the end pointed toward me.

"You'll get cold," I said, dazed, too confused to know what I was saying. Suddenly I was feeling the cold all too intensely, but I couldn't take my eyes from the object in his hand, the kitchen knife. I wondered if he'd taken it from the bungalow. I wondered if Belushi had ever used it to cut onions.

Benji looked around him, at the pool, the other hotel rooms, the majesty of the Chateau rising up around him. "Don't you just love this place?" he said. "It's everything I hoped it would be. It's like an enchanted kingdom. And the people, Hilda, the people who have been here, who have lived here." He looked back over at the bungalow. "Died here."

Suddenly there was the sound of glass breaking from inside bungalow 3, and someone laughed, loud and sharp, cutting through the silence.

"You're right, Hilda," Benji continued. "Those people in there, they aren't my friends. But you are. You were always my best friend, more than that. Even when we're apart, we're together. You know?"

"I'll always be your friend, Benji. But I have to go now."

"Why?"

"Because I'm scared. You're scaring me."

He stepped forward, knife still pointed toward me. "Don't be scared. It's just me."

"I have to go. Please."

He stopped. "You know, we could be like him."

"Who?"

"Belushi. We could be like all of them. Imagine it, Hilda. Imagine having people remember you, talk about you, visit where you died. You would become a legend. *We* could become legends. Forever."

I looked around for something to grab, something that would be strong enough that if I swung it I could bring Benji down. But there was nothing, just a few large potted plants that looked too heavy to pick up. "I don't want to be a legend, Benji. I want to live."

"Do you?"

"Of course I do!"

"Hilda, your parents are dead. Your mom and dad, they left you. Don't you want to be with them? Isn't that what all this is about?"

"No, Benji, I want to live. Please. Don't do this."

He stepped toward me, and I could see millions of goose bumps appearing along his skin like tiny insect bites. He was right: I did want to see my parents again. But not now. Not like this.

"Hilda, people would talk about us forever," he said, inching closer. "We could become ghosts. We could do it now, by this pool. We'd be famous."

I tried to scream, but nothing would come out. The knife came up, flashed in front of my eyes, and a desperate yelp escaped from my throat.

"No!" I squealed as the blade flashed past. I threw my hand up to my throat. There was no wetness, no blood, just the softness of my own skin. I breathed out. Benji's eyes were wide, manic.

"You don't want this," he whispered, and put his hand on my throat, softly, lovingly. "I'm sorry. I would never hurt you."

Tears started to brim in his eyes, and I put my hand on his cheek, still wary of the knife, a knife which was now by his side and could easily be plunged into my stomach. "Everything's going to be okay," I said, and pulled him in to me, held him, and he held me back, his hands shaking.

"I know," he said, releasing me, and turned to walk away. He was a few feet away from me, standing by the pool and looking into the water, when he suddenly held out his arm as if he were crucified, lifted the knife, and cut long lines into his flesh.

"No!" I screamed, and raced to him, but the knife came up again, this time in the other hand, and he cut along his other arm, holding it out so the blood could drip off his skin, like water drops on a windowpane.

"Help us!" I screamed. "Somebody, help me!"

A man flew out of his hotel room in a white robe, his wife cowering behind him, and when they saw Benji standing there, his arms red with blood, the woman screamed.

"I'll call nine-one-one!" the man yelled, racing back inside. Benji aimed with the knife again, cut a clean line across his stomach, and a thin trail of blood rose to the surface.

"Stop it!" I screamed, "Just stop it, Benji!"

But Benji wasn't there. His eyes were glazed, rolling back in his head. The blood was running fast now, making large puddles next to him. Some of it had run off his hand into the pool, making the water turn red. People started to pile out of bungalow 3, then stopped short behind me when they saw what was happening.

"Holy shit!" a guy screamed, almost falling over himself. All the girls behind him started to scream, and Benji just looked around calmly, surveying the chaos he was causing with a quiet look of contemplation. An image flashed in my mind: Sissy Spacek in the movie *Carrie*, standing at the prom, surveying the damage she had caused, pleased with the destruction. Hotel staff started to appear, and the man who had called 911 ran out of his room holding a bundle of bedsheets, tackled Benji from behind, and knocked the knife out of his hand. He pinned him to the ground, grabbed the sheets, and started wrapping them tightly around Benji's arms and chest.

"Holy shit, it's Benji," someone from the party cried. "That crazy motherfucker."

Suddenly I heard the wail of an ambulance, as if it had been waiting in the wings, and a moment later three paramedics rushed in with a stretcher and yelled at everyone to get back. I stepped away, blending in to the crowd, watching as they opened Benji's eyes and shone a light into them. The decision was made quickly: they picked up the stretcher and raced him away toward the front of the hotel, and before I could follow, the place was swarming with police officers.

"Okay, nobody's going anywhere," one of them announced. "We need statements from all of you."

"I was with him," I said, stepping forward, bewildered that it was over with so quickly. "He's my friend."

A police officer wearing a no-nonsense expression pulled me aside. In the chaos they all looked the same in their stiff blue uniforms. The only things distinguishing them were their name badges. "What's the kid's name?" the one called Roberts said.

"Benji. Benji Connor."

Roberts pulled out a notepad and whistled to one of his colleagues who was talking to a guy from the party still wearing his toga. The officer jogged over. I looked at his name badge. Johnson.

"She was with him when it happened," Roberts explained to him, then turned back to me. "Did somebody attack you?"

"No," I said quietly. "He did it to himself."

"Suicide attempt?" Johnson said.

I slowly shrugged. What exactly was it that had just happened? Johnson persisted.

"Has he tried anything like that before?"

I shook my head, kept my mouth closed. I stared into the distance, at the doors of the hotel through which they had taken him. Roberts studied me, concerned.

"Sweetheart, do you want me to find out where they took him? Want me to take you there?"

I thought for a moment, then shook my head slowly. No.

"Then can you give us the details of his next of kin?"

I gave him Mrs. Connor's cell number. They asked me a few more questions: was I his girlfriend, did we have a fight, had he taken any drugs, all of which I answered no to.

"He was sad," I said, as if that explained everything, and Roberts looked at me like I was crazy. A maid came out with a mop and started to clean up the blood, swirling it in big, ineffective circles so it just smeared across the courtyard, and everyone went back into their rooms. A sign was placed next to the pool saying it was closed for cleaning. The party in bungalow 3 went quiet. Benji had given everyone a hell of a show.

Johnson's cell phone started to ring. He scooped it out of his belt.

"Okay, thanks," he said, and snapped it shut. "Your friend is going to be just fine," he said. "The cuts are superficial. Nothing serious."

Nothing serious. I didn't know if I was relieved or not.

"You want me to call someone for you?" Roberts asked.

"Could I use your phone?"

"Sure."

I took his phone, dialed a number, and waited while the other end rang. The pool was once again deserted except for a couple of cops still lingering, and some guys from the party who were sitting by the pool, answering questions and looking miserable. Finally the phone picked up.

"What?"

"Hank?"

"Who else would it be?"

"Um, do you think I could come over?"

"It's sorta late, isn't it?"

"I just, um, need to talk to you."

All that blood. All that blood running down Benji's arms.

"I need to talk to you, too," Hank said.

"Why?"

"It's time."

"Time?" I was still dazed. "Time for what?"

"Just hurry. Please."

Hank had never said "please" in his life. I snapped the phone shut and handed it back to the officer. No, Hank. Not tonight. Not now.

"You need a ride?" the cop asked.

I shook my head.

"Suit yourself."

I picked up my heels and ran through the foyer of the Chateau and down to the boulevard, bare feet hitting the hard pavement. I thrust my hand in the air to flag down a cab, and as we sped away I became aware of the flash of cameras and the paparazzi who had chased me down, convinced I was someone else.

39

When I arrived at Hank's apartment, it looked like no one was home. The lights were off and the curtains drawn. Jake's were drawn also, but I could see the faint light of a reading lamp coming from behind the blinds. As I climbed the stairs I strained to hear the sound of Hank's television, constant and reassuring, but there was only silence. I crept toward the door, feet bare, heels still in hand. When I tried the doorknob it turned. Hank had left it unlocked for me. I opened it and padded inside.

I had to squint to see in the darkness. I saw a small sliver of light emanating from Hank's bedroom. I pushed the door open. Hank was lying in bed beneath the covers, his breathing shallow. Beside him on the bedside table was a lamp emitting a glow so dull and flat it barely illuminated his face.

I remembered the scene from *Apocalypse Now* when Martin Sheen confronts Marlon Brando at his compound in the jungle. All you can see is the top of Brando's head, bald and glistening, the rest of his body obscured by the darkness. At this moment I felt like

Martin Sheen in that movie, come to kill Brando while the natives dance outside. Brando had a hard life. His son Christian shot his own sister Cheyenne's boyfriend in Brando's living room in Beverly Hills. Christian was convicted of manslaughter and Cheyenne hanged herself at her mother's house in Tahiti. Everyone paid the price for the crime; everyone was punished.

All this raced through my mind as I watched Hank from the doorway. I wasn't even sure he'd heard me enter. His mouth was wide open and facing the ceiling. His eyes were closed. I was about to leave, thinking with relief that he had fallen asleep, when I heard his voice in the darkness.

"Sounds like you were having a fun night," he said.

"I hope it's about to get better, but from the sounds of things, I don't like my chances."

"Close the door. Did anyone see you come in?"

The single lamp gave the feeling of being inside a cave. "The CIA was trailing me for a while, but I gave the cabdriver a fiver to lose them."

"This is no time for jokes."

I sat on the edge of the bed, squinting to adjust to the light, and Hank sat up. He was a little skinny, but otherwise he appeared strong. As he pushed himself up on his arms, I could see the long, thin scars of his suicide attempt running up his wrists like reeds on a river bed and thought of Benji. The scars cut right through the blurred tattoo on his wrist, and I saw for the first time what the bandages at the hospital had been covering. In the middle of the tattoo the skin glistened wet and pink, looking infected. It was as though he had tried to cut it out.

"What's the crisis, Hank?"

He pointed to the wall, as if that explained everything. For the first time in the darkness I noticed stacks of old newspapers sitting in the corner of the room, piled high. It dawned on me that the newspapers in the living room had never been thrown out, just moved into his bedroom.

"What do you know about vigilantes?" Hank asked.

"That's a hell of a fire hazard, Hank. You drop a lit cigarette and this place would go up like the Wicker Man."

"Not a bad idea. Fire would be clean, leave no trace."

"What do you mean, vigilantes?"

"What do you know?"

"I don't know a thing."

"You know a lot of things about a lot of pretty screwy stuff."

"If by vigilantes you mean people taking the law into their own hands, can't say I've met many. Are you trying to tell me you're Batman?"

"I'm not the hunter, Hilda. I'm the hunted."

"No, you're a paranoid old man. By the way, if you think people are out to get you, you shouldn't leave the front door unlocked."

"It doesn't matter now."

I smoothed down his bedcover, tucked in the corners. "Well you seem perfectly fine to me, apart from the obvious dementia, so if you're looking for someone to stick a pillow over your face, you'll have to find somebody else. Try Jake. He'd probably find killing you therapeutic."

"Shut your yapper and get me one of those newspapers," he said, pointing to the corner of the room.

"Can't we turn on a light or something?"

"No lights. Just the newspaper."

"Fine," I said as I stood, "but if I trip and fall, I'm suing your ass."

I walked over to the towering pile of newspapers, stumbling on an empty beer bottle as I went. "Now I'm more scared of being crushed to death," I said, looking at the mountain of newsprint in front of me. "Which one?"

"Christ, the one on the ground. Do I have to draw you a map?"

I bent down and picked up a newspaper off the floor, separate from the others. It was the *Los Angeles Times* from last Saturday. The headline was about a spate of carjackings in Long Beach. I threw it to Hank like it was a Frisbee. He rustled through the first few pages, found what he was looking for.

"There," he said, jabbing at the article so forcefully he nearly poked a hole through it. I snatched the paper back, scanned the article.

"JWA in the US?" I read. "What are they? Your favorite band or something?"

"Justice War Alliance," he said in a hushed voice.

"You mean like the Justice League of America? Is Superman their leader, too?"

Hank's eyes dropped, drifting to something invisible on the bedspread, but I could tell he was just avoiding my gaze. I looked at the article again, reading more closely. Apparently some group calling themselves the JWA had been hunting down war criminals since the fifties and dispensing their own special brand of justice. On first reading it sounded like something from the TV show *Get Smart*, about a vigilante organization executing Indian burns and wedgies on the bad guys. But Hank was taking this very seriously. I could feel him watching me as I read the article, waiting for my reaction. I looked at him, my face blank, and I could see his disappointment. He'd been hoping this was the moment when all his ramblings and his failed suicide attempt finally made sense, but I was only more confused. I put the paper down on the bed but kept looking at it, not wanting to look at him.

"So what?" I said. "Sounds like an urban legend to me. Anyway, what's it got to do with you?"

"I've read the paper every day for nearly fifty years, looking for any mention of them. Last week a German was taken out on the freeway with a sniper rifle. The car crashed into a wall and when the cops dragged the guy from the wreckage they saw they had a goddamn homicide on their hands. They'd blown this guy's brains all over his windshield. I know it was them."

"Do you know what this guy did? Why the JWA were supposedly after him?"

"He threw people against electric fences at the camps. To see what would happen."

"So he got what was coming to him."

"Some might say."

"Is this why you're hiding out in here? Because you think some vigilante group is hunting you down? You're a Holocaust survivor, for Christ's sake!"

Hank scratched at his arm. His nails were jagged and cut into his tender skin, causing blood to rise to the surface. "I was only eight when I went into the camp. I wasn't a Jew, or a homo, or even a Gypsy. I didn't have to be there. You know why I was there?"

I sat down on the edge of the bed, shook my head.

"I was there because I was a stupid son of a bitch. Threw stones at the Nazis as they goose-stepped into town. I still remember braining one. Four of them chased me down into an alleyway, picked me up, and dragged me off. Threw me on the back of the wagon with the rest of them. No one saw it happen, and if they did, I guess they couldn't have done anything anyways. I didn't even get to say good-bye to my parents."

"That was brave, Hank," I said. I imagined a valiant young boy taking up arms against the invading forces, striking a blow while the adults were too complacent and scared to retaliate. Hank just laughed.

"Brave, hell. I was just a little shit. Threw rocks at everything in those days. I'd had my ass beat just days before for throwing stones at the Hooper shopwindow."

"Why doesn't that surprise me?"

"Remember this ain't no movie, Hilda. This ain't no *Schindler's List*."

"Obviously."

"Sometimes your life can turn on a dime just for some stupid shit you done. I get taken from my family because I'm a stupid, shit-head kid who doesn't know any better. I didn't deserve to be there. That's how I felt anyway. I wasn't part of the grand plan; I was just collateral damage. It made me angry. But not at the Nazis, no way. I was angry at the people in the camp. The other kids. The ones who were *meant* to be there. I kept away from them, sat on my own, ate with my back turned to them. I wanted to show that I was different, that it had all been a stupid mistake, and I wanted the guards to see that. They'd let me out and I could go back to my parents, but it didn't happen. Days and weeks and months passed and still I was there. Soon I forgot what my parents even looked like."

I didn't know what to say. I felt frozen to my spot on the bed, wanting to run away but desperately wanting to know the truth.

All of Benji's horrible predictions about Hank seemed to be coming true, as did all of Jake's warnings. I tried to imagine what it was like for a boy in that situation, how he would feel, what he might do to survive.

"At first it wasn't so bad, all things considered. We got three squares a day and they put us to work. As the war dragged on, things started to deteriorate. That's when people started to disappear in the middle of the night. The guards made us fight for food. We'd stand in circles and kick the living shit out of one another, just to get a scrap of bread. I was a pretty good fighter, but it was tiring. There was more food to go around when kids just disappeared. Poof!"

Hank threw his hands up like he was a magician dispensing of a rabbit in midair.

"Because I was quiet, and a loner, the other kids didn't pay much attention to me. They didn't know I was watching them. Didn't know I was *plotting* against them. Like some stinking, slimy sewer rat. Like the worst kind of dog."

I put my hand on his. "You were a kid," I started to say, but Hank cut me off, shaking his hand free.

"Kids are cruel—is that what you're going to say? Kids do the darndest things? I know what I was. I knew right from wrong."

"No, you didn't. You were a child in a *concentration camp*. How the hell would you know the difference between right and wrong? A whole country didn't know the difference!"

The light in the room dimmed a little, the bulb of the lamp running out. It was as if all the energy in the room was being sucked out by every word Hank said, as if the planet were growing darker just for us.

"I started to watch them," he continued. "Listen to their conversations. Some of them were planning an escape. A girl called Mary, her brother, Eli, and some other kid. They were always whispering in corners, hiding behind their hands. They were going to try to squeeze through the fence at night. I told the guards."

He looked at me for a response. I stared at the bedspread. There were oil stains and smears of blood from where his cuts were healing.

"Mary, Eli, and that other kid—they disappeared. The guards said I had done well. I got extra scraps of food and was allowed to take breaks while everyone else worked. It was a damn sweet deal. I started thinking about what else I could tell them. I spied on people. Looked for anything that would be worthwhile to tell. If some kid stashed a crust of bread beneath his pillow for later, I made damn sure those guards found out about it, and the crusts became mine. But sometimes there was nothing to tell. Sometimes I had to make shit up. I got more crusts. More kids disappeared."

Hank looked at his hands.

"I've lost count of how many kids disappeared."

A helicopter flew overhead and for a brief, wonderful moment the room was bathed in its spotlight. I remembered a history class in which we watched a documentary about the Holocaust. All those stick-thin bodies piled to the sky, eyes wide and unblinking, flies on their faces. My reaction had been one of incomprehension: How could this have happened?

"Then the war ended," Hank went on, "I got out, got to see my parents again. But it wasn't the same. Nothing was. I left for America. I tried to forget. But the longer I lived, the more it became clear to me the terrible, terrible crime I had committed. The terrible thing I had done. When you become an adult, you look back on some of the shit you did as a kid and think, 'Gee whiz, I was pretty messed up.' If you're lucky you get the chance to correct some of those wrongs. You see the fat kid you never invited to any of your birthday parties, the pimply girl whose pigtails you pulled. You get to say sorry. Sometimes they accept your apology. For me, it's too late for any of that. They're dead."

I understood what he meant. When I became friends with Benji it was partly because of a misguided sense of compassion. I didn't want to be the kind of person who picked on, bullied, or ignored the strange kid. I wanted to be the one who became his friend, who tore away at the inadequate exterior and found a diamond beneath. Looking back, I saw it was patronizing to Benji, and wrong. Sometimes there isn't a diamond beneath. But that's not how I felt about Hank. I wanted to believe he was a victim of circumstance.

Hank said, "When I got to LA, those dead kids followed me around like an army. But they weren't my protectors. I worked on movie stars' swimming pools. I screwed beautiful women. I tried to forget any of it ever happened. But every time I saw a group of kids let out of school, there they were—Mary, Eli, all the nameless faces. I saw them everywhere. In the end it was easier to see them at the bottom of a bottle. Then I started to see *them*. The JWA. They were tracking me. I was as good as dead."

All the elements were coming together, obscure pieces of a deadly jigsaw puzzle. "You think they're coming after you? For what you did?"

"Do you think they'd let a guy like me keep walking around? After what I did? It's only a matter of time before those cocksuckers show up on my doorstep."

I didn't know if Hank was being paranoid or if there was some truth to what he was saying. Either way I knew where this was heading. Suddenly the suicide attempt made perfect sense. I knew Hank well enough to know that if he had to go down, he was going on his own terms.

"You don't have to do this," I said. "This vigilante stuff sounds like bullshit."

"Like a movie star stabbing himself with a pair of scissors?"

"That happened. Look it up. Vigilante groups running around offing people? I don't think so."

Hank looked away. His voice was tired, his breathing labored. "It doesn't matter. I'm tired of living with it. With all this death. I've seen enough death to last me a lifetime."

"What about me?"

Hank reached out and touched my hand, and I started to cry.

"It's okay, kiddo."

"Don't make me say good-bye to you, Hank. I can't say good-bye to people anymore. It's killing me."

"Death ain't so bad, Hilda. There are worse things."

"I won't do it," I said. "I won't do anything."

"Exactly. That's exactly what I want you to do. Nothing. Just stay here until it's done. I don't want someone busting through the door and saving me like last time. Pain in the ass, that was."

He reached over to the bedside dresser and grabbed something I hadn't noticed before: a bottle of painkillers. Reaching down again, Hank pulled a bottle of vodka out from underneath the bed. "Can I have a minute?" he asked. "I can't swallow pills that well, 'specially if someone's gawkin' at me. I'd rather not choke to death."

"I won't let you do this," I said, even as he screwed the lid off the pills. "I won't let you." But then the pills were in his mouth and he was waiting for me to leave the room and I did. I stood up and walked out. There was nothing else to do.

I went into the bathroom, the same bathroom Benji and I had taken photos in, tarnishing with our darkness what should have been a beautiful California day. We had called ourselves *enthusiasts*, but we were worse than that. We were tourists, rubbernecking at the accident on the side of the road, straining to see the blood and despair on the highway as mothers screamed for their children and lives were torn apart. We were tourists of human wreckage.

I looked at myself in the mirror, my stupid panda eye makeup and lipstick that was too red, my attention-seeking pink hair. I was pathetic. The bathroom filled with ghosts. Bernie Bernall, his scissors poised over his heart, tears on his cheeks. Benji with his digital camera, photographing taps and fixtures, sucking the soul out of the room. Then, worst of all, there was me. The pretender. I'd stared death in the face, seen it careen through my family as surely as the truck that smashed my parents' heads from their shoulders. I wanted so desperately to show that I wasn't scared. But I was. I turned on the tap and splashed water on my face, and as I did Hank called to me from the bedroom.

"Hilda! Get back in here."

I went back in and sat on the bed. Everything looked the same: Hank was sitting in the same position, the room was still dark, the sheets were still dirty. There was one major difference. The pill bottle was empty. Hank closed his eyes.

"Just another old dead guy," he said quietly. "If I was Cary Grant, maybe somebody would give a damn."

"I give a damn, Hank. I'm your biggest fan."

At that he laughed. "You're a riot, kid. It's been nice having you around. You can have my videotapes."

"People watch DVDs now, Hank. *DVDs*."

"Fine. Don't have the videos. Christ."

I laughed through my tears and wiped my nose on my wrist. Hank's eyes closed a little, then opened again as if he'd been startled awake.

"Get out of here, would you?" he said. "Can't a man get any sleep around here?"

40

I DIDN'T GET TO SAY good-bye to my parents. There was just a hospital room and a bed that I woke up in and Aunt Lynette sitting beside me, weeping. I reached up and felt my face; instead of skin I touched bandage. I kept thinking my parents were going to walk through that hospital room door, worried sick, sorry they had been away so long. They never came. Five days later I went home. Every day I waited for their car to pull into Lynette's driveway. It never did.

41

WENT INTO THE KITCHEN and made myself a cup of tea. There wasn't anything good on TV so I put one of Hank's videos in the player, a Marilyn Monroe film I hadn't seen before. It was a musical, light on the laughs and heavy on the dance numbers. Marilyn looked tired. As she danced her feet kicked with a little less vigor and her eyes had lost some of their sparkle. I remembered a story about how when Norma Jean first became Marilyn Monroe she had to ask an autograph-seeking fan how to spell her own name. By the time she died she probably had no idea who she was at all.

It must have been some time during the movie that Hank slipped away. As the credits rolled and the screen went black I went into the bedroom to check on him. He was lying on his stomach, and even from the doorway I could see that he wasn't moving. I picked up my heels, turned off the television, and left the apartment.

Downstairs Jake's blinds were still drawn. I knocked on the door. I few moments later he appeared in tracksuit pants, eyes puffy, hair sticking up. I walked inside, walked to his bedroom, and lay down on the bed. A second later he joined me, and together we slept, a sleep so sad and so deep I would have been happy never to wake up, because when I did I would have to tell Jake what I couldn't yet put into words. Hank was gone, and for one night, lying in Jake's arms, I wanted that loss, like Hank himself, to belong to me alone.

42

WE BURIED HANK ON a beautiful California day, when the sun was shining and the sky was a vast blue expanse, as perfect as the ceiling of a sound stage. The only mourners were Jake, Lynette, and me. We found out that Hank had a son named Phillip, a stockbroker who lived in New York City. He wasn't interested in coming to the funeral but ended up paying for all the arrangements. Hank had never mentioned he had a son, and I'm sure there was plenty more he never divulged to either me or Jake, but it was still a surprise to hear. Just another sad story to add to an old man's miserable life. I told Lynette all about Hank after he died—well, not quite everything—and when I told her how often I had visited him she beamed proudly.

"You really are a sweet girl," she said, getting teary. "And all this time I thought you were probably on drugs."

I went to the hospital to visit Benji, not the hospital they took him to the night of the party, but another one, with large bedrooms and beautiful gardens. When the doctors suggested Benji should spend a few weeks under observation, his parents made sure he went to the best facility money could buy. It was more like a resort than a hospital, with nurses who would bring you food whenever you wanted, just like room service. When I walked into his room he was sitting on the bed, legs crossed and reading a magazine, looking like a young boy. He was wearing a striped red shirt and chinos, and his hair was nicely combed. His sleeves were long, covering the places where he had cut himself.

"What happened to your hair?" he asked when he saw me.

I twirled a few brown strands between my fingers. "I got sick of the pink. Made me look like a freak."

"I kinda liked it," he said. "It made you stand out, well, more than before. But this is good, too. Natural."

"Brown is my natural hair color."

"I know. We've known each other for a long time, remember?"

"I guess so."

Benji sat up and winced, placed one hand protectively on his stomach.

"How's it all looking down there?" I asked, motioning to his stomach and the places he had cut himself.

"A little tender, I guess. I've got so many bandages under here it's like I'm from *The Mummy*."

Other than that we didn't talk about the night at the Chateau. Benji already appeared stronger and healthier despite the injuries. He was also softer, and calmer.

"What are they feeding you in here?" I asked.

"It's all healthy stuff. Organic. They think diet plays a big part in, you know, making your brain work better. What you feed yourself, you feed your brain, and your brain's not going to function too well on hot dogs and candy bars."

"In that case my brain's a coffee and Danish. I wonder what that says about me?"

"It's really interesting stuff, Hilda. I think you'd actually like it here."

I flicked through the fishing magazine on Benji's bed.

"I'm sorry about Hank," Benji said. My heart leaped a little at the mention of his name. I'd sent Benji a letter saying that Hank had passed away after accidentally taking too many pills. Since he hit his head he hadn't been the same, I explained, and he must have forgotten that he had already taken his pain pills earlier in the evening. I told the same story to the paramedics, and no one ever questioned it. I guess the hospital thought it wasn't worth digging too deep over a guy like Hank, much to my relief.

"Thanks, Benji," I said.

He paused. "I really did like him, Hilda," he said sadly.

"I know you did."

"Mom thinks we shouldn't be friends anymore," he said, looking down like he was ashamed. "She says you're a bad influence."

I laughed, and luckily Benji laughed, too.

"They think this death stuff is bad for me, too," he said, his smile fading. "They went into my bedroom, put all my things into boxes."

I knew what things he meant. His beloved artifacts. It was so sad to think of them thrown into a box and shoved into a closet, away from where they could be appreciated, admired, contemplated. I doubted Mr. Connor had taken any care with them. Benji's treasured bits of wood and slivers of rock were probably destroyed now.

"That sucks," I said.

"They're probably right. Maybe it's time to get a new hobby."

"I can't really imagine you collecting stamps or building model airplanes."

"Me neither."

I put my hand on his leg, and he flinched, but I didn't pull away. "Don't worry. I'm sure all your stuff will still be there when you get back. You can take it out when you're ready."

We spent the rest of the day strolling around the grounds, making fun of the other patients and pretending we were in *One Flew Over the Cuckoo's Nest*. Benji picked up a trash can from the hallway and ran at the window with it, acting like he was going to bust out, and two burly guards raced over and almost tackled him before he could explain he was only joking around. Needless to say, they didn't think it was very funny, but Benji and I did, and we laughed harder than I had laughed in a long time, my sides aching. When I left Benji that afternoon, he had color in his face, and his eyes looked a little brighter. I decided that even if it was against Mrs. Connor's wishes, I would visit Benji again before the summer was through.

Slowly, over time, Jake and I came back to each other. I let him set the agenda: we went to art galleries, street festivals, and rock concerts. We went bowling and to the movies and talked about celebrities who were still alive. Jake abandoned *The Life Upstairs* and started writing an action film with an environmental message that already had a studio interested. I decided to get a part-time job to fill in all the summer hours I would normally spend on the Internet trawling for dead celebrities, and ended up working at one of those franchise coffee shops in the Valley. The whole scene was pretty laid-back, and I could have even kept my pink hair if I wanted to. There was always a cool CD on rotation, and the bright fluorescent lights and cushy sofas hypnotized me into a feeling close to contentedness. Some days Jake would come in and work at the sofa in the corner, and I would sit with him during my lunch break and talk about his script and the characters, offer him ideas of my own. I grew to really love the coffee shop. I was more than happy with where I was, in my green apron and hat, mastering the art of the perfect espresso while Paul McCartney tunes played over and over in the background. It was fine for now. Jake was ambitious enough for both of us, and I was happy to coast along for the moment, just enjoying the experience of being alive, being around people, being free.

The Manson Family parole hearings continued like some grotesque charade. I heard about it from the customers talking over lattes and from snatches of headlines from the newspapers they left lying around. I wasn't too interested anymore. Everyone knew they would never be let out, hell, I'm sure even they knew. It was just another opportunity to give Charlie and his followers the spotlight, macabre fodder for a slow news day. I thought about the family members who had lost their loved ones and had to listen to this crap every four years. It seemed unfair. I continued making lattes, sprinkling chocolate powder on cappuccinos, as Charlie made his pronouncements about judgement day. To Charlie I was one of the squares who had been blinded by the man. I didn't care. It was nice to be like everyone else for a change.

I didn't tell Jake any of what Hank had confessed to me. In some ways what had happened to Hank was unspeakable. Some days I would play the story over in my head, coming at it from different angles. Sometimes Hank came out as the tragic victim of circumstance. On other days, when I was feeling dark, he was a murderer. I went around in circles so many times that in the end I had to put it aside and let it be. Sometimes that is all you can do.

One day Jake called and asked if I'd like to go to the mall with him. He had a meeting with a director about his screenplay and wanted to buy a new suit for the occasion.

"We can do that in the morning," I said. "But then there's somewhere I want to go. I have something I want to show you."

"Let me guess. We're going to the Hollywood sign to see where that chick jumped off."

"No, Jake, I've already seen that. That's so old-school."

"Wait, I know. The restaurant where Robert Blake ate dinner with his wife before shooting her."

"Before *allegedly* shooting her, and no, that's not it, either."

"So where are we going?"

"You'll just have to wait and see."

That afternoon, after buying suits at Macy's, we drove in Jake's convertible to a small cemetery in Topanga Canyon. It was on a clearing beside a thick forest, the grave markings small and discreet, so as to not affect the natural landscape. We pulled up and Jake turned off the engine.

"I knew it," he said. "More death."

"This is different." I closed the car door and wandered up the clearing. I hadn't visited for so long. It was as peaceful and beautiful as I remembered. Tiny yellow flowers had covered most of the ground, some of them creeping over the gravestones, enveloping the gray marble in vibrant color. I knelt on the ground and cleared the overgrowth away from a stone. I felt Jake behind me, a few feet away, unsure of whether to come closer. I turned around.

"Come on. Sit down."

He sat beside me. "Is this who I think it is?"

I ran my hand along the stone. "Mom and Dad, this is Jake."

There was no crime scene tape, no tour guide with a megaphone, no high fences keeping out souvenir seekers. There were only stone markers on the ground, each one indistinguishable from the next. I didn't know if my parents could hear me, but it didn't seem to matter. I lay down on the grass with my hand resting on their marker, and Jake lay beside me and held me, and at that moment we were just people who had lost people, who would one day be lost to others. I pulled the pool tile from my pocket and pushed it into the quiet earth, where it could wait for me. Everything seemed okay.

AUTHOR'S NOTE

LOS ANGELES IS A town of mysteries and secrets. It is a place where stories converge and collide, where history is not only constructed but reconstructed on a daily basis. Time and place in the novel have been compressed to paint the fullest picture of Hollywood's veiled history. Every effort has been made to verify the many stories told in *John Belushi Is Dead*, but in the end the absolute truth, as you will have seen in these pages, is more often than not unattainable. Sometimes the ending is just the beginning.